MW01594757

Pole Shift

by
Albert S. Tukker

You can find more information about,
and works by Albert S. Tukker at
http://AlbertSamuelTukker.com

ISBN 978-0-557-02474-2

Copyright ASTukker 2007

In loving memory of my father,
Raymond Dale
3/12/1933 - 6/2/2007

Chapter I

Three years before the 'Equinox...

I was in a cabin in the mountains, rented for the night. I stood at the front window, unable to keep thoughts at bay. This was a get-away. An escape. But it wasn't working. Not even the stranger behind me helped. My thoughts continued.

Fourteen hours ago I admitted my wife to the hospital. This time I knew she wasn't coming home. It was the way they moved about her, the things they said to her, and me. The doctors weren't giving it much hope. There simply wasn't anything to do, except keep her as comfortable as possible. This time should be the end of her suffering, of both our suffering.

I shook my head, then drew on the cigarette.

How often, on the way home from work, had I thought, 'Will I find her dead tonight?' How many times in the morning was her face a death mask? Three and a half years I watched as she slowly deteriorated. Waiting for the inevitable. Waiting for her to die.

There really wasn't anything else I could do, anything anyone else could do, except try to make it as comfortable for her as they could, and I wasn't doing all that great of job. The stress was wearing me down. I wished we were rich so I could take her places, let her live before dying. But I had to work sixty hours a week just to earn enough to pay the rent and something on her medical bills; and now it looked like I'll be working the rest of my life just to pay those.

And for what kind of life, anyway? She suffers for three years: tired, fatigued, sick, fragile. She maybe had three, four weeks of decent days all total. Thirty days out of twevle hundred and sixty-three. Just to die anyway. What kind of quality of life was that?

Good for the hospital. Good for the doctor. Their bank accounts increased substantially while ours was ransacked and emptied. All of that money just for them to extend her suffering. And for what? So she could lie in bed, barely eating, feeling sick and lousy? Sit and stare at television because she was just too tired to do anything else?

And knowing the entire time that it was all in vain. There was no cure, only a temporary prolonging of the inevitable. No matter what anybody did, the disease was going to kill her. Three years was a long time to think about things. Her funeral plans are more elaborate than our wedding. Hopefully her life insurance will pay off the bills. Did we have life insurance? I had to check.

It gave us both a lot of time to think.

How long had I lived with the guilt of waiting for her

to die? When had I given up hope? The first time the tumors grew back? The second? I inhaled deeply, the cigarette tip reflected in the cabin window, casting a red glow over my face. I suddenly wished it was a joint. "Sure is a shame I can't run to a convenience store and pick up a pack of J's," I exhaled to myself.

Behind me in bed, a young woman laid naked. And I couldn't remember her name. As I let more smoke out, I remembered what the doctor said as we stood outside my wife's hospital room:

"She'll be out until she goes, Mr. Woods. With the level of pain she's in, pretty much all we can do is keep her sedated and comfortable."

"What happened? She complained of heartburn this morning, but other than that she was fine. She even had some energy," I looked the doctor in the eye. "She was smiling."

The doctor shrugged. "Her body simply got tired of fighting. It's simply time. I'm afraid we can do little more than ease her suffering now."

"This..," I paused, my mind racing at all the possibilities. Before I could continue, the doctor spoke again.

"I'm afraid so. She could last a few more hours, she could last a few days. I'm sorry, Mr. Woods."

I pushed open the door and entered my wife's room. I sat by her for an hour, holding her hand. I watched the monitors; all the hanging bags; all the tubes and wires. I gently tried to arouse her.

She mumbled.

"Should I tell your sister?"

She mumbled, barely moving her head in a nod.

I leaned forward and kissed her lips. They were cold and tasted salty. "I'll let you sleep." Her eyes closed and she slipped back into a drug-induced sleep. I let go her hand and left the room.

"I hope you don't take this the wrong way, Doc'," I said when I came out of her room, "or if your religious or not. But if He's going to take her? Take her. Stop making her suffer."

The doctor just stared blankly at me.

I thought I saw agreement in the doctor's eyes. "I have to go, Doc'. I can't sit and wait. I've watched too long. I'm going to let her sister know she's here. She'll come sit with her." I looked back through the window of the intensive care room to my dying wife. "I'll take off after I know she's on her way."

"She's so out of it. She doesn't know where she is," the doctor said quietly, "let alone who's in there with her."

I turned back towards the doctor. "I'll be back in the morning." Again, to her window. "But, I have to go. You have my cell?"

The doctor nodded. We headed down the hall together.

"You gonna keep her like that?"

"She'd only be in pain if we lessened it any."

"Won't that kill her? Keeping her doped up like that?"

The doctor shook his head. "She's dreaming.

Probably some wild dreams, but she's just lying there dreaming.

"If she were feeling pain, it could extend the dying process. At this stage, this is the best we can do for her. She doesn't feel anything, and her mind is set free."

"How do you know?"

"EEG."

After several steps, I pondered aloud, "How do you know they're not nightmares?"

I shook my head again, inhaled again, then put the butt out. I turned around and looked at the woman on the bed.

What the hell is her name?

"Get in."

"Thanks," she said as she slid onto the seat. When she closed the door, I got a whiff of her scent. A light scent. Musk. She'd been sweating. "How far ya' going?"

"Hesperia," I replied flatly. I had no idea where I was going, I was just driving. I wasn't even sure if Hesperia was ahead of me.

"Anywhere near Twenty-Nine Palms?"

I was quiet for a moment, then nodded. "Sure. No problem."

We rode in silence for awhile, and when she felt sure I was absorbed in the act of driving, she turned and studied me. After several minutes she blurted, "What'cha running away from?"

I turned my head slightly and looked sideways at her, then focused back on the road. I was never any good at lying, and my mind was full with what was

going on back at the hospital. "My wife. She's..she's
dying of cancer."

"You say it like it could be this very moment. Just a
phone call away."

I looked straight until an oncoming car passed,
then took a long glance at her. Her face was soft, her
eyes warm. She seemed sincere and I needed someone
to unload on. I reached into my jacket and retrieved my
cell phone, showing it to her. "She's been sick a long
time. Might not last the night. Might last a week."

I looked out the window of the cabin and into the
depths of the woods. It was night, raining hard. The lightning
and thunder had awakened me. A flash reflected my image in
the window. No shirt, and my jeans were zipped, but not
buttoned. I wiggled my toes. My feet were bare. I reached to
the table beside me and grabbed another smoke. My reflection
jumped at me again when the lighter flamed. I put the lighter
down then ran a hand through my hair. The stranger behind me,
we decided to share a room two hours ago over trucker's
coffee. What the hell is her name?

I stepped over to the door and opened it, the screen
door letting in a rush of cool, moist air and the noise of the
night, letting out the cigarette smoke. I went back to the
window, my thoughts churning the recent past. An inquiry into
when I started praying, wishing for her death. Was it when I
grew tired? Tired of watching her decay? Tired of seeing her in
pain, in the hospital, in my nightmares? Just, tired?

And she was tired. It was obvious how tired she was;
painfully so. But, she smiled when she could.

But why not wish for her recovery? Why not that?

I inhaled, watching the glow on the window. Wouldn't that have been like wishing you could flap yours arms and fly? Like wishing you didn't have to pay taxes? Like wishing you... would never die?

I leaned over her to talk to her, my mouth next to her ear. I asked her how she felt. We had been there nearly two hours and she had been injected with increasing strength painkillers the entire time. She was now floating in and out of deep and light sleep, both drug-induced. If you caught her at the right moment, you could get a response out of her. Her response this time was a bit of a surprise. In a weak, slightly shameful voice, she said, "I'm ready to go. I want to die."

"Okay. I understand." A tear welled up in one eye. I looked down at her chest. "You put up a good fight, Love. I know you're tired. Hurting." At that she nodded her head slightly. "Good. You just rest, then. There's nothing more for you to worry about. You go whenever you're ready."

"I wanna go now."

"Just relax. The medicine should be working soon."

I ran my hand through her thin hair. "Go to sleep."

"You gonna stay?"

"Yes," I lied.

She gave me a sorrowful look.

I kissed her on the forehead, then on her cheek, then her lips. "'Night, my Love."

I hadn't called her 'my Love' since our second year together. And just how long had it been? Twelve? Thirteen? I knew she realized this. And it was the last thing I said to her. Does she know now that I meant it?

"Thumper? Where'd you go?"

Damn my pinched nerve. She was what? Twenty-five, maybe 'six. Tall, thin, small hips and breasts. What the hell is her name? I heard her stir the bedcovers.

"Thumper? You okay?"

She was getting out of bed. I put the cigarette in the ashtray and waited. She came up to me from behind, not a stitch of clothing on her, and slipped her arms around me. Her naked breasts mashed into my shoulders blades. They were warm and soft. She laid her head against the nap of my neck. "Thumper?"

"I can't control it, you know." I was talking about the way my left leg jerked when I reached orgasm. "I've tried to stop it, but my leg cramps something terrible."

"I think it's cute."

"Cute?"

"Sexy."

"Phfft."

"Well, it is kinda neat. Sure is a good indicator."

"Of what?"

"Your reaction to me."

I reached for the cigarette. I have to tell her. I had told her I spent the last three and a half years watching my wife die. Yes, hopes were raised; more than once. But this last year was the worst. The last six months will haunt me for the rest of my life. I had to tell her that she was a much needed escape. She was . . . needed. But that was all. The last few hours were great, but I needed to get back to the city. First, I had to remember her name!

"I'm cold. I'm going back to bed. You coming?" she asked as she skittered away.

"In a little while," I said to the window, watching her reflection. Nice butt. I shook my head. I've got to get back to the hospital. "Soon as I'm done smoking."

When I had left the hospital earlier, I had walked to our car, not really any plans in my head. Maybe find someplace to eat. Next thing I knew I was on the freeway headed out of town, no destination in mind.

It spooked me at first; not remembering how I got on the freeway. I had lit a cigarette, rolled down the window, turned on the radio, then turned it back off.

I drove because my wife was dying. I drove because I didn't understand what I was feeling. I was sorry she was sick; sorry she was dying. But, now that it's imminent, a relief was coming over me. A weight, crushing, smothering, overwhelming, was being lifted. I drove, just for something to do, just to drive. How long before I got *the* call?

And where was I planning on going anyway? The desert wasn't calling me like it usually did. My favorite spot was a secluded outcropping of rocks that wasn't accessible by car, unless you knew the tricks. And I knew the tricks. But it wasn't appealing tonight. I drove to forget. I drove to remember. I turned north.

The moutains came into view ahead of me and I knew where I was going. The cabins at Cathedral Peak. We had spent many years going there on vacation. I had shown it to my wife during our first year together and she fell in love with it at first sight, just as I had years earlier.

An hour past midnight I had picked up the young hitchhiker and we stopped at a cafe for a sandwich and coffee, and ended up here. What the hell is her name?

9

I looked at her reflection in the window. Is that why I brought her here? To relive the past? Replace my wife by bringing her here?

No. I was on my way for the solitude. She just...happened. I sucked down another drag. What is her name?

I looked at my cell phone on the table. I should plug it in so it can charge. I should turn it on so I can receive calls. I should go back to the hospital. I should climb back in bed with Michelle. I put the cigarette out and lit another.

Michelle! I looked at her reflection. She looked asleep. Did she know this was never going to go any where? Did she know I desperately needed someone, for a few hours? Just a few hours. Something told me she knew.

I was worn out. Drained. Before my wife was diagnosed, we were considering a romantic vacation. Then they found the cancer; in her liver, lungs, kidneys, colon, almost fucking everywhere. That was three and a half years ago. And after she was diagnosed, sex always felt wrong. Like we shouldn't do it until she was better. Like, I could get infected. But she was...insistant. Once a week or so. So I wasn't starved for sex. So why Michelle? I glanced at her reflection. She looked...cozy. Why now?

I drew hard on the cigarette, making it hot. I smashed it out and sat down at the table. I was tired. Exhausted. I looked out the window and watched it rain. Guilt creeped into me as the night drew deeper. What was I doing here? It would kill her if she found out about Michelle. I chuckled. 'Kill her if she found out'. Then Michelle stirred and I looked at her reflection for a moment, my mind suddenly blank.

I wasn't proud of myself. A one night stand while my wife lies doped up and dying a hundred miles away. I was going to Hell. Now most definitely. I chuckled again. Like I believed in that kind of boloney. But if that were the case, I had been doomed to Hell since I lifted a bag of beef jerky from the neighborhood store when I was twelve.

No, it wasn't religion that brought the guilt. It was experience. Brought on by having been wronged himself. And I felt I had wronged my wife. And Michelle. How could I look at either now? I should get back to town. Before. . . before it happens.

I turned in the chair and looked at Michelle. So, why was I here? My wife will never know, but that didn't matter. Throughout our marriage I had had a few opportune times I could have cheated and she never would have known. But that wasn't the point. I would have known. Like now.

And it's already starting to eat away at me.

But she was dying, if not already dead. I glanced at the cell phone. It was still off.

The phone rang. The motel room phone. I looked at the clock/radio - 3:04.

"Hello."

"I thought I might find you there. You know her name yet?" It was Lisa, my wife.

I jerked awake, my head snapping up from the table. "Holy shit," I stammered. I rose quickly and stumbled, the blood a little slow to my head.

I walked to the bed and grabbed my shirt. I put it on, then picked up my underwear and socks and stuffed them in my jacket. After slipping my shoes on, I slipped a hundred-dollar bill under the motel phone, to help Michelle in her travels. I palmed the cell phone and left. I was headed back to the hospital. I turned on the cell phone and watched it go through start up. When it displayed the time - 3:13 - I started the car.

As I drove, my mind wandered, floated. The end was close, real close. Her own personal version of the end of the world. Then, I could live again. Start thinking about what to get rid of and what to keep. Rearrange the furniture. Move pictures. Redo shelves. Live alone, again.

I hadn't let himself think of these things for the last three years, always expecting her to come home, even though I knew one day she wouldn't. I always tried to keep her involved with things, so she felt a part of them. Like, I let her pay the bills, one of the few things she could do, physically. But that's why the finances got so awry. With her medication and the side-effects, she just couldn't do it right. But she wouldn't tell me, I had to find out when the shut-off notices were hung on the door knob.

But now, with what the doctor said upon admitting her, and the way she looked; gaunt, pale, my mind started wandering over things I could now do.

Twenty-two minutes later my cell phone rang. "Hello?"

"Mr. Woods?" It was the doc'.

"Speaking."

"This is Doctor James.Your wife passed away about three minutes ago."

"Oh geesh." I glanced to digital display on the car radio. 4:17.

"She passed peacefully."

"I sure hope so, Doc'. You did what you could for as long as you could." I glanced at the passing sign. "Um, I took a drive. A long drive. I'll be there by dawn."

"We'll have everything ready for you. The hospital and I would like to offer our condolences."

"Thanks, Doc', but it was expected."

"Her sister was with her when she died."

There was silence for several moments as I dodged traffic and wiped away tears. "Thanks, Doc'. I'll see you in a few hours."

"Goodnight, Mr. Woods."

The cell phone bounced in the seat as I cranked up the radio volume.

She's dead. Finally at rest. At peace. Gone. Home no more...home no more...the house is going to feel so. . . empty. I turned onto the interstate.

Chapter II

I watched the sky from the window seat booth in an all night diner, as if to see her float by. Squatted clouds on the horizon filtered and shaded the disc of the morning sun into deep hues of red and orange.

She was gone. Dead. Lifeless. No more to warm me on cold nights. No more sex. No more the silence as we gazed at TV. No more blundering. No more fights; few, but furious. No more someone to talk to, with.

I had called the mortuary after talking to the doctor and arranged to have them pick up the body. I would see her again at the funeral home later. At the funeral home I made the arrangements and the announcement in the morning paper. I had left there half an hour ago. I called her parents. I was to meet them at the mortuary later.

Now, I needed breakfast. Later, when the sun is a bit higher into the day, I'll go home and start packing up her things.

Back in the hospital room, as I was putting the contents from the dresser into a box, my cell phone rang.

Great. Here come the condolences calls.

"Hello?"

"I need a ride."

I paused. I knew that voice. "Michelle?"

"How could you just leave me here?"

"I..."

"And what the hell is the money for?"

"A...a taxi?"

"There aren't any taxis up here. I need a ride, Thumper."

"The name's," I swallowed. "My name is Forrest. Forrest Woods. And.."

"Hi, Forrest."

"Hi. Uh, Michelle, my wife died while I was driving back to see her."

There was that silence of mixed emotions from both ends of the telephone. She thought I was cute and passionate and pitiful. I thought of the mindless sex and the 'lying next to' as we slept.

"I'm sorry."

"It wasn't your fault. But thanks. The doctor said she went peacefully. At least her sister was there."

"You weren't, though. You were driving back after. . . me."

Silence.

"You okay, Thumper? Forrest?"

"Yeah."

"You want to be alone?" She asked, knowing the answer in her tone.

A moment of silence. "No," I said, surprising her. "Look, the viewing's tonight. Then we have to get to the crematory before nine. I can be up there by midnight."

"I'll be here."

"Thanks."

I hung up the phone.

* * *

It rained that night. A heavy rain that lasted through the wee hours. I had gone out to the porch after Michelle fell asleep and watched it rain.

I had taken my tray out there and smoked a joint as the storm rolled through. I had used my cell phone and called my brother in Nebraska. We chatted for an hour. It was the end of summer and they had had their share of cloudbursts. We swapped thunderstorm stories and reminisced about our childhood. It was after we had hung up, after the rain had stopped and I had smoked another joint that I saw the blue firefly.

It could have been a trick of the light, a trick of the eye, a trick of the mind. Then it flashed again, blue. I anticipated it's track, seconds later being rewarded with a start-to-finish blue glow. Never, ever, have I seen a firefly other than green. Never.

I watched it fly through the trees, staying in the area for over an hour. I nearly called my brother back to tell him, but he wouldn't have believed me, and the cell phone didn't have a camera. I watched, though. Stunned at the simple beauty of it; awed at its singularity; humbled at its life of celibate solitude. It must be the same as being a foreigner in a country where you have no idea of what is being said. I felt empathy for the lonely thing.

Then I realized I was the only one seeing it. The other cabins were all empty. It was the off season. The weather's cooler and there is more rain, and a lot less people. I thought about waking up Michelle, but decided against it. Any movement on my part could scare it away. So there I sat, in the moutains of Southern California, alone, watching an anomaly of nature. My mind drifted to memories of Lisa as I watched. But not just the good memories, all the memories. And, for some reason, all the fights and disagreements we had now seemed so picayune and petty.

About a half-hour later, the blue firefly was joined by several green ones. The greens didn't get very close to the blue one, and the blue one seemed to know to keep it's distance. A pang of sympathy welled in my throat as it flew off.

I awoke on the front porch at dawn, the east side of the cabin. There was a mist hanging just above the ground and glistening rays of sun that peered through the clouds and trees. I needed to decide what to do now that she was gone.

The firefly from the night before stayed in my mind. Something told me it was more than just a freak of nature. What, exactly, I had no idea. I rose from the wicker couch and went inside. It was time to go start my life over.

*   *   *

After dropping off Michelle in Twenty-Nine Palms, I drove back to Los Angeles to an empty house. It felt different when I walked through the front door. Almost as if I didn't belong there. I guess in a way I didn't any longer. This had been our home, for better or for worse. Maybe because it turned out for the worse that it didn't feel right anymore. I threw the keys on the end table and went to the bedroom.

I removed all of her clothes from the closet and dresser and stuffed them all into boxes, then took the boxes to the garage. I went back to the living room and gathered all the nic-nacs she had collected over the years and boxed those up, too. I continued throughout the house, packing up all that had been hers. By the time I was done the garage was half-full of boxes full of her things. It was late and when I turned from the garage after locking up, I saw the blue firefly. It was near the door, off to the side by the hedge.

I'm certain it was the same firefly I saw at the cabin. There couldn't be two of them. It stayed by the garage as I walked to the house, crisscrossing in front of the door as if the boxes inside the garage meant something to it. I took one last look at the bug, then went inside.

I made a sandwich in the kitchen, took it to the recliner and turned on the television. After flipping through the channels while I ate, I settled on the Weather Channel. I fell asleep in the recliner, all the lights in the house and the television on, wondering about the blue firefly and why it followed me home, my mind drifting to Lisa as I dozed off.

I woke the next morning and started going through the desk drawers. In a folder of hers marked, "Recipes", I found life insurance papers that she had taken out shortly before we were married. This she had kept up with and it was paid up to date. I nearly fainted when I saw the amount she had taken it out for - a quarter of a million dollars. I put the papers down and just sat, my mind blank when I saw that I was the beneficiary. I was stunned. She had kept this a secret all those years. But why? Did she know something back then?

It was then that I decided what I was going to do. I was going to sell the house. With the proceeds from that and the insurance money, I would pay off all of the bills, find a place in the country, and try to make a living selling photos. Even if I didn't sell any pictures, I could still live comfortably for sometime.

Chapter III

I moved to the high desert shortly after Lisa's death. I found some land about twenty miles north of a little town called Bagdad in Arizona. Forty miles west of Prescott, one hundred miles southwest of Flagstaff, one hundred miles northwest of Phoenix, it was out in the middle of nowhere, a little over six thousand feet above sea level in the Aquarius mountain range.

I was independent, cut off from the "grid". My electricity came from an array of twelve solar panels and a two-kilowatt windmill. Excess was stored in two banks of twenty-four batteries.

I grew most of the food I ate and my well supplied nearly all of my water. There was also a creek three miles to the west. All organic waste material was dumped into a composting bin from which I acquired fertilizer for the garden and methane gas for cooking and heating, including an inline water heater. Cold storage was a cellar below ground; twenty feet down to its ceiling to mantain the proper temperature. A simple life. What I wanted. What I desired.

My home is built from the soil excavated to put the first floor five feet down and the cellar twenty. I extracted the clay and put it in long sandbags to make the structure, stacking the bags one atop the other to form an arch. I built one main dome with four arched vaults, like a four-pointed star, with the eastern vault connecting to another dome that is my bedroom. There is also an utility dome that houses the batteries and convertor for the house current, accessed by a narrow vault off the north arch.

The land around my home was open, a mountain range fifty miles to the north, lying in the shadow of Mount Hope. The landscape rugged to the south, eventually sloping to the Sea of Cortez three hundred miles away. To both east and west were rolling hills of sand and cacti.

My closest neighbor was eleven miles away, and I never knew their name. The town of Bagdad was a day away on horseback. Grocery shopping took me two days. But that was fine. It became an excursion, an adventure. I rarely used the jeep I picked up anymore.

Other excursions I took lasted for weeks at a time. I'd pack an extra horse, take my two dogs and go. I had a thousand acres, one and half square miles. Only one side was bordered by unsold property, the short side. The rest belonged to the government; the backside of a national forest. That's where I did most of my exploring. I would set up camp on my property, then take a day junket into the park.

While on my excursions, I would take my pictures, and

simply enjoy the surroundings and life itself. The pictures I sold as calendars, postcards, posters & T-shirts. Thusly, I made my living. My pictures sold worldwide and my internet business was picking up. My land was paid for, I had no debts other than annual taxes, and enough in savings to retire. Which, at the age of thirty-six, is pretty much what I was. I had been lucky, in some ways.

Even though I moved to the desert to escape from it all, I still used technology in my simple life. A special solar panel powered my laptop computer, the panels for the household were state-of-the-art. I used a satellite phone to connect to the Internet. A computer ran the electronics inside my utility dome, keeping the voltage and current at the proper levels in the batteries. I had a computer connected to my telescope (I also took pictures of the heavens). I had a hundred disc CD player, with its own dedicated solar panel and battery. And a transistor radio. The battery recharger is also solar powered. But there's no television. I do, however, have a DVD player. I like movies.

It was the solitude, the isolation, the silence that drew me to the high desert, not some apocolyptic prophecy. And, like I stated earlier, it was after my wife died. I wouldn't be here now if she hadn't passed away.

Following me to Arizona was that blue firefly. I saw it the first night I stayed, and then off and on as I built my house. I didn't see it often. Sometimes one week would pass, other times five or six. It showed up when I brought the horses home. It was there the night I finished my house. It was there on the anniversary of my late wife's birthday. It was there when two stray dogs showed up that I adopted. It would show periodically, often coinciding with a date involving Lisa. It kinda spooked me, though, and caused some mild concern. Was I the only one seeing the blue firefly?

For three years I experienced the storms and mild earthquakes before it happened. Nobody seemed to know what was coming. The global shift in weather patterns, the stronger and more frequent storms, the stronger and more frequent earthquakes, nobody correctly put the pieces together.

I had stopped smoking two years before what happened, happened. I didn't know what it was at the time, but the night it happened I'll never forget. I remember wanting a cigarette really bad the next morning.

Chapter IV

It was late, just into the wee hours. The air was cool, in the lower sixties, and the sky was clear. The stars, as usual, were spectacular. The Moon wouldn't rise until just before dawn. The news over the last few days were warning of an intense storm and I wanted to be ready. The harvest from my garden was due to start in a week and I had done what I could to protect everything. I had just come up from the cellar, checking on provisions, and that blue firefly darted in front of me. Then the wind picked up.

Before heading to the cellar I had started a fire in the firepit outside and it now cast quick shadows that strobed the horses panic prancing. The dogs cowered and hung on my heels. Then there was a jolt.

It came up through my feet and nearly snapped my head off. Then I was on the ground, pinned with my dogs by a trembling that undulated through the Earth. In the dance of the fire I saw the wooden tool shed fall in on itself. Cacti and small trees danced a shimmy, many until they snapped in half. Small boulders and large rocks slid and bounced. I saw my horses stumble and forced to the ground. My dogs whined and yelped like frightened pups, still frozen at my feet. Myself, I was unable to move as I witnessed the terror unfolding. Then the moon raced across the sky at an ungodly speed, the wind kicked up, and all Hell broke loose. I swear I heard demons laughing.

The trembling seemed to last forever, but only until dawn. During those endless hours I heard terrible crashes and thunderous cracks. Lightning split a cloudless sky that quickly filled with choking dust and silt. The lightning pierced the dust with dull cracks, illuminating the low ceiling and all below it. I saw great movement in those brief moments of flash. Great movement of the land itself. Solid desert floor rolling like an ocean swell. I naturally disbelieved what I saw, instead blaming the illusion on the brevity of the light and the ground vibrating beneath me. An optical illusion I concluded.

I was pinned to the ground by the vibration that had followed the trembling. It made my entire body numb. Several times I believed I was going to die; the vibration seemingly to stop my heart, then jerk starting it a moment later. The intensity of the vibration gradually decreased, and my heart pounded without interruption, but the grip of the vibration over the rest of my body was unrelenting.

The new dawn rose as I lay motionless. The sun came up further north than I've ever seen. The mountains to the north are taller, piercing the sky with a new profile. What the hell had happened?

Before I could stand my horses got to their feet and bolted out of the broken corral. I checked my home. Only one vault was undamaged. The main dome and two others were heavily cracked, the dome also had a gaping hole in the side. One vault, the kitchen, lay in rubble.

The land around me was disarrayed. Broken plants littered the desert floor as far as I could see. In the distance I could see movement. I stared in disbelief as it seemed to head towards me. I glanced around for a weapon, knowing that at the least, I would have to dig out my guns. The dogs started to bark at the horizon. Whatever was out there was upwind. I would know before them. Minutes later, after an unbearable amount of time fidgeting and fretting, the movement became recognizable - it was my horses.

As I headed towards them, I righted my sundial. At noon I would have to remember to set it. As I went about cleaning up and salvaging what there was, I recalled the newscast I had watched the day before.

It was internet via satellite link. They were wishing everyone the best of luck at their location. The coming storm was going to be global in nature, something to do with solar flares they tried to explain, but it was obvious that either they didn't know what was going on, or simply weren't telling us because it was going to be extremely bad.

They thanked everyone for staying calm. The few incidents of large scale rioting had been quelled. Relief areas were scrolling across the bottom of the screen. If you survived and could get to a relief area, there would be food, water, blankets, clothes - items for survival. That, of course, if the relief area survives.

Then the President came on.

"My fellow Americans and people of the world. I encourage everyone to stay calm and stay indoors until the storm passes. Government scientists have assured me that this is not, I repeat, this is not due to global warming. It is being caused by unprecedented and massive solar flares the scientific community has never before witnessed.

"There are relief areas setup around the country for those who may need assistance after the storm subsides. We firmly believe that many will not need assistance, and that we will all come through this with only minor damage and inconvenience.

"As all you of know, I am a deeply religious man. Why God has chosen to do this is beyond our comprehension. But God is merciful and works in mysterious ways. And I, leader of the free world, do not question him. I will be praying for all of us.

"Thank you and bless you all."

Merciful? Then why he is doing this?

I haven't heard anything since. I haven't been able to connect to the 'Net, nor make a phone call: satellite, cell, or two-way radio. Nothing is working. It seems that every piece of electriacl iquipment I have is toast, useless. The jeep won't even click.

*　　　*　　　*

After cleaning up and around my house, I took a look at the garden. Most of the plants were unsalvageable. The ground had shook so hard that the roots were pulverized.

Nearly all of the carrots and potatoes were mush. The peas and beans faired better off, but the amount of destruction left me concerned how I was going to eat in the not too distant future.

Next I checked my well. The water was muddy, full of sentiment, and had a foul smell. I would not even be able to strain it to clean it. And there was no way to discern how long before it cleared up.

I grabbed my hat and hiked to the stream, both dogs following along.

The topography to the stream had changed. Plants and trees were broken and laying on the ground everywhere. There was a new hill and huge rocks had fallen from cliffs. I was amazed at the force that had done this, and just as amazed at what had fallen and what still stood.

An hour later I was at the stream. It was in worse condition than the well. I wouldn't be able to retrieve water from it neither. We returned home. I would need to figure out a way to survive the coming weeks.

Chapter V

In the days since whatever happened, happened, the Animal Kingdom has gone through a shift in hierarchy. I watched a flock of pigeons attack and kill a rabbit two weeks ago. A large herd of rats chased down and killed a coyote in my presence yesterday.

Ticks were an annoyance before it happened. Now they're fatal. They've become predatory, fearless, vicious, innumberable, and they hunt in packs, or should I say armies. Huge swarms of millions, blanketing the ground like a creeping black shadow. I've seen the shadow cover an acre. Any warm-blooded creature they find sleeping or slow is dead within hours. My oldest dog fell victim early one morning. She went peacefully. In the world before now, she would have been spoiled until she died. In this one, she became tick fodder.

I have seen two humans dead by such means as I've explored the area around my home. Who these two were I had no idea. Perhaps one a neighbor, perhaps travelers. Each a horrible site.

The first one was about three miles northeast from my home. It was shriveled and gaunt, a mummified appearance. It was all that was left after the ticks were done. The blood was gone from the body. It looked dry, powdery. There wasn't a tick to be seen, though. But the ground around the corpse looked as if it had been raked with a hair brush.

The blood gorged ticks were still attached to the second one. This one seven miles south of my home. I think he or she was my neighbor from that direction. There was a younger couple living about ten miles due south of me, and they had a toddler. He was Highway Patrol, she was a freelance writer for women's magazines.

Covering the person lying on the ground were the swollen, gorged bodies of the ticks, pulsating in unison with the fading heartbeat of their host. They were as big as pinto beans or bigger, their color a greenish-grey. A grotesque raisin.

All I could do was watch, mesmerized by the death scene playing before me. There were so many of the nasty little things that I could not see the dying soul beneath. I could not tell if it was a he or a she. But I could hear the moans, and an eternity later, the final sigh.

When the pulsing stopped, I covered the body with dry brush and set it aflame. I added more brush as it burned and listened to the bloated ticks pop and hiss with boiling blood until there were no more pops, no more movement. Then I moved on.

I went the few more miles to my neighbor's home and found the father and child, buried in the rubble that was once their house. The animals had been there and had eaten what they could reach. The father's right arm, the watch still ticking away on his wrist, was all that was left to identify him. The toddler was easier to discern because of the size. There was little left of the child. I scared away the rabbits chewing on the childs remains. I didn't find the wife. I assume it was her I found earlier. I buried the remains in one grave.

As I placed rocks over the grave it struck me; when did rabbits become carnivorous?

When I returned home that day, I didn't have an appetite. I kept my dog close and a fire by the horses burning all night.

As I watched the fire, I wondered why I survived, and how many others did. I stayed awake most of the night and watched the heavens.

The Moon looks to be in a new orbit now, further south in the sky. You can see her size change almost hourly. She rotates faster so you can see all her fascinating faces. The stars are different, too. The constellations are skewed, tilted.

I wondered what else had changed, about my brother in Nebraska, about the few people I knew and cared about.

It wouldn't be too much longer and I would find out.

Chapter VI

It's been thirty-one days since whatever happened, happened, and I'm packed and ready to go. Just where I'm going, I'm not sure. South, I guess. In search of others and food. Maybe even a new place to call home.

Also, I've got this urge to see the ocean again. It is over two hundred miles to the Gulf of California; I estimate ten days to get there. The town of Bagdad would be my first stop. But I was concerned; after all this time, anything electronic worked. And, silly as this may sound, I have not seen the blue firefly since that night of chaos.

I've packed up two horses with food, some clothes, a rifle, revolver, and ammunition, then let the other two horses go. The rifle was a Marine M40, an Remington 700 sniper rifle with a 3-9x40mm scope. My pistol was a revolver, a Colt Python .357 with a six-inch barrel made in nineteen-fifty-eight. I had been thinking about this for over a week, decided yesterday to go. Spent most of the night getting things ready and packed. Went to sleep after three and awoke an hour after dawn. The horses are tied up out front, the dog laying in the shade, waiting.

It is going to be difficult leaving here, even if it is just for an excursion. With things the way they are now, the chances of getting back are slim. I doubt there will be any convenience stores to stop and pick up a snack. The wild has returned to nature. But, I don't have much of a choice. My well is still filthy and the stream hasn't cleared at all. Perhaps by the time I return one or both will be useable, but I need to find water soon.

With the revolver on my hip and the rifle on the horse, I set out. I checked the sundial as I rode by: eight in the morning. The town of Bagdad was my goal by night fall.

*   *   *

I reached Bagdad just after sunset, the loom of the sun still shining over the horizon. I almost turned around and went home. The town was demolished. Not a building stood. Telephone poles were laying on the ground, the stumps looking like fence posts placed too far apart. Cars and pickup trucks were either crushed beneath a building, crashed into one, or simply parked, one or more door open, covered in dust. All sorts of trash was blowing around: paper, cups, plastic bags, a lot of plastic bags. Grass and weeds had grown between the cracks in the pavement; sidewalks and streets. Nature was reclaiming what Man had taken away.

I sat there on my horse silent, listening for anything,

anyone. After a few moments of staring at the destruction, I hollered out for anybody. Silence. I yelled again. More silence. Bagdad, population five thousand three hundred and four, was a ghost town.

I found shelter in a corner in the ruins of the bank and made camp. Then I searched out the auto parts store and grabbed all the motor oil cans I could carry. I returned to camp and poured a ring around it, hoping to keep the marauding ticks at bay. Throughout the night I heard rustling and animal feet as they scurried about the ruined town. That eased my mind a bit on the ticks and I fell asleep with my dog at my side.

At dawn I searched the town. I didn't have any hopes of finding anyone, but I wanted to salvage what I could: canned goods, bottled water, anything useable. As I wandered the streets, sifting through rubble, I found corpses everywhere. Nearly every demolished building I searched had at least one body in it somewhere. The stench of death led me to the remains. It didn't take long before I avoided the smell.

I found quite a few canned goods in the towns main grocery store, more than I could carry. Most of the water jugs were busted, though. I only found three gallons. I stashed what I couldn't take with me in the open bank vault, filled my canteens and put the last gallon of water in with the canned goods.

After breaking camp I continued south. Figuring in my head as I rode, the next town I would come across was two days away, Yuma another five, the Gulf of California seven. The destruction was just as massive the further south I went; trees snapped close to the ground, rocks and boulders scattered everywhere, hills and mountains I knew to be there gone, others anew. My map was almost useless, and using the sun for navigation was tricky. It's path through the sky had changed. I didn't understand it. What the hell had happened?

By noon I was smelling ocean air. Something wasn't right. There was no way I could smell the ocean this far away. Was the destruction and rearranging more severe than I had so far witnessed? And, although I have not seen anyone else alive, which in this neck of the woods wasn't really surprising, the scene back in Bagdad wasn't giving me much hope. I wondered just how alone I was as I proceeded toward the ever stronger smell of ocean air.

I made camp that night just south of the Arrastra mountain range, near Ives Peak. As I heated some canned vegetables, I stared at the mountains. Nearly all of them were peakless, like they were cut off by some massive chainsaw. It was quite unnerving. The force, the power that removes mountain peaks, whole mountain ranges entirely, left me alive. And so far, totally alone.

The devastion was making the going slower than I had anticipated. I probably wasn't going to make Interstate Ten tomorrow, but the day after. Yuma was probably a week further on, the ocean a good ten days more. I poked the fire and went to sleep.

*   *   *

On the second day after leaving Ives Peak I crossed Highway Sixty early in the morning, the small town of Aguila just as devastated as Bagdad. There was nothing to salvage. Everything was ruined. And still I hadn't seen another person.

It was now midmorning and the sight before me had me awestruck. I was at the edge of a precipice and some sixty feet below was what had to be the ocean. The waves were breaking at regular intervals, bigger and more severe than I remembered them to be. If this was truly the ocean, then the upheaval was a lot worse than I had seen so far.

I had not even reached Interstate Ten. Everything south of here, well, what use to be south, had to be gone. Yuma had to be gone. I wondered if California finally slid into the ocean, too. I wondered how much of southern Arizona was gone. Nogales? Tucson? Casa Grande? Phoenix? How much was gone? How much was left?

Isn't wasn't quite noon, but my desire to do anything, let alone go on was gone. I moved away from the edge and found a campsite. I could hear the breakers below, smell the salty sea air. I was going to have to think. What was my next move?

This was all too much to comprehend. What the hell could have happened that half a state would fall into the ocean? Wait. What happened to Baja California? Mexico?

Should I make that my quest? Search the continent? It was already obvious that the planet had tilted. The track of the sun and stars confirmed that, but what else had occured? Was this the apcolypse? The Rapture?

I don't believe in organized religion, so if it was the Rapture, naturally, I would be left behind. But I don't remember the Rapture story including mass, global destruction. And where the hell was anyone else?

I began to wonder if I was the last person on Earth. Then a bit of rationality struck. The country was pretty big. The planet was pretty big. There were other continents. Surely not everyone had perished. But I have been traveling nearly three days and had not seen another living person. Anybody south of me was surely gone, but what of elsewhere? I didn't leave my home until a month after that night. No one had wandered by. No government authority, state or federal, came looking for survivors. And nothing on the airwaves. I never felt so alone in my life, not even after my wife died.

Then a bizarre thought filtered through my mind; if my wife hadn't died we would have been in Los Angeles when this happened, and both of us would probably have died in the holocaust. So, why was I spared?

I became apprehensive, and more than just a little scared. I was going to have to be careful. I couldn't risk getting hurt. And I would need to be extremely cautious if and when I came across another human. I already knew that past conceptions of the animal kingdom no longer applied: carnivorous herbivores, pigeons that hunted in packs, and marauding legions of ticks.

With a fire going and supper simmering, I relaxed against the saddle and petted my dog. Night fall was several hours away and I was contemplating on which way to go next when my dog perked her head up, ears straight, nose quivering as she sniffed the air. I sat up and scanned the area. I couldn't see anything, no movement, no silhouettes of man nor beast.

Then my dog jumped up, her hair bristling, her muzzle snarling. I stood, revolver at the ready, and strained to see what had her riled up. Still, I didn't see any movement. The land was pretty sparse of vegetation and anything moving could be easily seen. I was about ready to scold her for getting us both worked up when I saw it. Movement on the ground, like a cloud's shadow, but the sky was clear. I gazed at it for a moment longer before I realized what it was - ticks.

I didn't have any more motor oil and the horde was heading right for me. I watched them for a moment, judging their speed. After a few seconds I realized I had plenty of time to break camp, pack everything up, and just move out of their way; and that is exactly what I did.

But the predicament was not going to go away that easily. The tick mass just simply turned toward my scent and followed. I headed eastward, along the cliff's edge. I wasn't sure where I was going and was trying to come up with an idea to keep the ticks away. The sun was setting behind me, too quickly now it seemed. I needed to find a safe haven so I could eat and rest.

An hour later I came across a junkyard, the cliff several hundred yards south. A final resting place for unwanted and worn out automobiles. Smashed specimens everywhere, once stacked, they had fallen over during that night. Row after row of smashed cars, piles of engines and transmissions. Scattered about were relics resting on flat tires. I was nearly past it when it dawned on me that I might find enough oil in the engines to encircle myself and my animals. I quickly scouted the area, then started the hunt for motor oil and something to put it in.

I was under car number three, about a gallon and a half of oil recovered, when my dog started barking and growling. It couldn't be the ticks, they don't move that fast. By the time I got out from underneath the car the threat was close. I stood to see a small group of people heading right for me. I counted five, three adults and two children. They were too far away to discern more than that, but I could tell each were carrying a rifle.

I moved towards the horses when a shot rang out. My pack horse stumbled, then fell to the ground. Instantly I was running, calling my dog to follow, cursing the strangers. I jumped into the saddle of my horse and kicked my heels. Another shot was fired and I heard the bullet whiz by like a metal mosquito. I leaned on the mane and took the first corner around the rusting cars.

When I knew I was out of their view, momentarily safe, I drew the rifle from the sheath and turned to circle back. There might not be very many of us left, but if they were going to start shooting for no reason, I was going to make five less of us before I left the area.

Slowing my horse, I dismounted as she trotted and gave her a pat so she would go on, my dog on the horses hoofs. Then I squeezed between the cars, headed for the strangers. A few yards into the maze I heard their voices. They were at the carcass of my pack horse, going through my supplies.

A few more yards and I could see them, all of them hunched over the dead horse, going through everything. I leveled my rifle at them, then hesitated. All they were after was food and water. I almost turned and left, but didn't. They were willing to kill me for what I had, without even asking if I would share. I wondered for a moment if they use to be business men, then shot the closest one. The others stood in shock for moment, then scattered into the labyrinth of cars. I shot one more before he or she disappeared behind a pickup truck, flipping the poor soul forward. The hunt was on. One adult and two adolescents left. I retreated into hunks of metal and started making my way towards them.

Moments later a bullet broke a car window by my head. "Damn!" I rolled on the ground and peeked over the hood of a Toyota. Somewhere in front of me was one of them. I stayed motionless, waiting for movement. What seemed an eternity later, but only a minute or two, I saw the silhouette of a head through the windows of small Chevy.

Squat walking, I moved in anticipation and waited. Not a moment later I had my opportunity as the stranger darted between cars. I fired and spun the teen around. A thunk and a thud told me my shot was good. I waited a moment longer. No movement, no sound. Two to go.

My heart was pounding. Adrenaline surging through my veins. This was not how I wanted to make first contact with my fellow man. It was too remniscent of the past. I decided to capture at least one of the two left. I had to know why they just attacked me. I had to know if there were more people, more like them.

The sun was getting close to the horizon. There was maybe an hour, ninety minutes of daylight left. I had to end this quickly.

Moving through the maze of junk cars I kept vigil, listening, watching for movement. Then I heard it, a wail of "No-o-o-o-o". It was female. Young. She had found one that I had shot. But which one? From the direction of the sobbing it had to be the teen by the Chevy. I turned back and crept close.

Taking aim at the back of the head of the young woman, I was putting pressure on the trigger when the last adult approached her. I was close enough to hear them talking.

"What the hell are you doing screaming like that? He's

going to know where you are."

"I don't care. Austin's dead."

"He was stupid."

"Yeah, just like you and your two friends are stupid. And Austin wasn't stupid. He was just a boy. He doesn't know anything about fighting."

"Don't call Jack and Billy John stupid."

"They are. Were. If Billy John hadn't shot that guy's horse they would all be alive. We could have asked for help. Asked if he would share what he had. But no, your stupid frien..."

I heard a smack. Skin against skin. I moved so I could get a better aim on the adult.

"Shut up, I said. Don't call them stupid."

The young woman remained silent.

"Get up. We've got to find this guy and kill 'im."

"You...you go ahead. I'm staying here with my baby brother. I'm going to bury him."

"Get up!"

I pulled the trigger. The man's head exploded and he dropped a moment later. The young woman screamed in terror.

I slowly rose, unsure of what she might do. I waited, impatiently, but I waited.

She screamed for a little while, then finally called out, "Don't shoot."

"Throw the guns in the clear."

A moment later, "Where's clear?"

I put a round into a patch of dirt to her left. A few seconds later two pistols skidded to a stop, followed by three rifles, one right after the other. "Okay, now stand up."

She started to rise.

"Hands above your head."

She put her hands on her head.

"You there. Young lady. I don't want to hurt you. I'm sorry about your brother."

She hitched her breath, choking back sobs. "Why'd you shoot him?" she hollered at me.

"Self-preservation," I said as I walked towards her. "I thought he was going to kill me."

"We didn't want to hurt anyone, you asshole. It was them. Those stupid hicks."

"And I was suppose to know that, how?" I was a few feet behind her. She stood beside the body of her brother, her back to me. Her brown hair was tied into a ponytail, reaching to the middle of her back. She was slender, a light blue shirt too big for her and tight black jeans. Tennis shoes, the white canvas kind on her feet. She couldn't be more the sixteen.

When she turned her head to yell at me she jumped, startled that I was right there. She fell over her brother. "Don't hurt me, mister. Don't hurt me."

"I have no intention of hurting you. I heard you two talking." I looked over at the man with no face. "Who were they?"

"That's Cody. Jack and Billy John are back by your horse. And I don't know who they are. Just some dumb hicks that found me and Austin after the Night of Shaking.

"Our parents died when our house collapsed. Austin and me were wandering the desert by ourselves for three days before they found us. We didn't have a choice but to go with them. We didn't know what else to do."

"What's your name?" I asked.

She looked at me defiantly. "What's yours?" she demanded.

"Forrest Woods. I'm a photographer. Well, use to be one, anyway."

"Forrest Woods? Hmph. You parents didn't like you, did they?"

"I was named after an old television star my mother liked."

"Oh." She was a head shorter than me, plain looking but pleasing to look at. "My name's Roberta. Roberta St Michael. Most people call me Berta."

"I'm really sorry about your brother, Berta. If I had known, I...I"

She looked to her brother. "I...I know. But to tell you the truth, I was getting scared of him. He liked those hick assholes. He even..."

I waited. Something was bothering her. Something painful. I wanted to prod, but didn't. I would wait.

"Nevermind." She looked at me. "Will you help me bury him. I don't want the animals eating him."

"Sure. There's a shovel on my pack horse."

Chapter VII

"How old was he?" I asked as we dug in the sand. The was sun was getting low in the sky, laying long shadows across the junkyard. I was getting concerned about the ticks, and the other creatures of the night. We would need to finish soon and get a fire started. Then I would need to finish collecting motor oil.

"Fifteen," she stated. "Two years younger than me."

I paused. "You're seventeen?" My tone was incredulous, but it just came out.

"Yes," she said defiantly. "My birthday was last month. Two days after the Night of Shaking. What a birthday present. My parents dead. Our home destroyed. And the rest of the world," she looked around, as if taken it in for the first time. "It's just ruined."

"Uh, happy birthday."

"Yeah. Thanks."

Ten minutes later I threw the last shovel of sand on the grave. Berta had found a four-way tire iron and stuck it in the sand at one end. It made a passable cross.

"What about the others?"

I looked over her head to the bodies of the three men I had killed earlier. It was funny, I felt no remorse. Austin caused a bit of guilt, but for the others, nothing. "I'll drag 'em further away and nature can do with them what she pleases." I turned back to Berta. "Want to say something over your brother?"

She paused, looking at his grave. She wiped some hair from her face. "Rest in peace, you little shit."

"Uh, amen." Something was going on. She almost told me earlier, but didn't. Now she calls him a little shit at his grave. I was getting curious. Then a coyote howled. It was miles away, but we had to get a fire started. Plus, I was hungry.

During the brief battle I had seen a pile of scrap wood. I pointed to some cars to my left. "Over there you'll find some wood." I pointed to some more rows of fallen cars that made something like a box canyon. "Start taking it over there. That's where we'll setup camp. I'm going to get some more oil, move the bodies further out, find my horse and dog, and retrieve the stuff from the pack horse.

"Get a fire going." I handed her a butane lighter, then set off into the growing darkness.

When I returned, with the horse Berta had a raging fire going. I didn't find my dog. I hope she was all right, but couldn't look for her, or dwell on her fate. She was an animal and could take care of herself. I told myself that she would be better off on her own, maybe even join up with a pack of dogs.

45

Berta had a small knapsack beside her when I returned. She must have retrieved it while gathering the wood. I was a little curious to what was inside, but didn't bother with it. I tied the horse inside the box canyon of smashed cars, then dumped the gear from the pack horse close to the fire. I went back out and grabbed the containers of oil: milk jugs, gas cans, and a five gallon jerry can. I poured out a perimeter that encompassed the horse and most of the campsite. We would be safe tonight, at least from the ticks.

Berta had several cans warming by the fire by the time I finished pouring the border against the ticks. It was starting to smell good. She was warming a can of peas, one of beets, and one of stew. As she stirred each can consecutively, I watched her, wondering why she wasn't more upset over the loss of her brother, and why she was so trusting of me.

"You gonna miss your brother?" I knew it was blunt, but something wasn't right. I had to know what was going on. I didn't want her taking revenge in the middle of the night while I slept.

She stopped fussing with the cans and sat back. She stared at the fire. "The morning after, after we found our parents, I knew I had to take care of Austin. Protect him, ya' know. We were scared. Scared we were going to die without help. But those three days before, before those hick boys found us, we were starting to make a go of things.

"Austin was listening to me. We were helping each other, supporting each other. I was beginning to believe that we would be okay. Alone, but okay. Then Cody and his friends showed up." She went silent, her eyes growing blank. "They fed us, gave us water, made us feel secure, then they raped me after Austin fell asleep. They raped me every night. By the second week with them, Austin was raping me, too." She put her face in her hands and bawled. Loud, body shaking sobs that left me helpless.

I had no idea what to do. I wanted to hold her, tell her that she was safe with me, that I wouldn't hurt her. But I didn't. I felt she would reject me. Shun away from being touched. I just sat there and watched her cry.

When her sobbing eased, I spoke. Stupid words, but I didn't know what else to say. "I'm sorry they hurt you."

"They turned my own brother against me!" she screamed. "Those fucking animals turned my brother against me."

I stood and walked over to her. I expected her to jump away, but she didn't. I squatted and put an arm around her shoulders. She nearly leaped into my arms. I put a leg out to catch us both from tumbling over, then held her close while she cried some more. I felt awkward. Confused. Like when I held my wife while she cried from the pain and depression.

Then I saw it. The blue firefly, blinking at the mouth of the box canyon of smashed cars. I wanted to show Berta, to see if she saw it too, but I let her cry, watching the blue firefly until it flew past the entrance.

Moments later Berta dried her eyes, wiped her nose on her sleeve, then spooned out the contents of the cans into hubcaps she had cleaned earlier. We ate in silence, me keeping an eye at the entrance. I was watching for danger, and that blue firefly.

I threw some wood on the fire after we ate, poked it like I knew what I was doing, then settled back against some tires. I was spent. Dinner was satisfying and I was full. I looked over at Berta. She was watching the fire. She caught my gaze and looked at me.

"We gonna be safe?"

"As safe as we can get. You wanna stand watches?"

"Do you think we should?"

I shrugged. We probably should, but I had been alone until now, with no one standing watch. "It would probably be a good idea. You want first watch?"

She nodded. I suddenly had a feeling of foreboding. Was she planning on killing me while I slept? Perhaps just stealing everything and taking off. "Wake me in a few hours."

She nodded again.

I laid my head back and closed my eyes. Sleep overcame me quickly.

*   *   *

I was being gently shook awake. "It's your turn, Mr. Woods."

"Hunh. Wha...oh, yeah. Right." Well, she didn't leave while I slept, nor did she kill me. "And call me Forrest."

"You want some coffe?"

Coffee? I didn't have any coffee. "Where'd you get coffee?"

"Had it."

The knapsack. "Love some. Thanks."

She poured a cup and handed it to me. She looked exhausted. She had also been crying again. "I want to thank you, Mister, uh, Forrest, for rescuing me."

Rescue? I never thought of it that way. "Uh, yeah. Sure. I'm really sorry about your brother."

She looked to the ground. "I want to forget about him. I want to remember him as the little annoyance he was before. Not the little son-of-a-bitch he became." She looked at me. "I don't want to talk about him anymore."

"Sure." I took a sip of the coffee. It was strong enough to make a trucker gag. "Good coffee. You get some sleep now."

She moved over to her blanket and slid underneath. "You gonna watch out for me, right?"

"Right."

"You're not going leave me, right?" The apprehension in her voice was blatant.

"No, I'm not going to leave you. I'll wake you at dawn."

"Forrest?"

"What?"

"What are we going to do now?"

I had no idea. That would give me something to think about while I watched the darkness. "You're going to get some sleep, and I'm going to stand watch."

"Tomorrow. What are we going to do tomorrow? And the day after? And the day after that?"

I stood up and looked down at the small, frightened girl. "I'll tell ya' in the morning. Now get some sleep."

I put on my holster, grabbed the rifle, and walked to the entrance of the car canyon. What the hell were we going to do?

Chapter VIII

As the sky slowly lightened, I lit a fire, then started to gather things up and pack them away. Berta lay sound asleep. She had several nightmares as she slept, thrashing and moaning as if she were fighting something, or someone. I felt bad for her. She had had it rough these past weeks. I hoped I could make it easier for her.

I made some coffee, and when the sun cleared the horizon, I woke Berta.

Breakfast was coffee and a some beef jerky. While Berta packed her knapsack, I loaded the horse. We would have to walk. The horse couldn't carry the supplies and us, neither one of us.

"Figure out what's next?" She had finished packing and stood behind as I lashed down the bedrolls.

"See how Phoenix faired. It's two or three days away. If it's still there."

"What's that suppose to mean?"

I stopped and turned to her. "That cliff over there wasn't there a month ago. It use to be land. Two hundred more miles of land before the Gulf of California. Now it's all ocean. We survived something that a lot of people didn't.

"What happened? I have no idea. But the world is tilted. The sun is in a different part of the sky, the stars are all wrong. Something really big happened. I have no idea what is left."

Her eyes grew wide. I could see terror in them. I hadn't meant to frighten her, but what was I suppose to tell her; that everything was okay, just a little screwed up?

"What are you saying?" Her voice trembled. I thought she was going to cry again.

"I'm saying that whatever killed your parents and moved the ocean three hundred miles closer fucked up the whole planet. I'm sure of it. Just how bad it is," I shrugged. I really didn't want to think about how bad it was. I just wanted to get going. See how Phoenix faired. See if there was more water, more food.

She looked to the ground. "I'm scared, Forrest."

"So am I, Berta. So am I." I put a hand on her shoulder. "You ready to start walking?"

She looked up at me, her green eyes searching for strength in mine. She nodded.

*   *   *

Late that afternoon we came across wreckage that had made a good sized hole in the ground. As we approached I thought it was a plane wreck. As we neared, it became clear it wasn't a plane.

"What is it?" Berta asked.

"I dunno. Plane, maybe." A few moments later we stood at the edge of the small crater. We had passed small pieces of burnt wreckage, small chunks of metal that looked as if they gone through a blast furnace, for about a mile. The closer to the crater, the chunks were bigger and more numerous. "Stay here," I told Berta, then made my way down into the depression.

This was no plane. The pieces and structure were all wrong. Maybe a satellite. Then I saw it, a helmet, the kind an astronaut would wear. I didn't remember the shuttle being in orbit. What else was up there that would be carrying people? Then it hit me; it was the space station. How many astronauts were onboard? Two, three, four? What a way to go, watching as the Earth neared and nothing they could do about it. I closed my eyes and shook my head, trying desperately to get rid of the image of them screaming into a microphone for help.

Had everything we sent up there come crashing down? Was there more waiting to come down?

"You okay, Forrest? What is it?"

I took a deep breath, then headed back up the crater wall. "Yeah, I'm okay. It was a satellite."

"It was big." She was observant.

"Some of them were pretty good size." I reached the top and turned back to the hole in the ground. Those poor saps. Burned to death on re-entry. I looked to the sky. Was there anything left up there spiraling its way down? "Let's get out of here and find someplace to make camp."

We made camp at an old mine at sunset. The buildings were like all the others we had come across, demolished as if in some massive earthquake. We found the entrance to the mine, but it was sealed. A cave in had filled the opening. It was useless for shelter. Camp would be a clearing, motor oil for a perimeter, and watches throughout the night.

As dinner simmered on the fire, Berta turned to me. "What happened, Forrest? What caused all this?"

I had no idea. I shrugged. "I durno. But something caused our planet to shift its poles. You can tell from the sun and the stars. What did it?" I shrugged again. "Maybe a comet or asteroid came close to us." I thought a moment. It would have to be pretty big to cause the planet to tilt its axis. "Maybe not. It would have to have been huge to effect Earth. They would have seen it coming. They would have warned us."

"Would they?"

I stared at her. Seventeen and mistrustful of the government. I could like her. "One would hope." They couldn't have kept something that big a secret. There was nothing about it anywhere. So, if not an asteroid passing close by, then what the hell did happen?

She stirred the contents of the cans on the fire. "How much further is Phoenix?"

"We should reach the outskirts tomorrow."

"What do you think we'll find?"

"Probably not a whole lot. If the damage is as wide spread as I think it is, we'll be lucky if we can find some more canned goods and water."

"You don't sound very hopeful."

"No. I suppose I don't. My wife use to call me a realist

and a cynic."

"You're wife?" She sounded dejected.

"She died of cancer about four years ago. That's when I moved to Arizona."

"I'm sorry."

"Thanks. But it was a long time ago now."

She stirred the cans, again. "Forrest?"

"Hmm."

"What's going to happen to us?"

"What do you mean?"

"If the world is as bad as you think it is, how are we going to survive?"

I hadn't thought about the future more than the next day since that night. Nor did I want to think about it. It was too frightening. Now I knew how the first pioneers must have felt as they headed west, unsure of what was around the next bend or over the next hill. The unknown before them and very little behind them. "I guess we'll just have to take it one day at a time. Like the frontiersmen of the Old West. An adventure."

"Yeah, right. An adventure for the rest of our lives."

She was right. If the devastation was worldwide, which I believed it to be, the rest of our lives would be one adventure after another.

"Where do you live, Forrest?" she asked as she handed me a can of stew.

"Up near Bagdad."

She looked at me dumbfounded. "Isn't that in Iraq?"

"Not that Baghdad. Bagdad, Arizona. It's spelled different. No 'H'. It's about forty miles west of Prescott."

"What are you doing here?"

I swallowed the bite I had just taken, using the few seconds to put my thoughts together. "I hung around my place for about a month. Waiting for my well and a nearby stream to clear up. When my water supply got low, it was either stay there and die of thirst, or go looking for water. I guess I just kept on going."

"You didn't live in Bagdad?"

"Hmm, no. I had a thousand acres all to myself. I was outside when it happened. It knocked me to the ground and held me there until morning. The things I saw in the sky though, I thought the world was coming to end.

"When dawn came and the world was still here and me still alive I wasn't sure what to do. I started checking my place out, then trying to reach someone. When I couldn't get a signal on my satellite phone, I tried the radio for news. But there was nothing. Nothing worked.

"I stayed around my place, figuring someone would eventually come by. State Patrol, National Guard, someone. So, like I said, when my water ran low, I headed out. I was heading to Yuma, then maybe the ocean. Found the ocean first."

"Then me."

*　　　　*　　　　*

As the sun was nearing its apex, we came across a small herd of rabbits feeding on the carcass of a horse. Berta nearly puked. I pulled my rifle from the sheath on the saddle and killed two before they scattered.

"Fresh meat for lunch," I told Berta.

She gave me a disgusted look. "I don't think I'm

hungry."

"I am."

"What would make them do that? I thought they only ate plants."

I shrugged. "I don't know. Everything's gone haywire since that night." I picked up the dead hares by their hind legs. "Rabbits eating flesh, pigeons hunting rats, rats hunting coyotes. Everything's crazy."

"You've seen rats hunting coyotes?"

"Uh-hunh. Near my place. There had to have been over a hundred rats attacking this lone coyote. I watched it for a little while, then put the coyote out of its misery. The rats didn't even jump when I shot the coyote. They just swarmed all over it."

"Ewww."

We made a fire and cooked the rabbits. The horse grazed on the sparse vegetation. We would need to find water soon.

Phoenix was several hours away, the ocean still on our right. I was beginning to wonder if Phoenix would even be there, perhaps having slid into the ocean, too. We were close enough that we should be able to see some of the taller buildings, but they weren't there. That didn't really surprise me, though. If whatever happened caused the ocean to move three hundred miles inland and remove mountaintops, leveling a city the size of Phoenix would be expected.

After eating, Berta kicked sand onto the fire while I packed up the horse.

*　　　*　　　*

Late that afternoon we were in Phoenix. I hate cities.
They stink of civilization. Even in ruins, the city stank. Worse,
no doubt, because of the dead.

Everything south of Glendale avenue was gone. It had
all slid into the ocean. Buildings were rubble in the streets.
Dogs, cats and rats ran through the rubble. Berta and I kept our
rifles at the ready. The horse nervously following our lead.

Here and there we found remains of the human
population. Decomposed bodies, bodies eaten by animals,
bodies rotting in smashed cars, mummified corpses the ticks
had reached. The place was a ghost town. There was no
evidence that anybody survived.

"Keep a lookout for a grocery store," I told Berta.
"Maybe we can find some food and water."

As we passed the next intersection, Berta said, "There.
Up that way."

I turned to where she was pointing. A couple of
buildings up was what looked to be a store front. We headed
that way.

It was a grocery store, all right. But there was nothing
left. The building that had stood beside it now lay inside the
store. We moved further up the street, hoping to find another
store.

"I can't believe everybodies gone," Berta said as we
passed another corpse.

"They're either dead, or they left. I wonder where they
went?"

"Who?"

"The survivors. Not everyone could have been killed."

"Why not?"

"There was too many people for all of them to have died that night." I stopped and looked around. The place was deserted. Buildings had fallen into other buildings. All of the wood framed houses had collapsed. If anyone had been trapped in the rubble, they were dead by now. It had been over a month since the Night of Shaking, as Berta called it. I walked over to a pile of debris and climbed atop it. "Hello!?" I yelled as loud as I could. "Is there anybody there!? Hello!?"

"Stop that," Berta demanded. "You wanna find more Cody's?"

She was right. I felt like an idiot. I didn't want to draw the wrong kind of attention. I climbed down from the pile of debris. "Sorry. I don't know what I was thinking."

"You weren't thinking." She looked around. "We probably should get away from here."

"Yeh. Let's get moving."

Three blocks up we turned right and saw a figure standing ahead of us, about two hundred yards away. We paused. I studied the figure. He didn't look like he was armed. In fact, he looked quite frail from this distance. Berta and I looked at each other. "You stay here. Keep me covered." I scanned the area. "Let me know if anyone else shows up." She nodded. I headed towards the figure.

I was twenty feet from him before he told me to stop. He was just a little man, about as tall as Berta. He had to be in his sixites, grey matted hair that touched his shoulders, a twisted beard that reached his bare chest. His camouflage shirt was in tatters, his blue jeans shredded below the knees, exposing skin covered bones for legs. His feet floated in oversize, new military boots.

He glared at me as we stood in the shattered street of the city. Rubble and remnants of buildings ran along either side of us, the center of the pavement nearly free of debris, the street behind him filled with fallen buildings. "Are you him?"

"Him, who?" I volleyed.

"The Messiah. Have you come to save me?"

I shocked him with my bellow of laughter. I didn't mean to, but it just burst out. I don't know where it came from. I excuse it to strain, stress, and getting caught off guard. I simply didn't expect him to say that.

He flinched and started to walk away. I stifled my outburst, shook my head to rattle things, then said, "No. I'm not your messiah."

The frail man stopped and turned. "Then who the fuck are ya'?!"

That's what I expected. "Names Forrest. Who are you?"

"It doesn't matter. Do you know why it happened?" he asked. He was glaring at me, daring me to know what he knew.

I shook my head.

"It happened because God was tired of the way we were treating his planet. He was ashamed of the way we were treating each other and our fellow creatures here. It's the Noah thing all over again." He looked around as if someone might be watching.

I shrugged. "That depends on your religious preference."

He glared at me for rebuking him. He looked around again, exposing his paranoia. "How many do ya' think are left?

A few hundred? A couple thousand? Ten? Just you and me?"

That was an awful thought, just him and I. But I knew better. Wait, couldn't he see Berta?

"And you know who caused God to be pissed at everybody? Caused most of the suffering and damage on this planet?"

I had no idea. Never even contemplated it. I didn't care. I wasn't religious. I shrugged.

"The white man! His civilization. His capitalism. His greed!" He stepped toward me and I backed away. "I'm beginning to think now that they're the devil," he said in a hushed voice.

I nearly laughed again. "Um, aren't you caucasion?"

Without pause he said, "No. I rejected the white man long before this happened. That's why I survived. I wasn't living in their sin." He stepped toward me, again. I backed away, again.

"The one their god warned about, was actually their god in deceit."

I stopped. "What?" Like I said, I wasn't religious, but I had read up on about all of the religions. Then it hit me; they always talked about watching for evil, because it can be so deceiving. The devil was suppose to be the 'Master Deceiver'. Wouldn't posing as a saviour deity be like painting a masterpiece?

"He's the Great Deceiver," the frail old man said.

"I can see your point." So, this would be like the masterpiece of conspiracy theories? "Have you seen Elvis, by the way?"

Then he drew a .45 from his back and pointed it at my

stomach.

"This close it'll go right through 'ya without killing 'ya right away. Give them coyot's something to listen to as they chew."

With reflexes I didn't know I had, I swatted the pistol out of his hand in a blink. It went off into the ground when it landed. I was on him by then, knees on his chest, pounding my fists into his face with the fury of revenge.

Some moments later I relented, bent over his bloodied face and caught my breath. Between my gasps I heard his gurgled breathing. He was still alive.

I thought about choking him, then caught movement to my left. I turned my head and saw a mass of ticks coming our way. I turned back to the old man and found several clips of ammunition in his pockets. I spit in his face, then crawled over to the pistol and picked it up. I looked at the old man lying on the ground once more. I pointed the pistol at his head. It was either this, or the ticks.

Then I remembered he was going to kill me just because. Revenge flung her mane again. I lowered the pistol. I kicked him in the ribs as I headed back to Berta. He moaned and gurgled profanity at me.

I calculated the time the ticks should arrive at the old man and turned around. They were almost on him. "Hey old man, ever been sucked to death?" I heard him gargle a scream as the first of millions crawled onto him.

"What the hell happened up there?" Berta asked when I reached her.

"Just some crazy old man that pulled a gun on me."
"Is he dead?"

I looked to where I left him for the ticks. He was just a black figure lying in the street. "He should be by now."

"What? What's that suppose to mean?"

My mind reeled. What was happening to me? Those four back at the junkyard. Now the old man. No remorse. No guilt. Where was my humanity? "I...I left him for the ticks."

"You did what? Forrest, how could you? What did you two you talk about? Why'd you leave him there to die?"

I gazed at her, not really looking at her. More like looking through her. I was at a loss. I couldn't explain my actions, to her, or myself. I shrugged. "Let's get moving." I started walking, back down the street, away from the old man and the ticks.

She just stood there. "Why'd you kill 'im?"

I stopped and slowly turned around, my eyes to the ground. "He pulled a gun." I pulled the old man's pistol from my back and showed her. "He was going to kill me. Why? I dunno. But he was crazy. Talking about how God did all this to punish the world for one race's sins. He was crazy. Death is the best thing that happened to him."

"I watched you pound on him. Was that the best thing for him, too? And you said you left him for the ticks. Is that the best thing for him?"

I wondered if she was really seventeen. I looked at her and her face softened a little. Could she see my dismay? "I...I don't know what came over me. After I knocked his gun away I...I just went beserk. And I know leaving him for the ticks wasn't the smartest thing to do. I should have just put a bullet in his head. But..." I left it at that. "You don't have to come with me, if you don't want to. I'll give you the horse and you can go your own way."

She stood there with blank look. After a moment she stuttered, "I don't want to be alone."

Chapter IX

We searched Phoenix until the sun slipped behind the horizon. We didn't find any food, any water, or anymore survivors. But as the sky darkened, we saw several campfires in close proximity to each other in the mountains east of Phoenix, not too far away. Maybe a couple hours walk.

"People," Berta proclaimed.

"Yeah, but what kind?"

We made our way to the campfires. As we ascended into the foothills, then the mountains, the damage to the area was less severe than down below. There were trees that had been snapped off near the ground, but there were more that only had the tops broke off. It was a welcome sight. The air cooled slightly as we climbed and the sounds of birds seemed to welcome us to the area.

We were both apprehensive as we neared the first campfire. Everything seemed to have gone haywire that Night of the Shaking. It seemed to have brought out the worst in people: Cody, Jack, Billy John, Austin, the old man, even me. Berta seemed unaffected, though. She was kind, wanting to help others, wanting to survive with dignity. I just wanted to survive.

We approached the first campfire with caution, trying to go undetected until we could discern their temperament. But that didn't work. They had posted sentries in the trees.

"Halt, or I'll shoot," came a young, male voice from above.

We stopped in our tracks. "We don't want any trouble," I called out.

"Over here," the voice yelled. "I've got two of them. They have a horse."

"Oh, shit," I whispered to Berta.

"Play it cool, Forrest. We don't know what the want. They might be as scared as we are."

Moments later we were surrounded. Men, women and teens. All with guns. We all just stood there, silent for several minutes.

"We're just looking for some food and water," I finally said to the crowd.

"Who are you?" came the reply, baritone and forceful.

"My name's Forrest Woods. This is Rober..."

"What are you doing here?" the same voice demanded.

"We need some food and water. We're starting to run low and didn't find either in Phoenix."

The speaker stepped forward, sihouetted against the fire burning behind him. He was bigger than me, by height and weight. He carried an automatic weapon. He had on a heavy jacket and a full brimmed hat. He eyed me up and down, then looked at Berta, then back to me. "That your daughter?"

I almost laughed. "No. I found her a few days ago."

"Found? What kind of idiot do you think I am." He turned to Berta. "Has he hurt you? Has he molested you?"

Berta did laugh. "No. He rescued me from some men who did, though. He's been," she looked at me, "quite the gentleman."

"I don't appreciate being laughed at, young lady."

"Then don't say funny things," she quipped.

"Quiet, Berta," I hissed.

The man looked at me, then back to Berta. "Spunky little cuss, aren't you?"

"Sorry. I'm just tired. It's been a long day."

He eyed us some more. "Come on over by the fire and we'll get a hot meal into you. We'll talk some more after you eat." He stepped aside, letting us go first.

We headed for the fire. I looked at everyone as we passed. I wanted to know who we were dealing with, and how many. I counted close to forty people, ranging in age from young teen to an old woman with grey hair and a sagging face. They appeared as frightened as us, still shaken from that horrendous night a month ago. They must all be from Phoenix. No wonder they still looked in shock.

I tied the horse up on a branch in the glow of the fire. Two of the younger girls greeted Berta and sat her down by the fire. They handed her a plate filled with food. I walked over to the man that had met us.

"I didn't catch your name back there," I said.

He stood up from the log he was sitting on. He offered

his hand. I took it. "Name's Lieutenant Hudson. Phoenix police. I'm kinda in charge of this group here. You can call me, Clint. Everyone else does."

"Good to meet you, Clint. Thanks for letting us join your group for the night."

"You plan on heading out in the morning, are ya'?"

"Wanna get back home. Guess I'm taking the long way around."

"Oh yeah? Where's home?"

"A little north of Bagdad. Got a few acres up there."

"My home's down there," Clint pointed to Phoenix. "In that pile of rubble."

"You have any idea what happened?"

He grabbed me by the arm and walked me out of earshot of everyone else. "I don't have a clue. All's I know that whatever happened, happened all over. We were getting reports from Tucson, L. A., El Paso, then everything went blank. Nothing but static. But before the radios cut off, they were saying how everywhere was getting shook up pretty good. El Paso was getting reports from as far away as SAC headquarters in Omaha, and they were saying how they were getting accounts from every major city on the globe. Everywhere was getting shaken really bad. Buildings falling down like kids blocks. Deaths in the hundred of thousands, millions.

"But they couldn't say what was happening because they didn't know." He looked around, making sure no one had walked up on us. "Some of the folks around here think it was the wrath of God. That he was mad because of all our sins. Like letting the gays walk around freely. For letting abortions happen. For not getting rid of the other religions.

"Bunch of fucking lunatics, they are. They stick to themselves, pretty much. Don't talk a whole lot about the wrath of God thing too much anymore. But they cause me some concern. 'Fraid they might want to create some sort of religious sect or something. Really strict SOB's, they are. Hope they don't cause you any trouble because of that girl you got with you."

"Like I said, we'll be leaving at first light."

"That what probably be for the best. Although you're more than welcome to stay. Now, let's get you something to eat, eh."

"Sounds good." As we walked, I prodded Clint. "So, what do you think happened?"

"Hell, Forrest, I couldn't even begin to guess. I thought it was just an earthquake. 'Til it kept on like it did. I was on a call, standing beside my cruiser and the next thing I knew I was plastered to the pavement, then the building I was parked next to fell on the cruiser. Inches more and it would have killed me. I got away with some bruises and a bunch of dust.

"I couldn't get up until morning. Everything was ruined. There wasn't a building or structure standing.

"When I got back to where the precinct use to be and found it and half of Phoenix had fallen into the ocean, I knew things were bad all over. Life was never going to be the same."

We had reached the fire. An attractive woman brought me a plate of food. Roasted meat, probably rabbit, green beans, and some bread. It smelled good. We sat down on a log as Clint continued on about the Night of Shaking.

"We searched for survivors for ten days. We found back hoes, bulldozers and other construction equipment, but none of 'em would start. They weren't damaged in anyway, they just wouldn't start. There wasn't anybody around who was mechanical, so we couldn't get very far into the rubble searching for people. I don't know how many were buried alive, dying in the makeshift graves.

"There was this one, though. Buried rather deep in the rubble of an apartment building." He looked to the ground. "Everything happened so fast. The buildings and houses came down so fast, very few got out." He looked around the camp. The people were off in their own niches: families, friends, age groups, those that thought alike. Berta and her companions were chatting away. "Out of nearly a million inhabitants, this is all that's left. That we know about, anyway. I suppose others could have gone their own ways, but it's not a hopeful sign of what's left."

He had changed the subject. He didn't want to go on about the person trapped beneath the apartment building, but he had my curiousity aroused. "Which one," I asked as I eyed the camp, "was the one you dug out from the apartment building?"

He turned to me, sorrow on his face. "We couldn't get to her. There was too much concrete on her. Too big. Too heavy. If we could have gotten something running, maybe we could have reached her.

"We tried everything we could think of: pry bars, jury-rigged cranes and pulleys. But nothing worked. She had told us when we found her about her baby." He wiped a tear from his eye. "We found the infant ten feet above her, dead. It's head had been crushed. But we couldn't get any closer to the mother. We tried for three days. Three whole fucking days. On the fourth day, there was no more sounds coming from the rubble.

She had died in the night." He stood and walked away. He was obviously disturbed by it.

So, too, was I. I put the half eaten plate of food down where he had sat and watched the fire burn.

Some time later, minutes maybe, an hour perhaps, someone yelled, "Look!"

I turned in the direction of the voice and saw a teenage boy pointing behind me. I whipped around and saw the blue firefly. I wasn't seeing things. They all saw it too.

"I don't believe it," a woman said. "A blue lightning bug."

"Aren't they all green?" someone asked.

"I'm gonna catch it," the teenage boy declared.

"No!" I blurted.

Clint strolled over to me. "You got something special with that bug?"

I didn't know what to say. Although I felt there was something special between me and the blue firefly; I didn't know what, so I couldn't say that there was. They would think I was some kind of lunatic. Then the boy darted for the firefly. I reacted instinctively and moved for the boy.

Clint stopped me with a hand on my shoulder, then the boy.

"Ricky! Leave the bug alone. There's been enough death lately."

I looked up at Clint. "Thanks."

Clint sat down beside me again as Ricky headed back towards the fire. I watched the firefly. "I first saw it several years ago, shortly after my wife passed away. It then followed me to Arizona, and I've seen it a few times since the Night of

Shaking. I...I think it has something to do with my late wife."

Clint was silent for several minutes as he, too, watched the blue firefly blink on and off in the trees. "I wouldn't know anything about that. But, it did show up on the side of the camp you're on." He looked at me. "You say it's been following you?"

I nodded. "It sure appears that way. First in...right after Lisa died."

"She your wife?"

"Late wife. Then when I moved to Arizona I saw it out there a number of times. Then when I left it showed up at my campsites.

"Only lately, though, have I been associating it with Lisa."

"Why's that?"

I shrugged. "Think about her when it shows up."

We watched the firefly until it left the area. Clint rose. "I'm gonna make my rounds, then turn in."

I stood. "Mind if I join you?"

"Nope. Could use the company."

We started out into the trees to check on the sentries. "Been having problems?" I asked.

"What kind you mean?"

"People problems. I mean, sentries and everybody in your group seems to be armed."

"About a week ago we had some men show up. There were six of 'em. Said they were looking for food and water, just like you. We let them in the camp and everything was fine. 'Til nightfall.

"I was waken up by one of the teenage girls screaming.

One of those men we had let in that night was standing over me, his rifle pointed at my head. The other four men were standing by the one raping Kathy. Guarding off others and waiting their turn.

"I sleep with my pistol by my hip. I grabbed it and shot the man over me through the blanket. I shot two of the others standing by Kathy, and the other two were shot by the group here. We pulled the man off Kathy, stripped him completely naked, put a bullet in his foot, and shoved him into the woods. Later that night we heard the coyotes get 'im.

"We've been posting sentries ever since. They'll be up in the trees all night, so you can sleep easy."

We had walked the perimeter and were back near the fire. I nodded. "Where should we bed down?"

Clint scanned the area, then pointed to a spot near where I had tied up my horse. "Over by your horse would be the best place."

"Looks good. I'll round up Berta."

*   *   *

We didn't leave in the morning. Berta wanted to stay another day and no one in the group voiced any complaints. After breakfast, Clint had a surprise for me.

"You feel up to an expedition, Forrest?"

"What do you have in mind?"

"Me and some of the men are going into Phoenix to pick up some marijuana from one of the precincts."

I didn't think I heard him right. A former police officer, not more than a month out of the job, and he wants to go pick up some weed. "Did you say you want to go get some weed? Uh, marijuana?"

"Yup. One of the older teens," he pointed to a lanky young man helping the women with dishes, "Oscar there, smokes it. Found out it keeps the tick hordes away from you. Something in it makes your scent unpleasant to the little critters. We smoke at least one joint a day to keep the ticks away."

I stared at him for a moment. "You're kidding, right?"

"Nope. We even started a patch of the stuff. That's if the winter doesn't kill everything. But," he looked to the sky, "it should be colder than it is."

"Um, you do realize that the Earth has tilted?"

"What do you mean?"

Was I the only one that noticed? "The axis has shifted. How much," I shrugged. "But no doubt the seasons as we knew them will change. It's November. Winter should be here soon."

"Yeh, you're right. We'll look for more blankets, too."

I looked at their camp in daylight. They lived mostly in tents, with a couple of rickety huts to store food. Maybe I would show them how to build a home like mine, out of the soil. I would keep an eye out for building materials on our expidition.

"Want to bring my horse?"

Clint eyed the saddle horse. "Sure could carry a lot more with it along."

Chapter X

On the way to the city Clint introduced the excursion team. There were five of us, including me. There was another former police officer, a younger man name Corbin Flaggs. He was close to my age, in his mid-thirties, but more muscular. His hair was still short, blond, and he had brown eyes. Fred James was in his forties, around Clint's age. He was lanky with brown hair that scratched his collar. The youngest of the party was Bob Jacobsen. He was in his late twenties, black hair as long as Fred's, but fuller.

We arrived at the Scottsdale precinct before noon and dug in the rubble several hours before reaching the evidence room. There wasn't much conversation as we dug. Everyone seemed numbed. I watched them as we searched, wondering what they were thinking, what they thought had happened. How many thought it was the wrath of God? How many thought it was terrorists? How many thought it was a government conspiracy? How many thought, like me, that it was simply Nature putting us in our place?

When we reached the evidence room we found twenty-five pounds of marijuana. We also found large amounts of cocaine, heroin and methamphetamines. We reburied the hard stuff before we left.

We had found some uniforms, and tying the legs shut on the pants, used them as saddlebags. We loaded the marijuana on my horse and headed back to the camp in the hills. We passed one of those big home supply stores on the way out and I talked them in to stopping to see what we could find.

As we searched the ruined store, I filled Clint in on what I had in mind, describing my home and how it had survived. He was very intrigued and supported the idea without reservation. Our search resulted in shovels, picks, axes and hoes.

Just before we reached the outer edge of the demolished city, all hell broke loose. Rats, hundreds of them, descended on us like a swarm of bees. They attacked us, biting at our ankles and climbing up our pants legs. Everyone started yelling and kicking and firing their weapons. Rats and men were screeching in pain and fury. The little bastards were hungry and wanted us for supper.

They went after the horse. It reared and snorted at the rats, kicking at them with it's hind legs, the ones it made contact with landing yards away, stomping others with her front hoofs. I quickly made my way over to the mare and swatted her on the hind quarter, sending her out of the melee.

When I turned around, one of the men was on the

ground screaming in pain. It was Corbin. Rats covered him. Fred and I kicked our way to him and started pulling off the vermin. Each one came away with chunks of the man's flesh. Each yank of a rat caused him to scream even louder. Blood was everywhere. As we pulled off one rat, two more would seize upon the opening. They kept at us, too. Between pulling off the rats on the down man and keeping them off us, we were losing the battle. When Corbin fell silent, we turned our attention on getting away, leaving him for the rats, and hopefully, that would be enough for them for us to make our escape.

I saw Clint make his way out of the drove of rats and to safety. The rats were headed to the dead man on the ground. The feast was on.

I made my way to Clint, the rest following. We all had bites and chunks missing on our lower legs, our pants legs were in ribbons. Fred and I also had bites on our hands and forearms. Blood pooled around us as we watched the rats devouring our comrade. We were all gasping and wheezing, shocked by what we just went through and still witnessing. Then someone shot at the rats, one of the creatures flipping off the corpse, half of its body gone. We all opened fire after that, sending the vermin into a frenzy between survival and food.

It was several moments later before we stopped shooting. The rats were either dead, or had fled the scene. Clint was the first to walk over the man on the ground. The rest of us followed, that car wreck syndrome, I guess. Everybody, but Clint and I, retched when they saw the body.

Corbin's clothes were in shreds. His entrails were splayed out to one side, his eyes and most of his face were gone. His genitals had been ripped away and the hole still oozed with blood. There were bite marks and hunks of meat gone from every inch of his body. I turned and walked away, following the others. Clint was the last to leave. I heard him muttering something before he did, though. A prayer, I assumed.

We bandaged our wounds with what we could find and went to find my horse.

*　　　*　　　*

An hour later we found my horse. She was down, laying on her side, deflated. Ticks. She must have stopped to rest. The blood drew the the ticks to her and they sucked the life out of her where she stood. I felt more loss for my horse than I did for the man we lost to the rats. It wasn't because I felt the horse was more important, just that I had known her longer.

I have always felt that way, that every creature was worth as much as the other. It was something my mother instilled in me as a child. Perhaps that is why I never had many friends, most people I met were anthropocentric.

Lisa had been different. She loved animals more than I did, but also was more tolerant of her fellow man. Maybe that's why I like Berta, she reminds me of Lisa.

We unloaded the horse, turning it over to get everything. The horse was relatively light with all the blood gone from it's body. We split the load between us, and made our way up to camp. Between the tools and the marijuana, we were weighed down pretty good. It would be well past sunset before we made it back.

77

Clint and I brought up the rear. Clint made a motion to slow down, to let the others get a bit farther ahead. I complied and soon we were back far enough that they couldn't hear us as we talked.

"We're pretty low on ammo now, thanks to those rats," he said.

"I had thought of that when we found my horse."

"We've had a few run ins with coyotes, but the fires at night keep them away." He looked ahead, then back to the horizon. "It'll be good and dark by time we get back. I hope the smell of our blood doesn't attract them."

That didn't make me feel any better. I already felt weak from the blood I had lost, and I worried about rabies or any other disease the vermin might have been carrying. Clint seemed to have read my mind with his next statement, though.

"We've someone back at camp that knows all about herbal remedies and healing. We all need to see her soon as we get there. Who knows what those rats were infected with to act like that."

"Could have been nothing. Is that the first you've seen animals acting weird?"

"Other than that lightning bug of yours, yes." He paused. "The coyotes go after one of the group if they stray too far on their own, but never come at all of us. Why? What have you seen?"

I told him about the rabbits eating a horse, rats bringing down a coyote, and pigeons attacking a rat.

"Holy shit," he muttered.

"Something happened that night besides the Earth tilting and buildings falling."

"Any idea what? None of it makes any sense. Animals eating things they normally wouldn't eat. Attacking animals that use to prey on them. And those rats back there, they had no fear of us. Just attacked." He looked to sky. "I've watched the sun all day. You were right, it is following a different path. What could have done that?"

"I dunno, Clint. I honestly don't know.

"Um, you've made other trips to the city, haven't you?"

"Yup. For food, water, clothes, supplies and marijuana. Why?"

"I take it you've never run into the rats before?"

"Not like that. We've seen some scurrying around. Some stray dogs here and there. But nothing like what happened today."

"So, you've always made it back before dark?"

"Uh-hunh."

I thought a moment. "Me and Berta didn't see any coyotes the other night. Maybe we'll be okay."

"Maybe. But you and Berta weren't bleeding, either."

We walked in silence, increasing our pace until we caught up with Fred and Bob. The light was starting to fade and we still had a ways to go.

*   *   *

It was dark by time we were close to the camp. Bob, who had point, stopped and hushed us. We all listened intently for the slightest sound. There were the usual crickets, a few birds, and the faint rustling of a breeze, but nothing ominous.

"What'd ya hear?" Clint whispered.

79

Bob took a moment to answer, still taking in the sounds. "Sounded like leaves crunching. Someone, or something, walking this way."

We strained our ears some more. A moment later we all heard it. Footfalls. Human footsteps. Someone was headed our way.

"Find cover," Clint commanded.

We scattered, each finding a tree or rock to hide behind. Weapons at the ready, we waited as the sounds grew nearer. As they got closer, we could tell there was more than one. I heard someone cock their pistol.

We waited, the footfalls getting louder. Then we saw a light, a torch, bobbing through the trees. Moments later we saw more torches, then the band of people holding them. They were from the camp. Berta was with them.

We startled them when we came out from our hiding places, but everyone was glad to see each other. Berta ran up to me and threw her arms around me.

"They were saying the guys were always back before dark. We got worried and came to look for you." She squeezed me. "I'm so glad you're okay."

"Me, too. Thanks for caring." Then I heard someone ask about Corbin.

Chapter XI

A month later, four long, vaulted structures nearing completion, I was ready to leave. They knew enough about the construction to finish on their own. I was growing restless. Besides, I had always been uncomfortable with people. Especially after Lisa died. And, the religious extremists were grating on my nerves.

Berta had grown attached to me. and I her, but she had opted to stay. There were those her own age here. She was with good people. I silently wished she was going with me, but knew with the dangers out there she would be safer here. I had grown fond of most of the group and was a little reluctant to go. But, I missed my home.

My wounds from the rat attack had healed nicely. The herb woman knew her stuff. She taught me what edible plants and roots I could find on my journey home. She even wrote up a list of herbal remedies.

I was going to miss having a horse. It also meant that I could carry less in supplies. I would have to forage for most of my meals. This left me a little anxious, but it didn't deter me. Life had become an adventure and I found myself alive because of it.

The night before I left, Berta and I shared a joint. Clint had been right about it discouraging the ticks. We had gone to Phoenix a couple weeks after we lost Corbin to the rats for whatever we could find. While we were searching, one of the guys with us fell asleep on a slab of concrete. No one had thought much of it and we went digging and looking. About an hour later, after we had moved about a hundred or so yards away, we remembered we had left him there. Clint and I went running back to find ticks surrounding him, but not on him. We yelled until he woke, then he slowly just walked through the mass of ticks. I was amazed.

When Berta and I finished the joint, we talked for several hours about how life had changed and how we were going to miss each other. When the others had went to sleep, I finally told her goodnight and laid down. A few minutes later she was next me.

"May I join you?" she asked.

She was seventeen. I was thirty-six. I was old enough to be her father. "I'd," I had to swallow. "I'd like that."

She crawled under the blanket with me. "I'm going to miss you, Forrest. I wish you wouldn't go."

"You can still come with me." Thoughts of lying down with her each night suddenly jumped into my mind.

"When you told me you leaving the other day, that's all I've been thinking about." She wiggled out of her pants. "I even thought about coming with you a few times. But..."

I ran my hand along her thigh. "But, what?" Her skin was smooth, silky, and warm.

She slid out of her shirt and started to unbutton mine. Her hands felt good on me. When she reached down to undo my jeans I asked again. "But, what?" I had to know before this went any further.

"I'm scared of..." she turned her head and looked towards the edge of camp, "out there. I really don't want you to go, either. I'm afraid of what might happen to you." She slid her hand down my open jeans. Her touch made me shudder.

"I can't promise you nothing's going to happen to me. But I can't stay here any longer." I placed my hand on her breast. It was small, but firm. She moaned slightly.

"Why?" She kissed my neck and help me off with my jeans.

"I don't know how to explain it. It's just not me."

We didn't talk after that.

*   *   *

The next morning I awoke to Clint and the religious sect standing over Berta and I. She didn't go back to her bedroll after we had made love and was curled up next to me. They all had stern looks on their faces, except Clint, he wore a slight smile.

"I have to ask you both to leave," Clint said. "Today."

"This morning." It was the leader of the sect, George Walker. He was a rotund, flabby man. "Now, in fact. We can't have this kind of promiscuity in our home." He took a step closer, his feet beside my head. "My God, man, you're old enough to be her father and here you are..." he paused, hesitated, as if the words were going to choke him, "having sex with this young girl. You should be ashamed of yourself."

Berta had woken and heard what Walker said. "Your just jealous," she sniped.

"You, you little whore, will speak when spoken to."

"Shut your pie hole. You can't tell me what to do."

Walker's face grew red with anger. His followers gasped in unison. He stood there for a moment, visibly trembling with rage, before he moved to hit Berta.

I reacted instinctively and pulled his feet from under him. He landed on his butt with a loud 'Oomph'. His followers moved toward Berta and I. Clint stepped up and held out his hand. "All right. There'll be no violence."

Walker's little group paused. Berta and I scrambled to get dressed under the blanket. Three of them helped Walker to his feet. Others from the camp started to gather, the commotion waking some of them, bringing others to our side of the camp. Soon the religious group was outnumbered. I hoped that they would not take their side. When Walker was back on his feet, his tirade continued.

"These two must leave here. They have picked the forbidden fruit and will bring the wrath of God upon us if we allow them to stay. They have committed blasphemy in His eyes. They have copulated out of wedlock. They have..."

"Shut up, George," Clint interrupted.

Walker glared at Clint. "You, sir, have no say in this matter. This is a matter of religiousosity. This is a matter between God and myself. And I, sir, am a messenger of God."

I was dressed by now and stood, putting myself between Berta and the group. I had heard enough. "You, sir," I started, looking Walker in the eye, "are an abomination. It was your god that destroyed everything." I waved my arm to indicate everything around us. "It was your god that put us all here, made you and me and Berta and all the rest. It was your god that fucked up by making us the way we are.

"And why would your god, all powerful and omniscient, choose only you to speak to? Why would he pick someone so spiteful, so judgemental, so malicious to preach his words of love and peace? You, sir, are like all the rest in history that have used religion for their own distorted purpose. You, sir, who couldn't get laid if the woman was blind and mentally retarded, make me sick."

"God will smite you for that!" Walker threatened.

"Fine!" I shouted. "Let him smite me right here and now. Prove to everyone here that he exists and has the power to smite at will." I was shaking, angry, pissed. I had disliked organized religion since I was a teenager. Over the years I saw it as a way to control people, to give those who had nothing hope that after they died all their suffering was for something other than propping up the rich.

Several minutes passed as everyone waited for me to drop dead on the spot. When nothing happened, I continued. "See. Your god is a phony. Something made up because you don't have the guts to believe in yourselves; because you don't have the guts to believe in each other. Because you need something to think you're better that everyone else. I got some news for you, Big Boy, you're just like everyone else. With the same wants, needs and desires." I couldn't help myself, I had to add, "It's just that some of us can get what we desire." Berta had finally gotten herself dressed and stood beside me.

"Holy shit, Forrest," she whispered. "What's gotten into you?"

I turned to her and whispered back, "I just couldn't take his ranting."

"All right," Clint commanded. "Let's break it up. Shows over. Come on. Everyone's got something they need to do, go do it." He turned to me after the crowd started moving away.

"George is going to be hell to live with for a few days now, but he'll get over it."

"I'm sorry, Clint. I don't know what came over me. Something he said just got under my skin and..."

Clint raised a hand to shut me up. "Don't worry about it, Forrest. He's had it coming since we came up here. Nobody's had the balls to say anything to him, though." He looked to the ground. "Not even me. Guess I didn't want to rock the boat." He looked back up. "It's been pretty unsteady, if you know what I mean."

"I understand, Clint. I just hope I didn't do any damage to the harmony of your camp."

"Nah. I think things will be better now." He glanced over his shoulder to Walker. "They might even pitch in a bit more now, instead of waiting for God to do something for them."

"You got a good bunch of people here. You'll do okay."

"You still leaving then, hunh?"

"I think it'd be best." I turned to Berta. "You still want

to stay?"

"No."

Chapter XII

We headed north. I figured we follow the foothills to Prescott, see what we could find there, then head back to my home and make a go of it there. Four days from Clint's camp we crossed Interstate Seventeen and plans changed.

In a clearing below us we watched as a group of eleven men preyed on one. They were about two hundred yards away.

"Can't we do something?" Berta asked. "Like what you did at the junkyard?"

"There's too many of them. Besides, it's too open." I studied the situation. "I could probably pick off one or two before they scattered. But then they would know where here. We'd be next."

She watched the scene for a little while longer. The one man was running, only to be knocked down again and again. "I don't care. We can't just watch them murder him."

"Maybe he did something wrong. Maybe he's the bad

guy."

"Maybe. But right now, they're the bad guys. Ten against one."

"Eleven."

"Well, if you aren't going to do anything, I will."

And I believed she would. "All right. All right. You think you can hit them from this distance?"

She shrugged. "Can you?"

"Yes." I scanned the area quickly. "You stay here. I'm going to move over there. When you hear my first shot, shoot and keep shooting."

Moments later I was in position. I looked to the clearing. I had to hand it to the guy in trouble, he was holding his own. I aimed the rifle, held my breath and gently squeezed the trigger. The man closest to the victim went down. I fired again and the next closest dropped. Then I heard Berta fire, a puff of dust rising into the air next to one of the attackers. By then they were all looking in our direction. A shot rang out from the clearing and I heard that now familiar metallic mosquito whiz by a few yards to my right.

I saw one of the attackers level his gun at the guy they were tormenting. I took quick aim and fired. He went down, his gun going off into the air. Berta fired again and dropped one of the attackers.

"I hit one!" she screamed.

"Shut up and keep shooting!"

The remaining seven scattered for the tree line behind them. I aimed and caught one in the leg. Berta hit another one, but the other five disappeared into the trees.

Minutes later we were in the clearing. The man that

had been victimized was beaten, but alive. As Berta tended to him, I walked over the one I winged.

"Please, mister. Don't kill me. We were only having some fun."

"Really? So were we. Where'd your friends go?"

"Hell, I don't know."

I jabbed the barrel of the rifle into the wound on his leg. He yelped in pain. "Tell me or I'll put a bullet in the other one."

"Camp is about a mile away. Through those trees there." He pointed to where the five had run.

"How many more are there?"

"A hundred."

I jabbed the rifle into his wound again.

"Christ, you sadistic bastard. There's just the five. Everyone else in Prescott is dead."

"What about him?" I tilted my head to the man they were just playing with.

"Some egghead that wandered into camp this morning. We barely have enough to eat ourselves and he's worthless, so we were going to have some fun with him."

"Yeah? Well," I put a bullet in his head, "playtime is over."

"Forrest!" It was Berta. "What the hell did you just do?" She was behind me.

"I put him out of our misery." I turned around and faced her. She was holding up the man we just rescued. "What? You wanted to keep him around?"

She was livid. I could see in her eyes that what I said made sense, but she was still angry with me. "How can you just shoot somebody like that in cold blood?"

I walked over to them. "I remember, not more than five minutes ago, someone yelling out, with a bit of glee in their voice, that she had 'got one'."

Berta looked to the ground.

"I guess we could have left him for the coyotes or ticks. I thought this would be more humane."

"I...I'd like to thank you two for what you did for me."

I looked at him as he shifted his weight, an arm around Berta's shoulders. He was about half a head taller than Berta, and just as thin. His left eye was swelled shut, there was blood coming from his nose, and his right ear. He appeared to have difficulty breathing, and he held his left arm across his abdomen.

"Looks like they beat you up pretty good," I said.

"It's not as bad as it looks. I bruise easy."

"We should get moving," Berta insisted. "Before they get their courage back and come back here."

"Yeah." I looked around. We had to go back and pick up our gear. I didn't want to head in the direction they went, nor back in the direction we came, which only left going north. "You got a name?" I asked the man as I took over for Berta.

He moaned as I put his arm around my neck, me being several inches taller than Berta. "Name's Alfred Rosten. Everybody calls me Alf."

"Alf?"

"Yeah. Stupid T.V. show."

"Well, Alf, we gotta get to those trees over there. You up to it?"

"Let's get going, before I pass out."

"I'm Berta. That's Forrest."

"I know."

*   *   *

We made it to the tree line without incident. The 'bad guys' hadn't returned to extract revenge. We walked for several hours north before finding a suitable place to make camp.

It was a shallow cave near a creek. The water ran fast and looked clear. I checked out the cave while Berta tended to Alf's wounds at the creek.

The entrance to the cave was small and I had to duck to enter it. It went back about forty feet into the rock, about ten feet at it's widest three quarters of the way in. I unloaded our gear, then went back outside to gather wood for a fire. Berta helped Alf into the cave and tended to his wounds while I started a fire.

The fire lit up the cave, warming it nicely. "Homey," Berta said. "I like what you did with it."

"Thanks," I ignored her sarcasm. "How's Alf?"

"I'm going to be fine. I just need to rest."

"Come on, Berta. Let's find us something to eat."

It was several hours until night, the sun halfway between noon and dusk. That's when I noticed the clouds on the horizon; ominous, tall and dark. "We'd better hurry." I pointed to the clouds. "That doesn't look too good."

"Wow," was all Berta said.

We found some edible roots, some berries and mushrooms, and Berta shot a squirrel, all within an hour after leaving the cave. We made our way back as the wind picked up. By time we slid through the entrance the wind was whipping up debris from the ground and throwing at it us with stinging precision. Moments after entering the cave the clouds opened up, unleashing a torrent of rain I had never seen before. Luckily, the wind was going sideways to the cave entrance and the storm didn't bother us.

We had been silent as we cooked, trying not disturb Alfred. I sensed she and I were pondering the same thing; how many more like this will we find? This had been two encounters now for her and I, this one we had the act of surprise.

A crack of thunder reverberated through the cave, waking Alf as I finished gutting the squirrel. Berta had the roots roasting next to the fire, poking at them and turning them periodically. I skewered the squirrel and balanced it over the fire.

Alf sat up and looked out the opening. He watched the storm for a few minutes. "Looks mighty fierce out there."

"Yeah, the wind was blowing pretty good by time we got back. Never seen clouds like that before. Tall, rolling, and dark like that."

Alf moved a little closer to the entrance. "Well, you can expect powerful storms like this for quite some time."

"What do you mean?"

"How much longer before it's ready?" Alf nodded at the cooking food.

"About twenty minutes," Berta said.

"I'll explain while we eat." Alf turned back to the opening and watched the rain.

*   *   *

"The squirrel's not too bad." Alf poked at the root in front of him. "What's this?"

"Root. Toasted and basted in squirrel drippings," Berta informed him. "Gives it that golden brown look."

"So," I swallowed, "what did you mean we'll have more storms like this one? What makes you so sure?"

"Where you guys from?"

"Bagdad, Arizona."

"Deming."

"I'm the, was, the weather man on channel thirteen in Barstow." He looked at the fire. "California is gone, you know. From the Sierra Nevada's west. Just...gone." He glanced at Berta, then steadied his eyes on me. "This has all been coming, you know. The storms getting stronger each year. The changing weather patterns. More frequent earthquakes and eruptions."

"You mean, like Rapture?" Berta asked.

"Um, more like Mayan."

"It wasn't a comet, right?" I asked.

"Um, no. Not a comet. Our solar system went through the gravitational wave emitted by the center of our galaxy. The Myan's had predicted it. But modern man disregarded it as ancient hoopla. After all, aren't we smarter, more intelligent, then those antiquated pagans?"

Berta and I looked at each. Neither were quite sure what he was talking about.

"You see, there's a massive black hole at the center of our galaxy. It's what keeps everything tied together. Keeps it from just spinning off into the universe. Now, the collaspe of the black hole has flattened it's gravitational pull. That's why the galaxy is in a spiral, with arms that contain the stars and their planets, like most other galaxies we can see. It's the gravitational plane of influence that we went through that caused all the damage. As we went through that plane of influence, we encountered a pole shift. It's happened before, and will happen again. It occurs every five thousand one hundred and twenty-six years. Roughly."

"What do you mean, roughly?" I took a bite of the root. The squirrel juices did help.

"It's a cyclic phenomenon. It's called the Galactic Equinox. Much like the Earth's own Spring and Autumn Equinox, but on a galactic scale. The Myan's knew about, so did the ancient Chinese and the Egyptians. But the Myan's were the most accurate in their predictions.

"The bad thing is, when everyone started using the Gregorian Calendar, it threw the Mayan's calculations off. Just how far, nobody knows.

"See, our solar system doesn't just rotate around the center of our galaxy, around that black hole, but follows a sine wave pattern as we orbit. One of countless solar systems, all having their own gravitational problems." He leaned to look out the entrance, then turned back to us, excited. "Have you noticed the moon?"

I nodded. Berta shrugged.

"It spins a lot faster now. Her faces changes every four to six hours. Completes her orbit about every three weeks, not four. Well, so far anyway. It's only been about two months. But the pattern's looking more familiar every passing week. Think it's closer, too. Just looks too big."

"How long will the storms go on?"

Alf shrugged. "Few years. A decade. Won't know until it happens. You do realize it all built up to that night when our solar system, our galaxy, our arm of the spiral, dipped through the Galactic Equinox and changed the forces, the effects of gravity on billions of galaxies and stars and planets, aligned in gravational harmony so strong that it nearly squeezes the life out of everything up and down that line, it's swath billions of miles in circumfrence."

"I thought you said you were a weatherman on tee vee?" Berta pointed out.

"Um, well, the study of the 'Equinox has been a hobby of mine since college."

"So, you knew this was coming?" I asked.

"Well, um, kinda. Remember, I said the Mayan coversions were miscalcultated. We thought it was going to happen in twenty twelve. Right around Christmas. On the Winter Solstice, to be precise." He shrugged. "It came three years and a couple of months earlier."

"Early?"

He shrugged, again. "What can I say? Western arrogance doomed itself. Too much technology. Too much waste. Too much hubris."

"What does that mean? Doomed itself?"

"Too much realiance on machines, computers, automation. Cars aren't going to run. Turbines aren't going to spin. Stereos, TV's, Ipods, nothing.

"What do you think happened that second night? After the survivors discovered themselves? Wha'd you think the morning after?"

I shrugged. I hadn't look back since then. No reflection, no trying to put the pieces, the reasons, the whys. "I guess I really didn't think the morning after. I guess I was in shock over what happened. I did wonder what the hell happened, but that's about as far as it went. As for what anybody else thought..." I shrugged. This theory of Alf's was interesting. Explained a lot, too. It was just a theory, though. But there's been no nuclear winter that's suppose to happen within weeks of a mental meltdown of our countries leaders.

Volcanics eruptions would explain the colorful dawns and sunsets. A polar shift is obvious to anyone that looks up. Orion, for instance, now crosses directly overhead.

"Uh, speaking of the couple months early thing, this would be December now, right?" I asked.

You could see his eyes drift as he calculated back. "What day is this?"

Berta and I shrugged in unison.

"Hasn't anybody been keeping track?"

"Find a housewife," Berta said. "She'll know day and date."

"Hell, all we need for that is a Timex that's still ticking."

"Um, well, no. Any electronic device is useless. And after two months any spring driven watch would have wound itself down. But the night it happened, the Galactic Equinox, was October twenty-first. A month past the Autumnal Equinox."

"Ooh," Berta blurted. "You seen the ticks?"

Alfred looked into the fire. "Lost my wife to 'em the day after. While she slept beside me." He got up and went to the opening.

"That's gotta be hard," I said to Berta.

She nodded. "And I thought it was bad finding my parents buried in the rubble of our house," she uttered to herself, just loud enough for me to here.

I remembered finding the tick victims. I jerked one shudder, as if somebody poked me. "Sorry," I said to Alfred.

Alf came about halfway back and stopped. "When you said, about it being more humane than the coyotes, yes. The ticks, after running into those guys a couple days ago, I think the way she went was better. Probably didn't even know it was happening."

Drifting off into death in a dream state, I thought, while the little critters sucked the life out of you wouldn't be that bad, really. Going quickly with a sensation of being knocked in the head hints on a big surprise. But what if you weren't asleep, or unconscious? What if you were awake, but immobile, when they found you? Sucked the life outta ya' as you watched. Helpless. I shook my head to fling the thought out of my mind.

I cut off another piece of squirrel, then told Berta to get the weed. "Did you hear about what repels the ticks?"

Alf shook his head.

"Weed."

"What?"

"Marijuana."

"I know what weed is. Are you serious?"

I nodded. "Saw it with my own eyes."

"And, you have some?"

"Enough for a couple months. Just takes a few hits a

day to keep the level up."

"Um, you know, I've always wanted to try marijuana. Guess I've got a good reason to now."

"Who's gonna say anything? From what I've seen there's not a whole lot left. Everything is wild, again. There's no civilaztion left. We gotta start all over."

"Quite possible." He eyed the joint Berta had rolled. "You gonna light that thing?"

Chapter XIII

The storm lasted two more days. Easing up enough for us to gather more food. Alfred did a lot of sleeping while he healed. On the second excursion Berta and I went on, I found some medicinal herbs for Alf. He wasn't showing any signs of infection and no fever.

On the third day inside the cave dawn came bright and crisp. The temperature had dropped about twenty degrees as the storm passed. Now it felt like December. But the sun was still pretty high in the sky. Then I remembered Alf talking about the pole shift. It was going to be wait and see on what seasons were going to be like. Wait and see how long the storms last. Wait and see on what normal is going to be. Wait and see on a lot of things. An adverture, everyday.

I stood just outside the opening to the cave. The creek was now a stream, a small river. The water was murky and faster. The sky was clear, the sun warm.

We had decided to head back south. Perhaps even stopping at Clint's camp. But if winter was now coming, I wanted to go south where it should be warmer. We were going to the coastline and follow it East. Find out how much land was lost.

Perhaps we could become nomads. Wandering around, discovering what's gone, what's new, what's left.

I heard stirring from the cave. Someone else was awake. I went back inside to find Alfred struggling to stand up.

"Still stiff?" I grabbed his elbow and helped brace him.

He nodded toward the entrance. "Outside," he whispered, then looked down at Berta. She was still asleep. We shuffled to the opening and out into the morning air.

Alf stretched and turned in the sunlight, warming different sides of his body at a time. When he quit shivering I asked,

"If you were in Barstow, how come your here now? I thought you said California dropped into the ocean. Up to the Sierra Nevadas. Wouldn't Barstow be inclusive?"

"It is, was." He turned and faced me, the sun on his right. "We were in Flagstaff. The guy who does, did, the weather in Flagstaff had the same hobby as me. We took a long weekend to visit with him. We were there the night we went through the 'Equinox.

"We were at the station and he knew how to bring up some of the satellites in real time. We watched as half of California, the Baja penisula, and good slice down Mexico's west coast just disappeared. The beach is now just a few miles to the west of Kingman, Arizona. The desesrts of California are now large expanses of water on our new coastline. The Mojave desert is now the Mojave sea. Florida and the Carolinas are gone, too.

"We saw a massive cloud; water vapor, smoke, or dust, we couldn't tell, over the Central Plains states. It could have been that oversize volcano they said was in Wymoing, or, just a really big storm.

"After that, that EMP hit and knocked out all the electronics in the place. In every place. We knew the satellites were worthless. Every single one had to be out. And if our equipment was any indication, then it wouldn't really matter because everything was toast. Equipment that wasn't turned on, or even plugged in, was fried.

"That was some big EMP to take out electronics with no power being supplied to the device. And, I'm pretty certain it wiped out everything electronic on the planet, from digital watches to nuclear power plants, spy satellites and missile silos."

"What's EMP?"

"EMP. Electromagnetic pulse. Like when a nuclear bomb goes off, it throws out this intense EMP that fries the circuitry of anything turned on at the time. And this EMP fried the circuits of things not even plugged in. The nuclear power plants and missile silos were made the most impervious to those types of attacks, and I can almost guarantee you they're toast, too.

"Then we realized that a lot of those satellites might just start orbit decay and crash back into the Earth."

"Wouldn't they just burn up?" I had the vision of that helmet at the space station crash site vivid in my mind.

"Not the bigger ones. And some are run with little

nuclear devices. Wonder if they burn up, too?"

I wished I had a cigarette. Even though it had been two years since I quit. They seemed mild now. Could cut my life span by ten or even twenty years. Hell, my life span didn't look longer than the next five years. I would probably die before the cigarettes even came close to killing me. The urge passed, rather quickly. "How far south do think you we can get?"

He looked me straight in the eyes. "Remember the shape of Texas?"

"Yeah."

"Can you picture where Dallas-Fort Worth was?"

"Uh, yeh."

"It's beach front property. From Dallas to El Paso to Albuquerque to Phoenix to Kingman; all beach front property. Nearly followed the Interstate system. We can get further south by going east of Albuquerque. We can go about as far south as Austin.

"Most of Mexico and Central America are gone, too. We didn't get to see much of Europe, only that the Mediterranian was huge. France, Spain and Italy, gone."

"All because of this Gravatational Equinox?"

"Galatic."

"Oh."

*   *   *

An hour later we were tredging through the wet forest. Alf slowed us down a bit. We didn't go as far each day, and it took us longer in the morning to get started. Alfred was healing, but was still stiff, sore and slow.

Six days later, when we arrived at Clint's camp, we knew something was wrong when we came across a sentry, dead at the base of a tree. Unfortunately, horribly, we found the entire camp that way. They had all been shot, some numerous times. Clint had five. Next to him a woman, Linda. Shot once in the head and her breasts cut off. I shook my head. What the...? We're they taking trophies? No, animals must have eaten them. Clint had bite marks. They all did. But not many. These were relatively fresh. Only a few days.

As we searched the rest of the camp, I noticed that the vaults were almost complete.

Then Berta pointed out the obvious, "Where are the women?"

I didn't mention Linda, but we soon found four others, five out of eighteen women. All with...trophies...missing. They were in a group, a pile. Animals hadn't done it, the attackers had. I saw Berta clutch at her chest. I felt a stirring, deep. The thought of someone taking a knife to her caused a black rage to swell.

"God help them if I find them," I muttered.

Berta heard me. "I thought you didn't believe in God?"

"I don't. That's the point."

"You knew these people?" Alfred asked.

"Yes."

"And you say the women are missing?"

"Yes."

"How many?"

"There was eighteen when we left, we've found five."

"Five?" Berta asked. "We only saw four."

"Linda was next to Clint."

Tears started sliding down Berta's cheeks. I had the urge to go to her, but instead held out my arms. She rushed to me. I held her tight for several moments, letting her cry some of it out. We had to get going, though. Before the carnivores returned.

A search of the camp resulted in a lever-action rifle with scope for Alf, but we also discovered that, except for some food, the only other thing they took were the women. Thirteen women abducted. But, by who? The why was almost too obvious. I had to find them. Stop the insanity before it spreads. The trail headed south.

"We could always go west," I suggested.

"You've already decided," Berta tsked.

"Which is?" Alf asked me.

"Put us out of their misery."

"You mean?"

"Yes, Alf. He wants to kill again." She gave me a look of ice. "He likes it."

"And you want to try..what? Rehabilitation? These guys have already decided. They want to rehabilitate you.

"Alf and I, well, they..uh..they want us dead. You saw what they did to the camp. All the men are there."

"Yes, I noticed that all the men were there. If we can't stop them, but try, I know where that will leave everybody. But we can't let them get away with it. If nothing else, we have to hurt them. Hurt 'em good." She rubbed at her chest, unaware she was doing it.

"Alf, how good of a shot are ya'?"

"Um, who missed back there? Uh, when we first met. One of your two's shot hit the ground."

I looked at Berta.

"It was me." She confessed.

"Better than her, not as good as you."

"I sure hope so."

"What do mean by that?" Berta asked.

I turned to her. "That he's not lying."

"I wouldn't lie about something like that. Not now. But these people are insane. This is barbarism we're talking here. Barbarism."

"Barbarism. Insanity. Evil. Who's to say anymore? The better shots? The more cunning? The more sneaky?" Suddenly I wished I'd never left home. Berta was right, I wanted to kill. But not because I liked it, but because of Abby, Clint, even Walker. From what we are taught from childhood, whoever attacked the camp were bad. Evil. And, yes, it felt good to kill evil.

"Do we need to find you a Bible and show you what they did was wrong?" Berta reproached.

I couldn't help it. "Wouldn't that depend on the page you were on and who's side you were reading about?"

"Ewww. I hate it when you do that."

"Eh," I shrugged.

"Why is this bothering you so much?" she confronted.

"Mind if we step aside here, Alf?"

"Um, no. Go ahead. I'll be here."

I grabbed Berta's hand and led her a few feet away. "When I first realized what they're doing with kidnapping all the women, I had the thought; just for second, not even a second. However long it takes for you to think, 'that would be pretty nice as the top stud'."

She hit me in the arm, my bicep. "Creep."

"It was just the one thought. Besides, that's not the problem.

"I was just thinking, there were close to forty people in that camp, all of them armed. I didn't see a strange face back there. Did you?"

"Maybe they took their dead with them. Or came back. We were gone almost two weeks."

"That could explain why the bodies aren't too chewed up yet. The animals have been getting scared off. They did look kinda..fresh, too.

"But the point is, that's quite a lot of people to kill and get away with it; with live captives."

"You," she ducked to see my face. "You think we're outnumbered."

"Almost positive."

"We gotta do it."

"I know. I want you to be careful."

"You can count on it. I want to get into your pants, again."

"I'm going to remember that."

"I'm planning on it."

The trail was obvious, but days old. How many was anybody's guess. We could be a week behind, or two days. We would need to be careful until this ended.

We followed the trail. Here and there we could see drag marks. They never lasted that long, which we took as a good sign; they weren't dragging the women.

A few hours down the trail we found the first body. It was one of them. One of them that died back at the camp. They had carted off their dead, only to leave them on the trail. He was in a shallow grave off to the side. Pigeons were digging it up, pointing it out to us. He was in his late twenties.

We found seven more in the next half mile. About a hundred yards apart from each other, the graves getting shallower and shallower. The last two bodies we found just had leaves covering them. They had gotten into a hurry. Was something chasing them? The animals seem to have gotten more brazen. Was the smell of death giving their location away? Pigeons alerted us to the first one, but the rest were undisturbed. If it had been animals forcing them to drop the bodies and go, the corpses would be mutilated. No, they were just in a hurry.

I took the number of casualties as a good sign. There should be just as many wounded. Our chances of succeeding were improving every hundred yards. We searched another mile before giving up on finding any more bodies. It was just that eight, unless we missed some before we started seeing them. Still, eight was a good number. Their numbers had to be close to the camps. With eight dead, at least that many wounded, their force was cut roughly in half.

We walked most of the night, stopping a few hours before dawn for some sleep. At dawn, we started walking again. Not too long after, we found another shallow grave. This one appeared to have died of his wounds, here. This is where he fell, this is where they left him. I was hoping to find more like this before finding them. We left the body as it lay and continued on.

A few hours later we found a stash of guns. Most were little machine guns, Uzi's. They left the Uzi's because they were out of ammo. That explained how they overcame the camp. Their numbers could be smaller than I previously thought. A couple of rifles and several pistols rounded out the cache.

Less than a hour later we found the next body. Another one died of their wounds. We found two more before dusk. They had simply fallen behind and dropped dead. That was twelve they were down.

I was getting a little anxious to catch up with them. Two days my rage had been brewing, simmering. Finding their fallen comrades like this only made me hate them more. I couldn't wait to put a bullet in somebody. Watch them drop. I have to admit, it is a satisfying feeling of power.

Maybe that's the key: Go to the other side, the dark side, and simply fulfill it. Then, when you're done, you step away and stand back in the light. I've done it twice now. The first time when I found Berta, the second when we rescued Alf. How many more times could I do it? How many more times would I need to?

Again, we walked through the night. A few hours after the moon passed it's zenith, we caught glimpses of a campfire ahead. We were still several miles away when we could see the fire clearly, while we were still tucked away in the trees. We stopped and waited, making a fireless camp. At dawn we should be able to count how many are left. So far, we haven't discovered a female corpse. That's thirteen to account for, the rest would be them.

As we watched their campfire, I began to wonder about the state of things. Such as these men we are chasing. There are strong signs that they believe they are superior to the rest of us.

The kidnapping. The massacre at the camp. The mutilation of the bodies. To kill for such reasoning is outright insanity. And I was, again, taking it upon myself on who would live and who would die. Just as they had.

What right did I have to make that choice? Sure the hell wasn't might. Not the three of us. Yet I was intent on passing judgement on as many as necessary to free those women. I had to wonder by what right.

Perhaps, the right of humanity. Have we not evovled at least that far? Is not what they have a done a crime against humanity? Especially when we don't know how many of us are left? No one, save the ones about to be killed, could argue my guilt. So why do I keep coming back to it?

Is it because, since the seeing the camp, I've noticed similar traits in me. I'm older than Berta, so automatically I'm suppose to be her superior. And Alf is smaller than me. In a world like this one is turning out to be, size matters. But, I don't feel superior, to either Berta or Alf. Nor do I think myself better than either one of them. It's much like the way I feel toward most things; live and let live.

"We could sneak over there and slit everyone's throat," Berta insulted.

"Don't be ridiculous. Tomorrow we see how many they are, how they're controlling the women? That sort of thing."

"Yeh, study 'em. See how they operate."

"Right. Then tomorrow night we sneak over and slit everybody's throat."

She hit me in the arm.

"That hurts, you know."

"It's suppose to; you're an ass."

"You want to take care of prisoners?"

"No."

"How 'bout if I call myself Fate, Alf can be Destiny, and you can be Bad Luck?"

"That's not funny."

"These kind of people don't quit, Berta. Their nuts. Crazy. Insane. They'll just regroup and come back with more followers."

Alf had overheard and stepped a little closer. "Roberta looks more like a Destiny. I'll be Bad Luck."

Berta threw a hand to her mouth to stifle a guffaw. I turned away and bit my lower lip.

"What?" he asked me. "You wanna be Bad Luck? Fine, I'll be Fate. Like it better anyway."

Berta hit him in the arm. "Shut up," she whooshed. "This isn't funny."

"No, it's not. It's good versus evil."

"And which is which?" I posed.

"They're the bad guys."

"How do you know?"

"The only ones that would condone such actions these people have comitted, would be the same ones that could commit them? Who would oppose such actions? Everybody else."

"How can you be so sure? We don't know how many white supremist, survivalist-type survived. A democratic vote could go the wrong way."

"Is he always this cynical?"

"Often enough."

"I'm just saying," I tried to explain. I also wanted an

answer. "There were those that thought that eugenics was just a misconception with bad PR. Those guys Alf ran into sure weren't afraid to show their dominance."

"It took all eleven," he boasted.

"We saw," Berta confirmed.

Alf looked at her, then looked at me, then back at her. "You two..."

"We two, what?" I straightened. I didn't want to hit him, but...

"Oh yeah, a number of times now," Berta offered.

Alf looked at me, again. I shrugged. "She acts a lot older."

"It's my idea. I've always liked older men."

"Behave, now. I could've said no."

"Yeah, right. How many is it, nineteen?"

She meant the difference in our ages, in years. I nodded in the moonlight. "You're cute, too."

I felt like strangling her for telling Alf we've slept together. Although it wouldn't be hard to believe. Berta is a pretty, young woman. And I clean up rather nice, so the possibility of attraction is there. Why we didn't until the night before leaving Clint's, I cannot explain. But that night she asked to lay next to me will be unforgettable.

Why her telling Alf should bother me, well, three months ago our relationship would have broke the law. Three months ago, murdering a small community and kidnapping the women would have broken the law, too. But biologically, she's a woman. So Nature's law isn't broken. And Berta and I agreed. Even asking politely. 'May I join you?' played through my mind.

But this was a brave, new world. Laws would be meaningless. But we evolve. Don't we? Common sense humanity knows that killing and kidnapping is wrong. Yet, we were on a hunt. And we were hunting humans. To kill them at hunt's end, for kidnapping and killing needlessly. Death for the sake of humanity. Murder to save the human race from itself.

I reached over and pulled Berta to my side. "You know, I really don't like it," I whispered to her.

"What? The age difference?" she whispered back.

"The killing."

She pulled back a little, to look into my eyes. I can't imagine what she saw in the dimness. "You don't, do you?"

"No. I wish we could just walk into their camp and say, 'Okay, enough fun. Let the women go.' And they just would. And when we got back to Clint's camp, they would all be there waving.

"But these people have done wrong on the level of humanity. As decent human beings, we have the duty to stop them from spreading. Or it'll all happen again like before."

She looked at me rather stunned. "You..you want to change the world?"

I snickered. "According to Alfred, nature's already done that. We just don't need that kind of people around to screw it all up again."

"What kind?"

"Mindless killing. Kidnapping. It's...it's..."

"Inhuman?"

"Actually, it's too human. That's the problem. We're still human. The Earth changes it's tilt. Animals change their behaviour. But man is still human."

"Don't get too down on humans, Buster. You're one, too."

"That's the paradox. That's the paradox."

She kissed my neck.

"You awake, Alf?" I said in hushed tone.

"Duh."

"Wanna wake us in a while?"

"Sure."

As I nodded off to sleep, I caught a glimpse of the blue firefly flickering through the leaves.

Chapter XIV

Alfred woke us at dawn. We stayed still as we watched the camp across the way. There was no movement. Had they left before sunrise? I asked Alf.

"Nope. The fire burned until just before dawn. I would have seen 'em leave."

"Okay. But if they've left, we should be moving, too."

"I'm telling you, nobody left. I..."

"There," Berta said, pointing to their camp.

It was a man, kicking dirt on the fire. Then another moved into the clearing. Then another, pulling the women behind him. The women were moving in single file. They had them tied up. A fourth man came clear and appeared to be in charge. After a few moments, he turned and headed away, the others following.

"I counted four."

"Me, too," Berta said.

"That's all I saw," Alf added.

"Let's get going."

As we walked, I did the math. They had been a force of sixteen. Sixteen against forty. But with the machine guns, it should have been a massacre. But Clint's group killed eight of theirs outright. Four more dying of their wounds later. Could this have been the attackers first raid? Perhaps my apprehension at the start of this was unwarranted. I wanted to catch up to the remaining four in a hurry.

"We should be able to catch them today," I said.

"What's the plan?" Alf asked.

"Get the women back."

"Yeah. But how?"

"By force."

"That's a duh. But, how?"

I knew what he was asking, but it wasn't possible to plan anything this early. "We'll play it by ear."

"What the hell is that suppose to mean?"

"When we catch up to 'em, we'll decide then."

"Why don't we just run up there and blow 'em away?"

I stopped walking and turned to Alf. Berta was off to one side. "If we just start firing away at them, they might open up on the women. We have to take them by surprise. Three, four seconds and it'll all be over with. We can take three out at once, leaving the last one for the quickest shot."

"That would be you."

I shrugged. "Does it matter?"

Alfred looked to the ground. "No. I guess not."

"Good. Can we get moving then?"

"You're the one who stopped," Berta pointed out.

We started walking again. We were careful to stay far enough behind so they wouldn't see us. That made it difficult to get close for an ambush, though. After several hours, we resigned ourselves on getting through the night. Until then, we would just follow them.

By dusk we were close to the ocean. We could smell the sea air. We were also out of the trees. We had been shadowing them in a parallel ravine for the last several hours when they stopped for the night. We were a mile away.

"We got anything to eat? I'm starved," Alf volunteered.

I looked at Berta. She just shrugged. We had been eating roots, raw, while we walked. But none of us thought to pick up any extra.

"Nope. We'll eat in the morning."

When darkness came we went to sleep. We would need to rise before dawn to get into position for the ambush.

Berta laid down next me. I put my arm over her waist and waited for sleep. But sleep was illusive. I kept thinking about what we were about to do and it was bothering me. The time back at the junkyard was reactive. The time with Alf was forced on me by Berta's actions. This time, it was thought out, planned, premeditated. We were going to kill fellow humans. Doesn't this make us as bad as them? Aren't we just as criminal as they are? Like rival gangs on a city street?

I heard Alf snore and turned to look at him. He was asleep on his back, mouth open. Then I saw the blue firefly. My mind went blank for a moment, then the firefly disappeared into the night.

A few moments after it left, my mind took a turn. Those men had killed to take from others. We were killing to stop them from doing it again. Stop them from hurting others. I told myself that that made it right. I repeated this to myself as I drifted off to sleep.

*　　　　*　　　　*

A blue filled my mind. I was in that realm of half asleep, half awake, and couldn't discern from were the light was coming. My mind tried to find a reason for it in my dreams, while my eyes tried to force me awake with the glow. For a moment I was in a blue gel, surrounded by the soft density of the viscous substance while Lisa's voice spoke to me in inaudible words. Then the blue glow disappeared, then reappeared. I opened my eyes to the blue firefly perched on the back of Berta's head.

I sat up quickly, but the firefly didn't move. I stared at it for a moment, then reached out to touch it; to make sure it was real, and it flew off, disappearing over the rise behind us. I looked at my companions and they were still asleep. I looked to the sky. The eastern horizon was a little brighter than the rest of the sky. Dawn was approaching. I woke Berta and Alf.

Thirty minutes later we were looking down at the camp of the four men and the women they held captive. Their fire was still burning and we could make out where everyone lay. The women were bunched together closest to us. One of the men lay close to them, but not too close. The other three were spread out around the fire. Everyone was asleep.

"Alf, move over there so you can get a clearer shot at the one on the left. Get a good aim on him, and when you hear me fire, open up."

Alfred nodded, then quietly moved a hundred yards to our left.

"Berta, you go to the right and take aim on the one on that side."

She nodded, kissed my cheek, then moved just as quietly as Alf to her position. When they were both ready, I took aim at the one closest to the women and squeezed the trigger. The rifle jerked with a loud crack, an instant later the man on the ground jerked.

Two more shots rang out in the dawn and I watched as both men targeted flinched where they lay. The last man awoke and stood, pistol in his hand. I took aim, but the women were awake and several stood up; right in my line of sight. I couldn't risk shooting for fear of hitting one of them. Then a shot came from my left and the man dropped where he stood. I waited, my eyes watching for movement from the men we just shot. Out of the corner of my eye I saw Alf stand and rush their camp.

When he was halfway there, Berta also moved on the camp. I waited, still watching. The women just stood there, as if waiting to see who was going to claim them next. I waited until Alf entered the camp and kicked each of the dead men. Satisfied that they weren't going to jump up and shoot any of us, I headed for the camp myself.

By time I reached the scene, Alf and Berta had the women untied. They were all grateful to see us, thanking us repeatedly. Then Susan, a young woman in her twenties, walked over to the last man shot and kicked him in the crotch. His body jerked from the kick. She stomped on his abdomen, then started kicking his head. Some of the other women joined her, the rest went over to the other bodies and began kicking the corpses.

I have never seen such hatred. They were dead, yet these women insisted on battering the bodies. We watched in dull shock for a few moments before Berta went over to Susan.

"He's dead, Susan. He can't feel anything."

"I can," she spat. "I can, dammit. He killed everyone at the camp then took us at gunpoint." She kicked the dead man's head again. "He raped me the first night. Raped me again last night." She brought her heel down on his face, the bones crunching. "Fucking, son-of-a-bitch."

Alfred and I quietly stepped away from it all. I thought it best to let them get it out of their systems, horrifying as it was to watch. As the women continued their assault on the corpses, Alf and I rummaged through the gear they had with them.

We found ammunition and some food, mostly canned goods, but there was also fresh roots and other edibles. We sat with our back to the camp and quietly ate, the thumps and thuds of feet hitting flesh reaching our ears between bites.

Berta joined us a few moments later, having given up on trying to stop the women. She sat beside me and opened a can of Vienna sausages. One by one, the women stopped their pummeling and joined us. When the last one sat down and had taken a few bites, Karen, in her early thirties, began telling us what these men had planned.

"They were going to start a Master Race, with them as the seed. That's why they raped us. We were to have their babies. Start the human race all over again."

"Fucking, arrogant, animals," Julie, also in her

twenties, added. "They thought they were the Chosen Ones because they survived. Fucking, stupid, assholes. We survived, too. We had all survived until they showed up with their stupid ideas."

"When they attacked the camp and killed everyone, I knew they were evil. But when they started preaching about how they were chosen by God to repopulate the world," Karen continued, "I knew they crazy."

"And we were helpless against them," Susan stated. "I never felt so helpless. So..."

"Weak," Megan finished. She was the youngest, a couple years older than Berta.

"It was really frightening," Karen said. "What they did at the camp will haunt me until I die." She looked at me. "I don't what it's going to do to the rest of them, but I won't be able trust anybody again."

All the women nodded in agreement.

"Somehow they came up with this idea that because they where God's special people, everyone else was meant to serve them. Be their slaves."

"Did they say who they were?" I asked.

"The guy in charge was a politician. A Senator or Congressman or Councilman or something. I think all politicians are mental. Megalomaniacs. All them. No wonder he believed what he did."

"A Senator? From where?" Alf queired.

Karen shrugged. "New Mexico, I think. I'm not sure he was a Senator, though. Just some self-serving politician that thought he was better than everybody else."

"Yeah," Julie agreed. "Bunch of fucking loonies. You'd

think that after what happened everybody would work together, not go on like it was before."

"People don't change that easily," Susan pointed out. "I wouldn't have thought that people like that would have lasted very long, though. Without someone else doing everything for them, I figured they be rotting somewhere. Dead from their own ineptitude."

"People like that can always find some sucker to do the work for them," I explained. "Who were the ones that were with the Senator?"

"One was his aide," Karen said. "The others," she shrugged, "suckers, I guess."

"I've already been having nightmares," Kristy admitted. She was in her early twenties.

"Me, too," Julie said.

Nods and 'Me, too's' came from all of them. This was the real world. No more shopping, watching television, chatting on the phone or gossiping in the beauty salon. Life was going to be a struggle. An adventure, everyday. Clint's camp had been a sanctuary. Life was rough there, but not ugly. Now they had seen the ugly.

"What are we going to do now?" Donna asked no one in particular. She was around Karen's and my age, maybe a little older.

Suddenly I felt all eyes on me. I looked at everyone, then said in the most confident tone I could, "I don't know."

"We could go back to the camp," Becky suggested. She was in her twenties somewhere, a little heavier set than the others.

"Great idea," Vicki seconded. Vicki was the only black

in the group. She was in her early thirties.

"That isn't such a bad idea," Susan agreed. "The vaults are almost done. We know the area. There's plenty of food in the forest and the garden is already started."

I thought for awhile. They were right. Clint's camp would be a good idea. It was already established, there was shelter, food, a water supply, and only a few days hike back the way we came. But I didn't want to stay once there. "Sounds like a plan. You think you can make it there?"

The women looked at each other. Karen spoke first, the natural leader, "I don't see why not."

Then Laura spoke up. "We don't want him there. He's a sinner." She was one of the religious extremist's that had banished Berta and I. "He's the reason our camp was attacked. He's the reason we were kidnapped. He's the..."

"He's the one that saved us, you stupid bitch," Susan interrupted.

"You don't call me a bitch, you little whore," Laura retorted.

"Whore? You were the one who was flaunting yourself at these guys. Saying you were here to help spread the good people."

"You shut up right now." Laura looked embarassed.

Barbara put an arm around Laura's shoulder. She too, had been a follower of Walker. "All of you leave her alone. She was just trying to survive."

"Oh, for Christ's sake. You're as bad as her," Julie spouted. "How many did you fuck?"

"Ladies! Ladies!" I said forcefully. "And I use that term loosely. I'll get you back to the camp, but I won't stay. I've already decided that.

"Now, let's collect as much as we can carry and start back."

As we gathered up guns, ammunition and food, Karen caught me alone. "You really going to leave after we get back?"

I stopped what I was doing and looked at her. She was pretty. Nearly my height, slender, light brown hair, green eyes and a medium size chest. "Yeah. I think Berta and I will just keep going, see what's all left."

"Isn't she a little young for you?"

I looked over at Berta. She was with Kristy and Julie, stripping the corpses of ammunition. "I don't think of it that way. We've been together over a month now. We've been through a lot. We've got a bond now. There's something about her."

"Yeah, she's half your age."

I looked Karen in the eye. What was bothering her? Did she want me? Or was she just being righteous? "Like I said, I don't think of it that way. She's an intelligent, young woman with a good aim and I like her."

Karen looked dejected. "I was just..." she let the thought go. Then she straightened. "I want to thank you, and Roberta, and..," she looked towards Alf.

"Alfred," I said.

"And Alfred for what you did. Rescuing us. You didn't have to."

I looked to the ground. "Yeah, we did." Then I walked away before she could ask why.

Chapter XV

Alfred caught up to me after I walked away from
Karen. "Have you looked up lately?"

"Wha'? No. Why?" I replied as I looked to the western
horizon. Storm clouds were building. Quickly. "Oh, shit. We
gotta get..."

Then the ground shook, violently, throwing everyone
to the ground. An earthquake. A big one. I tried to stand but it
was futile, the shaking was too strong. Some of the women
were screaming, others started crying. Berta made her way over
to us on hands and knees.

"What's happening?"

"It's the Equinox," Alf said. "It's not over, yet."

"How much longer is this going to go on?" I asked.

"Should only be a few more seconds."

"Not the quake. Everything."

Alf shrugged. "Could be years."

Then the ground gave way just yards from us. The sound was horrendous, like the world was splitting in two. Half the women we just rescued disappeared. Susan, Kristy, Julie, Barbara, Laura and two others just dropped from view. Their screams lasted several seconds as they fell with the ground. My heart beat like it was going to burst. A few more yards and we would have been gone, too.

Moments later the shaking stopped. I got to my knees and looked at the results. There was a cliff not fifteen feet from me that wasn't there minutes ago. I cautiously stood, expecting the ground to start trembling again. I eased my way over to the edge and peered over the side. It was coastline. A hundred feet down the water was still churning. There was no sign of the women.

I felt a knot in my stomach. They were gone, just like that. A minute before they were here, now they're gone. And there was nothing anybody could do. I felt so helpless, just like when Lisa was dying of cancer.

"Forrest!" It was Alf. "We gotta find shelter. Fast."

Shelter? Who was he kidding? There was no where to go. The land was open. The tree line was miles away. Taking refuge between rises wasn't a good idea. If it rained like it did ealier, we could be hit by a flash flood. We had to get to higher ground and weather the storm in the open.

"On top of the dune. Before the rain starts," I called out. "Gather what you can on the way." I looked to Berta. "You ready to get wet?"

"The...the women. Kristy, Julie, where..?"

"They're gone, Berta. We have to get moving."

Thunder cracked, sounding as if on top of us, then the rain

came. In an instant everyone and everything was soaked. The lighter items floated over the edge of the newly formed cliff within moments. Karen and the other five women had their arms full and were headed up the embankment as the water quickly rose. Alf, too. The water was already over the top of my feet. I grabbed Berta by the arm and the bag by us and nearly dragged her up the embankment behind the others.

On top of the dune we all just stood in the rain, in shock over the loss of the others. The raindrops were huge, pelting us mercilessly. Berta was against me and I held her tight. She was shaking, but it wasn't from being cold. The rain was warm. She was trembling because of what happened to Kristy and the others. She had been over by Kristy when the earthquake started. If she had stayed there she would be gone too. I squeezed her a little tighter with that revelation, then turned to the water. It was rising fast.

"We need to get moving," I shouted over the downpour.

"Where to?" Alf replied.

Everyone looked around. The ground by the cliff was disappearing fast, washing over the edge by the yard. On either side of us the water was rushing by, too fast to cross. The only option was back the way we had came. But we couldn't see more that twenty yards the rain was coming down so hard. If we ran into trouble, we wouldn't know it until we were on it. But our options were limited. The water was rising and taking more of the hill with each passing minute.

"That way," I pointed along the dune we were on. "You wanna lead, Alf?"

Alfred nodded. He picked up a bag and started out.

Karen was behind him, followed by Megan, Becky, Vicki, Donna, Berta, then me. The going was slow and arduous. The wind had picked up and blew the rain into our faces. It stung. Thunder continued to rumble, lightning flashes accentuating the dim daylight. We trudged along for an hour before we got off the dune.

Alf had found a path that led to the trees, still several miles away, but there was no rushing water. If the last storm was any indication of what to expect, it would be raining for a couple of days. We needed to find, or make, shelter.

By late afternoon, the rain still pounding us, we made it to the trees. Many were snapped off near the ground like everywhere else, only a sparse few remained intact. But we found an area we could make a shelter and we started bringing branches and logs to a crisscross of fallen trees and made a haven from the weather. It wasn't waterproof, but it did keep out most of the rain. We had to crawl into it and could only stand on our knees. It was cramped and low, but large enough for the eight of us and a small fire.

As the fire warmed everyone, Megan and Becky heated up a couple cans and roasted some roots. I could feel Karen's eyes on me while I held Berta as she slept, her head on my chest. She was still shaken by the earthquake and how close she had come to being killed.

I had grown very fond of Berta in the relatively short time we had been together. I don't know if it was because she reminded me of Lisa, or because of what we had gone through together. It didn't really matter, though. With the way things were now any chance at the smallest piece of happiness was welcome. Maybe that's why Karen's gaze bothered me. Maybe that's why she was staring at us; she wanted her little piece of happiness. Or perhaps she thought it was wrong for a man of my age to be with someone so young.

"Is there something bothering you, Karen?" I asked quietly. I didn't really want to start anything, but her stare was getting on my nerves. Things were bad enough without tension within our little group.

"I'm just trying to...are you a pedophile?"

I thought about for a moment. I suppose three months ago I would be considered a child molestor, but in today's world it was a difficult call. "Do you think I am?"

"Y..," she looked to the fire. "I con't know. She's what sixteen?"

"Seventeen."

"A few months back you would be thrown in jail for being with her."

"A few months back I wouldn't have thought about being with her. In case you haven't noticed, things have changed."

"I've noticed. It just seems you've taken advantage of it."

"You're not jealous, are you?"

"What?" she seemed insulted. Not that I asked, but that I had figured her real motive. "No. I'm not jealous. I'm just not sure it's right."

"What's not right is what those men did to you and the rest. I have no intention of hurting Berta." I then told our little group how Berta and I met. By the time I was through with my short story, night had arrived and the food was ready. I gently woke Berta.

As we ate, I prodded Alfred about the Equinox. "So, this Equinox thing is still effecting our planet?"

"Ours and a crapload of others. Everything is connected. Our gravity effected the moon, both effected Mars. Jupiter effected us. Stars millions of miles away effected their solar system, that effected the next, etcetera, etcetera. It cascades along the gravitational line, growing, compounding, causing all sorts of mayhem and chaos.

"There's a theory that's how Venus came to be in our solar system. During one of the Galactic Equinox's it was pulled from another system and got trapped in ours."

"What are you two talking about?" Donna asked.

Alf explained the theory of the Galactic Equinox while I listened again and we all ate.

"It wasn't an asteroid?" Karen asked when Alf had finished.

"No. Or a comet."

"What do you mean it caused a pole shift?" Donna asked.

"The axis of the Earth was tilted about twenty-three degrees off the ecliptic," he started.

"Oh, yeah," Vicki interrupted. "That's what causes the seasons."

"Quite right. But now the axis is considerably less than it was."

"How much?" Vicki prodded.

Alf shrugged. "It's hard to say, but I don't think we'll be having seasons like we used to. It's also why we're having these enormous storms and the earthquakes. The planet is trying to realign herself."

"So, how much longer is this going to go on?" Karen asked.

"The Mayan's predicted that the effect would pre-date the Equinox by several years and continue on several years after."

"This could go on for years?" Becky asked, the dejection in her voice blatant.

"I'm afraid so," Alf confirmed.

Although the rain had been continuous, the thunder and lightning had stopped, until a loud crack of thunder shook our impromtu structure, the corresponding lightning illuminating the gloomy interior. Everyone, including me, jumped.

A moment later there was another burst of thunder, the preceding lightning striking a nearby tree. The groan of timber giving way to weight was the only warning we had that something was amiss. Another moment and the struck tree fell on us, instantly killing Vicki, Megan and Karen. The fire was extinguished. Alfred was pinned, his legs trapped underneath a pile of logs and branches. Berta had been hit in the head and was knocked unconscious. Only Donna, Becky and I were unhurt.

Becky went into hysterics when another flash of lightning showed us the carnage. Donna grabbed her and crawled outside, trying to calm her down. I pulled Berta away from the demolished shelter and laid her beside Donna and Becky, then crawled back inside to free Alf. He was concsious.

"How you doing?" I asked him.

Through clenched teeth he replied, "My left leg is broken and it hurts like hell. My right is just stuck." He panted. "How's everyone?"

Lightning flashed again and I saw who didn't make it. "Donna's with Becky outside and she's hysterical. Berta's out cold, but I think she'll be okay." I started yanking and tugging at the timber on Alf's legs.

"And the others?"

I paused. "Dead. I don't think they knew what hit 'em."

"You hope."

"I hope," I muttered and I continued to pull at the logs and branches covering Alf's legs. I was afraid that if I pulled the wrong one, more would come tumbling down on us, but I wanted to get him out of there. A flash of lightning helped me choose what branch to grab. "Can you move yet?"

Alfred pushed with his arms and moved about two inches. "Not yet."

I cursed not having a flashlight as I continued to feel my way around. I grabbed something soft and Alf yelped in pain.

"That's my leg, you idiot!"

"Sorry," I said, then went on removing the smaller branches. Several minutes passed before I cleared enough away to discover a large log over his legs. I was going to need help. "Donna!"

Donna stuck her head into the squashed shelter. "What?"

"I need help lifting this log off Alf."

"What? I can't see a thing."

"No shit. Follow my voice." A moment later a hand touched my thigh. "That's me."

"No shit."

"Come 'round behind me." I felt her hands on my butt,

then my back as she maneuvered behind me. "You find the log?"

"Yeah, I got it."

"Okay. On the count of three, lift. Alf, you pull yourself free."

"Sure thing."

"One. Two. Three." I pulled up with all my strength and the log budged. Then Donna joined and the log moved.

"I'm free," Alf barked.

Donna and I dropped the log then pulled Alfred out. Becky was whimpering in the darkness. Berta lay silent where I had left her. A flash of lightning showed Becky, knees to her chest, arms around her legs, huddled beside Berta. Donna went over to them while I splinted Alf's leg.

As I splinted his leg I felt an unnatural bend below his knee. A flash of lightning allowed me to see it. Luckily, the skin wasn't broken.

"We need to set that leg of yours," I told him.

"I...I know. Got any whiskey?"

"I wish." I grabbed a small branch and broke it over my knee. "Here. Bite down on this."

"That's suppose to help?"

"It does in the movies."

"Christ, I don't want to do this."

"You want it to heal that way?"

He looked at his leg, then up at me. "No. Let's get it over with." He put the stick in his mouth.

"Donna, grab his shoulders." While she moved towards Alf's head, I positioned the splint. When Donna was in place, I took a firm hold of his ankle, then looked Alf in the eye. He nodded. I yanked. He bit the stick in two, then passed out. His leg was straight. I felt around the break and it felt as though it was set. I re-splinted his leg.

The next morning it was still raining. No one had slept, Berta was still unconscious and Alf was just coming around. Becky was back in control. Alfred's broken leg looked bad, but it was straight.

I looked at the two women. "We gotta get out of the rain."

"How's Roberta?" Donna asked.

I looked over my shoulder at her. I was worried. I turned back to Donna. "I don't know. You'd think she would have come around by now, with the rain and all."

"How are we going to move her and Alfred?" she asked.

I thought a moment. "Ever hear of a travois?"

"Isn't that what the Indians use to use?" Becky asked.

"Yup."

"Know how to make one?" Donna asked.

"I've got a pretty good idea how they work."

We pulled the bodies from under the tree and buried them. After a short break, I went to work on the travois.

By the time I had the first one finished, Alf was saying he just needed a cane. I made him a set of crutches.

Chapter XVI

      With the rain still pouring, Donna helped me put Berta on the travois. We covered her the best we could with some extra clothes. Becky helped Alf stand and then with his crutches - two crooked branches with clothing lashed to one end for cushion. Donna took the lead, followed by Alf and Becky, with me bringing up the rear, Berta dragging along behind me on the travois.

      Thunder and lightning was sporadic, and each clap made us all jump. Time was hard to judge without the sun, but after several hours we stopped to rest. I gently laid down the travois and checked on Berta.

      She was pale white. I touched her face and it was cold. I grabbed her wrist and checked for a pulse. There wasn't one. I put three fingers on her juggler, still no pulse.

      "No-o-o-o-o!"

      The others gathered around me, silently staring as I

wailed. She couldn't be dead. It was just a knock on the head. She didn't even bleed that much. I couldn't understand why she was dead. I wouldn't believe it. I kept my hand on her neck, waiting for the pulse to beat.

The rain continued. The wind started to pick up again. Still, I crouched beside Roberta, my fingers on her neck, waiting. Waiting.

Several moments passed before Alf hobbled beside me. "I'm really sorry, Forrest. I know how much she meant to you."

I jolted straight up. "You have no idea what she meant to me." I was shaking with emotion: anger, grief, shock. I didn't mean to snap at him, but another person I cared about just left me and I had to lash out at something, or someone. "Cancer took my wife a few years ago and I thought that was just how life is. Then that night everything was destroyed took what I had made for myself after she died and I thought that was just how life goes. Then I save Berta from some animals and figured that's just how life is going to be. Then some more animals kill Clint and his friends. Then the Earth herself takes the women we just rescued from those same animals and I figure life is a bit more cruel than I thought. Now Berta is dead because a tree fell during a storm," I threw my arms up and out. "This storm. And you want to console me by pretending to know how much she meant to me. Go fuck yourself, Alf. Just go fuck yourself."

Alf looked me in the eyes. "I'm really sorry for you Forrest. Really, I am. But we've all lost a lot lately. You're not the only one going through a living hell. So, you can just go fuck yourself."

It was like a slap in the face. I looked down at Berta,

tears streaming. I sniffed back some mucus and wiped my nose on my sleeve. "I'm...I'm sorry. I didn't mean to take it out you. It's just..."

"I understand, Forrest. We all do. None of this is easy."

I behaved like an ass. A self-centered ass. "Thanks." I looked down at Berta again. "You go on ahead. I'll catch up in a little while. I'm going to bury her."

"We'll stay and help," Donna offered.

I looked at each of them, each nodding when I caught their eyes. "Thanks."

*   *   *

After we put as many stones on Berta's grave that we could find and carry, we set off for Clint's camp. It would take several days to make it there, especially with Alfred being hurt again. I had to admit, I admired the guy. He had been beat up pretty good and came back strong, and now has a broken leg and is keeping a decent pace, considering. He might not be very big physically, but I now knew he had a strong heart.

As the light began to fade and still no luck in finding shelter from the rain, we had resigned ourselves to walk through the night.

*   *   *

Dawn brought clear skies and a beautiful sunrise. The air was clean and fresh, the sun warming it and drying our clothes. We were all exhausted and searched for a place to rest.

When the sun had climbed about an hour above the

horizon, we found a rock outcropping that was bathed in sunlight. It would make for a hard bed, but it was better than muddy ground. We climbed atop the biggest rock and stretched out on the cool stone.

Alfred eased himself down and laid back on one of the bags. Donna and Becky claimed a spot to Alf's right. I was to Alf's left and stayed sitting for a while, trying to gain a bearing.

We were close to the path we followed down, but I couldn't discern how close. I sure didn't want to miss the camp, even though we were still a good three days away. What we were going to do once back at Clint's camp, I hadn't the foggiest, but we would at least have some shelter. I laid back against the bag I had been carrying and closed my eyes. As I drifted off to sleep, the sun drying and warming me, I wondered if ticks could climb rocks.

Screams woke me. I opened my eyes to the sun directly overhead. More screams. A woman's scream. I sat up and looked towards Donna and Becky. Donna, who had been on the outside, was being attacked by coyotes. It was Becky who was screaming. Alfred woke when I did and we both stared in shock at the sight for a few moments before we came to our senses. I grabbed my rifle and stood. Alf grabbed a pistol and fired first.

He hit one of the animals in the shoulder, spinning it off Donna. It's yelp pierced the scene, shocking Becky into silence. I aimed, then pulled the trigger. The coyote by her head was forced back and fell, dead. It was hard to tell how many there were, but Alf and I fired until we were both empty. I counted four coyotes running away, then walked over to Donna's body and counted five more. They must have grabbed her by the throat with the first bite because no one heard her scream. Her body was horrifying. Her neck was ripped open, bites were out of her arms, legs, and abdomen. Huge chunks were missing from her thighs and abdomen. I turned to make sure Becky wasn't looking and she was standing beside me.

"We need to bury her," she hushed out. A moment later she added, "What's left of her."

I nearly agreed, then thought if we left the body for them to finish, they wouldn't track us out of hunger. I quickly countered myself that if they thought they could get away with eating a human, they might not hesitate to attack next time. "Yeah. She's needs buried." I looked around for a suitable spot, wondering how big of stones do we need to put on top of it? "We'll leave the coyote carcass', though. They can go ahead and eat there own. Show them what's it like to be human."

I moved to climb down and start digging when an idea struck. "You wanna' dig or filet the coyotes?"

"Are you serious?" Becky seemed astonished. "I'm not touching those filthy things."

"I'll slice up some coyote meat," Alf offered. "You two get Donna buried. Deep."

I suddenly wondered if we had buried Roberta far enough down. Were the stones big enough? "Let's get started," I ordered Becky.

"I won't eat it," she dared. "They killed Donna."

"And if we pass up a meal and grow weak they could end up killing more of us."

"I still won't eat it."

"Fine," I finished. It wasn't harsh, accusing, or patronizing. Simply a matter-of-fact statement. "Now dig."

*   *   *

Four days later, the weather clear, sunny and warm the entire time, no animal attacks, no tick incursions, nothing to speak of, nothing to write about, we arrived back at what once was Clint's camp. That's all I ever knew it as. I turned to Becky. "Did you guys have a name for this place?"

"We just called it Phoenix."

I looked to where the bodies had been. They had all been dragged away. Parts were left behind, however. A hand here. Fingers and toes over there. One head, but it had been chewed beyond recognition. "We should have buried them," I muttered.

"Why didn't you?" Becky accused.

"We wanted to catch up to you."

"You should have buried them."

I did some rough calculation. "You would have been a day further south. Then all of you would have died in the sea."

She looked at the grisly scene. "Maybe that would have been better."

There's always hope, I thought. After Lisa died I found the desert. After the Equinox, I found Berta. "I dunno. We've always got hope."

"Hope for what?"

"Tomorrow."

She smiled, but only for a moment. "Maybe."

I wondered what Alf thought about Becky. "Alf?"

"Hunh?"

"How's your leg?"

*　　　*　　　*

Over the next two weeks, while Alfred's leg healed and we completed one vault, we discovered that Becky had liked Alf better than me from the first day. Something to do about Roberta. But that was fine because I was planning on leaving before Berta died, even more so now. The day Alf came out to the worksite without crutches or a cane, was the night I left.

"Don't you at least want to wait 'til morning?" Alf questioned.

"It's a full moon tonight. I'll be all right."

"You have enough supplies?" Becky offered.

"Plenty." I glanced out into the woods, then back. "There's plenty out there, too. Just gotta know where to look."

"You gotta leave right now?"

I tried to understand Alf. He should be happy I'm going. No competition for the girl, even though her choice is blatant. No interference. Alf and her can build their own garden of Eden. "You've got plenty of ammo. I've showed your local food sources. You get a big batch of roots dried, in case things get bad for a few days. Weeks. I dunno. Just be ready for about anything, man-made or otherwise. And you know what I mean by otherwise."

Alfred nodded. His expression did not show any confidence.

"You'll be fine. Just, just take care of each other, watch each other's backs. You know how to do what's necessary to survive."

"And just what are you going to do out there?"

"Either go home," I looked out into the dimming light. "Or see what's left."

"Now? Wait 'til morning."

"I'll be fine."

"We'll never know," Becky pointed out. "You can't call or write."

I just shrugged. "Guess you'll just have to hope that I am."

Chapter XVII

As I walked away from Little Phoenix, I wondered how long it would be before I had the chance to come back and see them. If I had a horse I could visit them every few months.

I needed to find a horse. This walking is nice, but it's so damn slow. But, it does give you a lot of time to think. I thought about all that had happened since Alf's Equinox.

All the destruction, all the presumed dead, all the dead I've seen and caused, the loss of ten miles of coastline in an instant, along with seven people. A tree branch killing one, coyotes another. Man killing man. There was still Alf and Becky. How long would they last? How long will I last? I looked to the sky. The moon was up.

According to Alf's calculations and observations, I couldn't count on the Moon for guidance. Not for a while, though he couldn't say how long. It's orbit changes nightly and he can't tell where it will settle, if it does at all. But he thinks the Earth's axis was shifted to almost perpendicular to the orbital plane around the sun. That means the seasons aren't going to change, he thinks. It's another one of those wait and see things.

There were a lot of wait and see's. Tomorrow is a wait and see. And the Moon, it's been slowing it's slide south. Tomorrow night it could stop. Then what? More earthquakes? And just how much longer are we going to have storms that last days at a time? The climates "recalculation", according to Alf. I'd settle for some kind of pattern. More than just it's probably gonna last a few days.

But I had at least a week's journey ahead of me to get home. Home. Funny word. Wonder if the water's cleared?

A blue flash caught my eye and I turned towards it. A moment later another flash, a little further up. It was the blue firefly. Was it trying to tell me I was going the right way? Or just running away from me? I stopped. Watched.

The firefly continued on, in the direction I was intending on going, flashing every few feet until it disappeared around a curve.

Was I to follow it? Or merely continue on as intended, puzzled over the coincidence?

I continued on, wondering what it was all about. After seeing the blue firefly my thoughts would stray back to Lisa if I drifted in any way, and walking caused my mind to drift.

I remembered all the fights she and I got into, big and small. They seem so meaningless now. But I still remember them. The nice things, the good times I remember hold more importance, more meaning.

I didn't see that firefly the rest of the night, and my

thoughts of Lisa dwindled until they were hidden, once again. I occupied my thoughts with staying alert for food and danger. I also tried to picture the globe, then straighten it. Then I spun it, wondering what the weather was going to be like, once it settled down, at my latitude. Without the tilt of the axis, there will be no more seasons. Just one long one. If you want a change of weather, change latitude. Too hot? Go north a few degrees. Too cold? Head south for a day or two.

The weather patterns, the movement of cold and hot air, cold and hot water in the oceans, was another one of those wait and see. Alf even thought there might be a chance that something else big might happen when we reach the other side of the gravitational influence. He said it wasn't a line like a string, but more like a ribbon. A thick ribbon, and when we go out the other side, we could see another pole shift. I sure hope he's wrong, but we won't know for about seven more years. He thinks. He got that from Christianity and the seven years of tribulation. Just another wait and see. I hope I'm asleep if it happens.

When the sky behind began to lighten, I found a suitable spot and stopped. I ate a few bites of roasted root, then laid back for a few hours sleep before dawn. I should be able to get an idea where I'm at then, but it should only take a few more days to get to Prescott.

*   *   *

Morning brought warm sunshine and high, swirling clouds. I munched on more of that roasted root as I watched the clouds sweep across the sky. I could see them churning, like someone was up there with a spoon stirring them into a continuous vortex, corkscrewing from east to west. I wondered what it foretold? There wasn't going to be anymore, 'Red skies at night, sailors delight' ditties to help predict the weather. I don't remember seeing clouds like these before. I wondered if Alf had?

I washed down the root with some fresh water from a puddle, then started walking. I hoped to come across Interstate Seventeen sometime today.

*   *   *

When I reached Interstate Seventeen later that afternoon, my approach was from a hill, allowing me to look up and down the highway for several miles in either direction. The grass and weeds coming through the cracks in the road made it look like a long, abandoned parking lot. Coming from the north I could see a solitary figure headed my way. I could easily meet him, or just as easily sit and wait until after he passed.

Berta, or Lisa, if either were here, would want to meet the figure. See who it is, what they know. If either were here, though, I would be even more cautious. I was tempted to run into whoever it was, see where whoever has been, seen. But why should I chance a meeting that could go bad if I can avoid it?

I was rather heavily armed. I carried a high-powered rifle, with scope, and a .357 revolver holstered at my hip, and submachine gun, seven millimeter, over my shoulder. Most of the weight in the pack I carried was ammunition. I had large knife hung in a sheath on my belt, another smaller one strapped to my right calf.

I wasn't too concerned about the actual meeting, although he could always surprise me, catch me off guard. Still, I felt confident for a face to face. But if I felt I couldn't trust whoever this was, I would have to make sure that I wasn't followed afterwards. That would mean staying up all night watching over my own campsite for three days, or until I could convince myself that whoever it is forgets me as I will try to forget whomever.

But what if that stranger had spotted me without giving it away. He could waltz right on by, then double back. I could be staying up a few nights either way. I had to meet him. At least to see what I was up against.

I scanned both directions of the road again. It was indeed a lone figure. I checked the revolver, then headed for the interstate and an the inevitable. It had to be inevitable, destined. In a world like this, where whole cities are wiped out, states, pieces of the country, just gone, what are the chances of meeting someone?

"Hey!" I screamed at him. I was still in the trees. Stepping forward to catch him had put me in shadows.

He stopped and looked in my direction.

I waved my arms. I doubted he could see me.

"Who's there?" he hollered back.

"Forrest."

"What?"

That tone didn't sound right. I thought I'd best clarify, "My name's Woods. Forrest Woods."

I could see him lean in my direction, but he just wasn't

seeing me.

"Is this some kind of a joke?"

"Shit," I muttered to myself. What the hell was I thinking? He can't see me, but hears a voice calling out from the trees that it's Forrest Woods, the guys going to think he's gone insane. I fired a rifle shot into the air.

"No! No! Don't shoot!" He dropped his packs and raised his arms. "It's not much, but you can have it all. Just don't shoot."

"Shit," I cursed myself. "Idiot," I muttered, then continued walking towards him. This was going to take a few minutes before he could see me.

"Um, um, I'm sorry," I yelled to him a few yards later. A little closed I called out, "My name really is, Forrest Woods. I'm not going to shoot."

"I...I...can I put my arms down?"

"Of course. I'm really sorry. I didn't mean to scare you."

I stepped past a tree and saw recognition in his full body jerk. He's seen me now. I was further down than he thought, turning towards me as I came into view. "I didn't want you to think you were losing your mind." I was almost to him now.

"Actually, I did think..." He knelt down and retrieved his gear. "Your Forrest, Woods?"

"Don't make me explain. It's not all that fascinating."

"You could have just waited until you knew I could see you before getting my attention?"

"I couldn't risk you were some trigger happy cowboy ready to shoot first and ask questions later."

"So, you gave yourself the upper hand."

"Guilty."

"'Cept that name didn't work all that well. 'Specially if you're like me; I haven't seen anyone in about six weeks. I thought I was going nuts. I couldn't see you, and then your telling me that you're forest woods, I was convinced I had cracked.

"You could have been closer, too. That was the longest three minutes in my life."

"I didn't even think what my name would do until I called it out to you, suddenly aware of what it must sound like. But you know how sound carries out here." I looked past him to where he had been trying to squint into the trees. "And, I was close enough to hit you," I held up my rifle, "if I'd been so inclined."

"Well, thanks, for not shooting me."

"I said I was sorry."

"Yeh, but I couldn't see your face then."

I swapped hands with the rifle and extended my right to him. "I'm, Forrest...wait, three minutes? I pulled my hand back. "Six weeks...how are you telling time?"

He pulled out a pocket watch. "Old school. Made in eighteen ninety-two. Runs fine. Just got to wind it everyday day." He then produced a pocket day planner, and a stub of a pencil. "I've been crossing out the day before the next morning since that night all Hell broke loose."

"Galactic Equinox."

"What?"

"Um, somebody told me that that night you call all Hell breaking loose, was caused by the passing of our entire solar system, through a gravitational wave given off by the black hole at the center of our galaxy. Happens every fifty-one hundred years. It's on a cycle." I spewed it out like some college graduate who knew what he was talking about. I had an idea of what I was saying, but the confidence was all Alf's. "He also said we could have another night like that if we haven't passed through the wave yet."

"That's an interesting theory. I've heard it before. Solar Equinox or something. I don't like the part about passing through the wall of this gravitational wave, again. How thick do they think it is?"

"He said it could be seven years from now."

"The tribulations."

"He mentioned those, too."

"Any correlation with the Mayan or Chinese calendar?"

"He, um," I was stunned. This couldn't be Alf's friend. Alf said he was dead. Yet he knew of the 'Equinox and some details. "He mentioned them both."

"I never got that deep into it. I saw a show about it on PBS or something and checked into it for a little while, but nothing major. I had some books we could have checked, but they're gone now. Everything seems to be gone now." He looked past me to the remants of the forest. Broken trees littered the hills. The mountains further on were lower, many of them capped, the tips broken off. Over half were flat-topped. Much of the rest had severe shifts on at least one face. He turned back to me. "That would explain the pole shift, though." He looked to his feet, then to the sky. "Velikovsky suggested that a celestial body large enough, passing close enough, could alter our poles, too. He thinks Venus caused it once. Except, I didn't see anything. Did you?"

"Um, who are you?"

"Oh, jeez. I'm sorry. I'm Felix Morgan. Did you?"

"Did I what?"

"See anything that night, or the day before? Or even before that?"

"See what?"

"In the sky. Anything big enough to shift the Earths axis doesn't just whiz by in a couple hours. It takes several days. We would have seen it in the sky, like we see the moon."

"Um, no. I didn't see anything."

"This Mayan Equinox thing is sounding more and more like the explanation."

"Galatic Equinox."

"Suppose to happen every five thousand years?"

"That's what Alf was saying."

"Alf? Alfred Rosten?"

Again I was stunned. "You know Alf?"

"Me? No. Knew someone who did, though. Guy I knew lived in Flagstaff. Did the weather there on tee vee."

I would have to tell him how to find Alf and Becky. Later, if I felt I could trust him. "Wow. This is weird. Alf was with the weatherman from Flagstaff the night it happened."

"No kidding?"

"That's what he told me."

"And Alf Rosten made it out alive."

"Was when I left him."

The sun was setting fast, as it was getting a habit of doing this time of day. The pattern was already seeping in. I had also noticed that the sun only reached a certain point in the sky each day. Never gaining, nor receding. It was now quick to rise and quick to set, but crawled across the same track in the sky each and every day.

"Wanna share camp tonight?" I bluntly asked.

"That'd be great. If I start talking to much, you just tell me to shut up."

"Count on it."

We talked about food options and who might be a better cook as we continued down the roadway, coming across what use to be a rest area just a few minutes later. Picnic tables, concrete lean-to's and outhouses, everything was flattened, although there were a couple of corners stuck up here and there. The cement picnic tables were strewn about the grounds. Some broken into pieces, others whole but lying flat.

We made a fire ring in front of the tallest corner and started in clearing the area for a camp as the fire took. Plywood and rusted sheet metal made for a roof, braced with a four by four and held down with pieces of concrete. Dragging the picnic table benches next to the wall created useable seats. While a couple cans of green beans heated up and a good size piece of root roasted, I studied my companion as we conversed. I thought I could like him. "So, what did you do for a living before that night?" I inquired.

"I use to be a processionist."

Oh great, he wants to talk politics. "A what?"

"You know the Earth is tilted?"

"Was." I remembered today's observations. No difference in the sun's path. I've been keeping track.

"Uh, right. Well, it also has a wobble that they've

tracked over millions of years and discovered this wobble makes a complete cycle every forty thousand or so. Our tilt varies from about twenty-two degrees to twenty-four and a half because of this wobble. It's called the ecliptical procession. It's only a couple of degrees and takes thousands of years to change, so, no one really thinks it has an effect on the climate. No discernable effect is what they called it. Years after believing that shit, we're suddenly told that is was a mistake. An oops.

"Couple a years ago we find out, we, being the grassroots support for the processionists, that they had known this 'no discernable effect' conclusion was backed by almost all in the scientific community from the beginning. They had gotten it suppressed all those years though, somehow. They still funded our gatherings and made sure the media was at each event. I guess even fools can cast doubt. And that's all they wanted, to cast doubt so the debate would continue about global warming and they could continue doing whatever it was they had been doing all along."

"Yeah. They're like that. I imagine most of those kind are gone. Crushed inside their big stone buildings, or underneath all that wood in their four-story homes. Even if they did survive the night, they couldn't have survived the last two months if everyplace is like this. Not on their own, anyway."

I thought of the men that raided Little Phoenix and kidnapped all the women. They had said the leader was a politician of some sort.

Still, I felt no guilt for killing those men, or the ones hurting Alf, or the one's that shot at me, nor the frail old man with the fast draw. And that absence of guilt worried me. I may have killed for all the right reason's, but there should always be guilt. Remorse of some kind. Especially now, when there's so few of us left.

"Albuquerque is smashed flat, by the way," he changed the subject, "if that's where you're headed. Gallup is a waste land. Anything Man put up, fell down that night."

"You from Albuquerque?"

"Nope. Little city called Las Vegas."

"Little?" I queried, thinking about the city in Nevada.

"Las Vegas, New Mexico. Just outside of it, actually. But it didn't fair any better than Albuquerque. Whole mountaintop came down on it." He thought for a moment, staring at the fire. "You know, there were glitches, little swaths every five thousand years or so, of extreme flucuations in the Earth's magnetic field."

"How big were these swaths?"

"Real narrow. Five, ten years."

That tribulations thing came to mind. "That five thousand figure, you remember when the next one is due?"

"Oh geeze. Uh, early this century. Twenty-ten, twenty-fifteen?" he shrugged.

"Alf said Winter Solstice, twenty-twelve. This is oh-nine. And it happened shortly after the Autumn Equinox."

"This is barely oh-nine. Tomorrow's New Year's Eve."

"Sirius reaches it meridian at midnight on New Year's Eve."

"Yeah. So?"

"We can tell how much the poles have shifted."

"Really? You remember what's suppose to be right above this star?"

154

"Actually, I think Orion is off to the right." I stepped over to the fire and checked the food. It was ready.

As we ate, the night deepening with each passing minute, Felix started to just talk.

"When I was with the processionists, I realized that I hadn't been thinking for myself. The bad thing is, is that it hadn't started there. Most of my life I've followed what others thought would be good for me. And any idiot could see that the processionists idea of climate change was faulty from the start. I left those baffoons and just poked around on my own for once. Heard about that equinox thing on some public tee vee show, like I said. I was still learning about it when it hit.

"There's also that theory about the rogue planet that orbits the center of the galaxy and passes by Earth every thirty thousand years. That was suppose to have stirred things up back in...June...of oh-one.

"Then there's the one that concerned our alien forebears coming back to take the creme of the crop. 'Cept, no one really knew what their standards were. They could have wanted leaders of nations, or the man off the farm. Supposedly, if you could decipher the crop circles, you could go.

"Personally, I thought we'd nuke ourselves before anything else could happen. I wonder what's going to happen to all those warheads?"

I swallowed my last bite. "They're suppose to be useless, according to Alf. That EMP thing."

I could see him kick himself mentally. "Of course. They shouldn't have detonated, either. They're all just a clump of radioactivity buried in a standing grave."

"What about the power plants? If they shut down, how

are the rods staying cool?"

"Oh Christ. With all the nuclear plants we have, all the plants around the world, they could release enough radioactive material to irradiate the whole planet."

"Oh nice. Survive the biggest shake up in five thousand years just to die of radiation poisoning because we're a bunch of fucking idiots."

He didn't like my attitude. "They could always have collapsed on themselve, like all the other buildings. That could contain the meltdown."

I didn't like my attitude. "You know where there's one at? So I can check."

"I think the closest would be Kansas. Wichita, I think. Up the thirty-five."

"Yeah. They should have collapsed." I bit a piece of root, pondering should I go check, or go home.

"No wait. Not Wichita. A little place called Burlington. Wolf Creek is the name of the reactor. It's south of Topeka about sixty miles. East of Wichita."

"East of Wichita. How far east?"

"Actually, it's northeast. 'Bout a hundred miles."

"I need to find a map," I muttered to myself.

"That first night," Felix suddenly restarted. "The morning after, I was reconsidering the ideas of the Solar Flarists. Some of their predictions were right on the money. Like the EMP. Wiped out everything. On, off. Plugged in, stored in the garage. Zap. Useless. Nothing is ever going to work again.

"They thought that every few thousand years the sun flares up and cooks the Earth. Only way to survive is in a cave or a nuclear bunker. Those guys were bonkers. I went to one meeting. Left early, too.

"But I never thought of the Galactic Equinox, until you mentioned it earlier. All the predictions fits. They're all there. And I bet we are still in the actual wave itself. Notice how fast the Moon is spinning and how much faster it goes across the sky?"

I nodded. "It also looks a little bigger. Like it's closer, too."

"Looks like it is, but I can't tell for sure. That's gonna do something to the tides if it is. And the tectonic plates, too. We had a big quake just the other day. Did you feel it?"

I stared at the fire for several moments. "Half of Phoenix is gone. It's not there. Half of it is at the bottom of the ocean, the rest is beach front property.

"We were a little southeast of Phoenix when the quake hit and the ground just fell away."

"Wait, wait, wait," he riveted. "Whose, we?"

I told him about Clint's camp and finding Alf. I didn't tell him about Berta and me. Then I told him about returning to Clint's camp and finding the massacre. I continued up to the earthquake. Those that made it past the earthquake, I told him, I left back at Clint's camp. All of them. They could explain to him, if he goes. I still may not tell him where it is.

"I haven't found a group yet," he stammered.

"Where'd you come from? Las Vegas, New Mexico?"

"That's where I live. Lived. I was in Amarillo the night it happened. My presentation hadn't gone as I would have liked, so, I was unwinding by putting miles on the rental car when I got lost. I was out in the middle of no where, sleeping in the backseat of the rental, when everything went to hell."

"You must have been totally confused when the car wouldn't start."

"That's when I started thinking about the 'Flarist's. Well, right after I tried the radio and it didn't work. I was shocked when I reached Amaraillo later that day. I had wound up only ten miles north on some rarely used county road. It only took me a few hours to get there.

"But I couldn't believe what I saw. Amarillo was flat. My first thought was nuclear bomb. But I quickly ruled that out. If I was only ten miles away, I would have been fried by the heat blast.

"And as I walked through the rubble, I noticed that it wasn't as if things had been blown up. It was more they just fell over, and not all in the same direction. I didn't find anybody alive, either. It took me two days to get all the way through and out the west side. I was headed for Tucumacari and the one-oh-four. That took me to 'Vegas.

"It was gone, too. Tons and tons of rock on top of it."

"How long have you been walking?"

"Since that first night. Hell, all I had was that rental car, and it wouldn't start. I had no choice but to walk home. Only to find it buried.

"So, I headed down to Albuquerque. See if it, or anyone, survived. Maybe find something useful, if nothing else. Made it as far as Kingman, Arizona. Well, what use to be. Everything's flat there, too. Just like Flagstaff, Gallup, every single one of 'em.

"I've only seen a few people, too. Seems nobody's walking the old interstate. Maybe that's why."

"Perhaps. I try to stay off..."

"Oh my gosh. Did you see that?"

Felix was looking directly behind. Of course I didn't see it. "See what?"

"A blue lightning bug."

"I've been seeing it since my wife passed away. Going on three years, now." I turned and looked for the firefly. A moment later it blinked. Blue as opal. "That thing showed up the night she died. Follows me wherever I go."

"You think it's her?"

I shrugged. "I don't know. Always makes me think about her. Guess because of the timing of it all. Like, your favorite song is the one that was playing when you met."

"Almost spooky."

"Nah. It always brings warm thoughts. Almost like carrying a picture around."

"But you said it follows you around?"

"I first saw it outside L. A. shortly after she passed. It followed me to a mountain range, then to Arizona. Shows up every few nights or so, just to let me know it's still around."

"How do you know it's the same one?"

"How many blue one's have you seen?"

"Including this one?"

I nodded.

"One." I could see him smile in the glow of the fire. "You seem to be a decent enough guy. So, this lightning bug's been following you."

"Decent?" I kinda half chuckled it out. "I'm not too sure. I've killed a lot of men since that big night."

"So have I. Some men are just evil, simple as that."

"How many have you killed?"

"I've had to kill three men, or else be killed. All on the road. All within minutes of meeting them. Did have one snipe at me, but he missed and I couldn't find him so, he doesn't count."

"So, how can you tell when they're evil?"

"When they try to kill ya'."

"Believe me, I wish I didn't have to kill all that I have. I really don't think there's that many of us left. I've been wandering around for about two months now and have only ran into that sparse few I told you about."

"Well, you're number nine."

I put the can down on the ground, empty. "So, what did you do before that fateful night? Besides finding yourself."

"I was a nuclear plant inspector. Federal level."

"Really? What was that presentation about in Amarillo? Nuclear secrets?"

"Um, ah hell, it doesn't matter now. I wanted them to stop producing spent rods until we could figure out what to do with it all."

"But, wouldn't that mean shutting down the plants?"

"Yeh. It didn't go over very well. One of 'em called me a terrorist. That's when I asked him if he had a swimming pool. He said he did. I asked him if he would mind if we stored some spent nuclear fuel rods in it."

"He called me a lunatic."

"I told him it was perfectly safe, as long as the water level didn't drop or get too hot. Which meant a continuous supply of cold water being added. He couldn't swim in the pool anymore, either. And he really shouldn't walk around breathing the air. All that evaporating water is radioactive.

"Even after we take the rods out, the water and the concrete would stay radioactive for thousands of years. Then I called him a lunatic for thinking people were going to stay placid when they found this out."

"Uh, who were you arguing with?"

"The head of NRC."

"The National Rifle Club?"

"The Nuclear Regulatory Commission."

"Holy shit."

"I just wanted more thought going into the waste problem than we're just going to bury it in a mountain. So, I threw my paperwork at the man I had just been arguing with, stormed out, and started driving."

Chapter XVIII

"I figured out what I was going to do while I got lost."

"Oh yeah, what was that?" I pulled out the joint I had rolled that morning and lit it off a flaming stick from the fire. Felix hadn't noticed.

"I had some land that was left to me by my grandfather a year ago. Up near Las Vegas. It was bought and paid for, and he had the foresight to pay taxes on it for ten years. I had some money in the bank and fired or not, I was still going to get some kind of pension. I was going to put a trailer or something on the land. Maybe build a house later. I would do okay. Maybe find a part-time job."

I smiled. I thought about my place for a moment. "Yeah. Sounds like a nice plan."

"What are you smoking?" He was indignant.

"Weed. What'd'ya think it is?"

"When did yo...how much do...put that out right now."

"What? Are you nuts?"

"I won't have that at my campsite."

"Ain't no cops around. Not no more."

"I'm not concerned about the cops. That stuff is dangerous."

"Really? What's it's suppose to do?"

"Mess up your brain. Makes you see things. Makes you think you can fly."

"That's acid. If you take it with a clean body, the trip is fine. Enlightening. Take it dirty, bad trip."

"What the hell are you talking about? Nevermind. Put that out right now, or...or leave."

I looked at him with a blank stare. It was all I could muster. The joint was half gone and he just now notices. "You don't want any?"

"No. I don't want any."

"Don't you know about the ticks?"

"Ticks? What ticks?"

"Hordes of the little critters. Zillions of 'em. They crawl on ya' while you're sleeping and suck ya' dry."

"See what that stuff is doing to your mind."

"Ticks don't like weed, for some reason. A joint a day keeps the ticks away."

"You're going to have to leave. You've gone mad."

"You're going to hate yourself in the morning if you don't finish this tonight," I held out the remainder of the joint to him. "We're in tick country."

"You're not scaring anybody. I want you to leave. Don't make me get physical."

He was serious. After all that good talking we did.

163

"You know, I was getting to like you, Felix." I got to my knees and gathered my things. "I'll come back and check on you in the morning."

"Don't bother. I won't be here. I'll be gone at the crack of dawn."

"Okay then, hope to not find you in the morning. Sleep well."

I grabbed a burning stick as I past the fire. "If you don't mind?"

"As long as it's one you put there."

I almost threw the stick at him, then thought briefly of just shooting him. Instead, I paused to study the stick. "It is." I walked to the far side of the rest area and found another corner, and a board for a roof.

*   *   *

The next morning, as the sun was just peeking over the horizon, I walked back across the rest area to check on Felix. When I arrived I kicked myself for not trying harder. Felix was deflated and grey. The ground around him had been combed with a fine brush. Ticks. Poor Felix. I wondered what made him so adamant the night before. Just a couple of drags would have done it. Three good hits and he would be alive this morning, without a hangover. "Fool," I muttered.

On the way back to my camp, I noticed the same combing of the sand going in the my direction. The combing stopped several inches from my bedroll. It was clearly outlined in the morning's rays. I would sleep a little more confident tonight.

I rolled a joint for tonight before packing up camp.
This was definitely going to have to become a habit; a joint
ready by nightfall, rolled after breakfast.

I walked back to Felix's camp and grabbed a few things
he had I could use. I picked up his satchel of canned goods, his
canteen, knife and pistol; a forty-five automatic. Three clips
and several hundred rounds were in with the cans. I also
grabbed his watch, his pocket calendar and pencil. I put a line
through the next day open. Today was New Year's Eve.

A clear area behind the turnout became Felix's grave. I
buried him about three feet down, then slid a table top on top of
his grave. I stepped back and read what I scrawled in charcoal
on the table. 'Felix Morgan, 31 Dec 2009 Man of vision'. I don't
know how long it'll last. First rain I imagine will get rid of it.

"Fool," I muttered. "Three hits and we'd be talking
now." I kicked dirt at the headstone. "Idiot," I called him as I
walked away.

I headed north, back up the overgrown freeway. The
first good looking break heading east I'm taking. I had to find
that nuclear plant and see how it faired. Burlington. That was
all the way across New Mexico and half way across Kansas.
How many days would that take? Weeks? I tried to calculate in
my head, but without knowing the miles it was impossible. It
would just have to be a wait and see. The day was bright and
the band of swirling clouds still slid overhead. I wished I had a
cigarette as I walked, then for a CD player.

*   *   *

This is my second day in New Mexico. I went through

Gallup to pick up some more canned goods, found four of those little bottles of water, and a folding map of the States. I had stopped several miles past Gallup and found a place to camp for the night.

As I look over the map at breakfast, I wonder why I'm doing what I'm doing.

If I would, could, walk a staight line, Burlington was about seven hundred and fifty miles away. At twenty miles a day...that was five weeks. Five weeks to survive and see if one of hundreds of nuclear plants is going to be safe for the next fifty years.

Perhaps I could make that my quest? Search out these nuclear power plants and erect some type of marker, a warning to future generations of the dangers found beneath the rubble. I put that thought aside. I wanted to see this reactor, then go home.

Maybe the weather will be different a few degrees north. Should be cooler. Not like the weather has done a whole lot of changing around here lately. Most days have been bright and sunny. It's warm, but not hot. And that band of swirling clouds? The further north I get, the more directly overhead it gets. It's fascinating to watch. I lost several hours one day just staring at it after stopping for something to eat. It feels strange to admit, but I have been enjoying the trek.

Since leaving Felix under that picnic table I haven't seen anything bigger than a rabbit. Cooked one the other night; had it for supper, breakfast, and even took a good size piece with me for lunch. The rest was left for scavengers. The blue firefly has shown up too, twice. Both times right before I fell asleep. Guess it was checking up on me.

After checking the map, I marked off another day on
the calendar. Today was the ninth. I locked at the map again,
tracing where I had come from. I found the rest area where I
left Felix. I got the pencil back out and circled the icon. Then I
wrote his name and date of death real small. I didn't know how
long I was going to be needing this map and I wanted to keep it
legible. I had made decent time, though. A little over twenty
miles a day. Of course, most days I walk over ten hours.

I dated Gallup, - 9 Jan 10, then folded the map and put
it away. I hefted the pack and stood, grabbing the rifle and
using it for support as I rose. I kicked some more dirt on the
coals of the fire and started walking. The sun, just now clearing
the horizon, was in my right eye. I was heading east-northeast,
straight to Burlington. I hoped.

The band of swirling clouds was like a visible latitude
line. If I could keep a thirty degree angle to it, I should run
right into Burlington in five weeks.

Five weeks.

*　　　*　　　*

Thirteen days out I was beginning to wonder if I was
off course. I should have come across Los Alamos at least by
yesterday, but the Continental Divide is a lot higher on foot. It
was getting dark and, as usual, it was getting dark fast. I
scoured the area for a decent place to camp as I picked up
pieces of wood for a fire.

When the light dimmed to the loom over the horizon
and it looked like it was going to be the biggest stump for
camp, I noticed a glow on the near horizon. It was blue in hue,

and it seemed to pulse. A long, slow pulse, like a breath. Radiation. I knew I had to get out of there. I dropped the wood and headed directly away from the glow.

For a moment, one moment, I had the unsettling thought of it being that firefly. Huge, laying on its back, legs up and bent. I shook the vision out of my head. It wasn't some monstrous lightning bug, but nuclear material reacting; fusing or fizzing or whatever it does. How much material did they have there to make that big of glow? Miles around is going to be useless for thousands of years. I didn't have my hopes up too high about Burlington now. But I will have to remember to approach it after dusk. See if it, too, glows blue.

Funny. I always thought it glowed green.

*   *   *

Four hours and ten miles later I was laying atop my bedroll watching the stars under the swirling clouds when a blue flash caught the corner of my eye. I flipped my head in that direction, thinking it was Los Alamos spreading somehow, when it flashed again. It was the blue firefly. For some reason, it's presence always put me at ease.

My thoughts drifted to Lisa, and that summer we spent in the back yard because she wanted to experience life off the grid. Two years before she had started a vegetable garden and the third harvest was coming on strong. The year before that we had a root cellar put in that still had vegetables from the first harvest, canned and ready to heat and serve for another two years. The installation of the root cellar caused such a stir in the neighborhood we made it on the local news. But it worked. Three months later we got rid of the refrigerator.

Then it occured to me, that was back in L. A. during the summer. I'm north of Albuquerque, several thousand feet up and it's the middle of January. I should be freezing my ass off, instead I'm laying on top of my bedroll in shirt sleeves. We have definitely tilted. If we're not straight up, we're pretty close.

I thought about that for a moment. The sun's rays were hitting us straight on, with no seasonal relief. How hot is it going to get? My home in the high desert could probably be uninhabitable. Much of the Plains could be too. I might have to think about living somewhere else in the morning.

*   *   *

Twelve days later, Interstate Twenty-Five two days behind me, I came across some grassland that had dropped into a basin. Literally. I had to climb down a fifteen foot cliff to reach it. The cliff goes off in either direction as far as the eye can see, the grass off into the horizon, and there's movement.

Something is in the grass ahead of me and to my left. I unlatched my revolver and righted the rifle when I reach the plain. The wind was coming from behind me so if it was an animal ahead, it should be smelling me soon enough.

Several paces into the grass and the thing raised it's head and looked my direction. It was a horse. It didn't bolt, which I took as a good sign. As I continued to approach, I hoped that horses haven't gone to being meat eaters too. What am I going to do if I get up there to find the horse snacking on the carcass of some animal? I approached slowly but steadily. I didn't want to give it a reason to bolt.

Some minutes later, feeling more like hours, I find the that horse had been eating grass. I was next to it, stroking its neck and feeding it some canned peaches. I looked the horse over as it ate.

It had some scars that weren't very old on its hindquarters. There were smaller scars across its chest and shoulders, and a few on its neck. Other than the scars, the horse looked in good shape. It had a bridle, but the reins had been snapped off. I removed the bridle and opened another can of peaches. While it ate that can, I stroked its back. Getting it use to my touch. Talking to it, getting it use to my voice.

A half hour later and another can of peaches, my last, I was atop the horse, bareback, grasping it's mane for balance and control. We were headed northeast. It should all be down hill from now on. I was soon to discover that that would be a mistaken assumption. Past experiences aren't reliable anymore.

Chapter XIX

Four hours later the horse and I came to another cliff, this one going up about thirty feet. As we approached I scanned both sides for an access route up, but didn't see anything in either direction. After looking up one way, then down the other for several minutes, I turned the horse and headed north.

By nightfall I still hadn't come across a way up, so I found a drawback that was about twenty feet deep and about fifty feet wide and made camp. At dawn I would resume the search.

After I ate and fed the horse a can of yams, I laid atop my bedroll and thought about the land we had just crossed. I didn't see a single tree, or stump, the whole trip. It had all been grass. Knee high and thick, like a carpet. Any walking through it was going to leave a trail, and I didn't see any other trails. And, since I kept my angle to the swirling clouds, I'm a little closer to being directly underneath them.

The clouds have been steady since the day I saw them. The band doesn't seem to move except to the east. There doesn't appear to be any north or south motion, but I'll know that for sure when I'm directly underneath for a couple of days so I can watch the stars behind them.

I comtemplated the horse. The luck on finding a domesticated creature this late in the game was too much to comprehend. The prairie looked to be pretty good size, stretching past the horizons. To have this animal nearly in my path in all this space on the day I came through was something like a miracle. Fate, destiny, karma, luck, whatever you want to call it, somebody put that animal there or put me on the right path to find it. Either way, it had me a little spooked.

Then I wondered if the blue firefly had anything to do with the horse? A moment later it appeared at the north side of the mouth of the drawback. That had been the direction I had been going before stopping for the night, so I took it as confirmation I was going the right way.

Or, perhaps it was indicating that it did have something to do with finding the horse?

I glanced over to the horse. It's dark brown color made it hard to discern in the firelight. It seemed content to be back in the company of a human. It wasn't tied to anything. I had left the bridle back where I found the animal, so it was just standing about ten feet away, free to go if it wanted to.

*   *   *

The next morning, February sixth, I awoke to find the horse still there. I walked over to it with a can of yams, I was only going to eat them as last resort, and fed them to the horse for breakfast. I had some roasted root, that stuff stays good forever it seems, and some water.

We found a highway just after noon, cutting into the cliff wall. The road was heavily damaged, but as we got closer, it looked more and more passable. At one point as we were heading up, I had to dismount and walk in front of the horse. I didn't get back on until we were out and back on flat land. I was so happy to be out of there. The horse was obviously glad to be out, too. I wondered just how long it was down there?

We veered east until we ran into another highway. This one I saw a sign for, laying on the ground next to the pavement - Fifty-Six. I checked the map. It was going in the right direction and with the sun starting it's acceleration to the horizon, I started looking for a place to camp.

About an hour later, the sun minutes from scraping the horizon, I came across Gladstone. There wasn't even a corner of a building left standing in this town. It was all flat. The few cars that weren't smashed by something, sat covered in dust with at least one door open.

We headed through to the other side of town and found a suitable camp site. The firefly showed again, moments before my eyes closed. Checking on me.

*   *   *

I found the ruins of Liberal, Kansas shortly after dawn ten days later. It was like all the rest everywhere else. Flat, demolished, destroyed. Everybody dead or gone. There was nothing to salvage, but I did find a state map at a gas station on the outskirts.

*   *   *

Five days later I was on the eastern outskirts of the ruins of Viola, Kansas. According to the map, Interstate Thirty-Five was due east about fifteen miles, Wichita northeast about twenty, Burlington another hundred, but ocean waves were crashing not more than twenty feet from me. If it's not the ocean, then it's one really big lake. I dismounted and walked over to the water and got a finger wet. I tasted it. It was salty.

"Holy shit," I muttered. The horse shook it's head and snorted. "It's seawater," I said to it. I got back on the horse and looked to the north. The beach pretty much ran due north, with a slight turn east near the horizon. I new what was south.

We started north. We had several hours before the sun set to see how far north the water reached. Did it stop before Burlington? After? Ever? Is there now an East and West United States, seperated in the middle by the Plains sea, hundreds of miles wide, connecting the Artic ocean with the Pacific?

I pondered how far I wanted to go as we continued on, deciding to decide after a nights sleep. I set looking for a suitable place to camp, wanting to give everything a rest and relax a bit before going any further. This changes a lot of things. My mind raced from thought to hypothesis, unable to concentrate on any as I watched for movement. There were so many questions that I couldn't answer. The only way to answer some was to go on an undefined journey. There was no way to know except travel it by horse. How long would that take? Would it make any difference if I knew or not?

At the intersection of Highway Fifty-Four I looked east. Water, nothing but water to the horizon. I turned west, headed for home. I didn't want to map out the world, I wanted to fix my home and get the garden started.

Just before the sun started it's downhill slide I came across remnants of a four-lane highway. Remarkably, a large, stone sign still stood naming the city of Garden Plain. That's where I made camp, next to that stone sign.

I cleared a spot near the center of the sign, moved some rocks to make a fire ring, put some wood in it, then headed into town. I had some time before sunset and I wanted to see what I could find. I had a horse again and could carry more things.

This town had had one grocery store, two gas stations, a truck wash, and one main street, the highway. My kind of town. Well, was. I didn't really expect it to be different, but I've got that hope; that I'll come across some town and it won't be damaged at all. Or, very little.

But Garden Plain was ruined. The grocery store walls fell outward, and the roof came straight down on the store. There was a lot someone could have reached without really trying, and by the looks of the racks and shelfs, somebody did.

I unlatched my revolver, then slid the machine gun around to the front. As I got closer, I could see that things hadn't been disturbed around here for a while. Still, I remained more cautious than usual. When we reached the store, I dismounted and looked underneath. The space was pretty narrow. I checked all the way around. Nothing was left. I got back on the horse and continued through town.

One of the gas stations blew up that night. There was

nothing left except a hole where the tanks use to be and pieces of lower framing for the shop. The metal sign for it, Ed's Gas & Smokes, laid next to the crater.

The other gas station faired better, but it had been scavenged, too. I did, however, find a small treasure in state maps. State maps show more geographical markings than the whole country map I have, elevations, hilly or flat, more towns and cities, that kind of thing. I found all the surrounding states, plus Texas, New Mexico, and Wyoming. It made my scavenger hunt worth it.

I headed back to camp, re-latching the revolver and put the machine gun back behind me.

Back at camp nothing had been disturbed. I started the fire, opened the last can of stew, then opened the Kansas state map. I would need to veer towards towns until I found some more provisions. Sometime in the near future, I will need to move to a place where I can grow a garden. For now, I'm headed home.

Later that night, as I was readying for bed, the blue firefly made it's appearance. It was on the west side of the camp, and when it disappeared in that direction minutes later, it left me with the distinct impression I was to go that way come morning. Towards home. I thought it a good idea, then lit the joint.

*　　　*　　　*

I followed the highway to the town of Pratt, arriving a few hours before nightfall. Shifting land had cut the town in two, twenty or thirty feet apart vertically. It took a few minutes to find a path up. It was steep and I had to get off the horse again, but once on level ground on the other side, I started scavenging.

I found twenty-two cans of edibles. Seven for the horse alone. More yams. That gave me about fifteen days, plus whatever else I could find on the way. At least I'm stocked again.

Water is still a challenge. I did find a few plastic bottles of water. Other than that, I have been letting the horse find it.

The next town was about ten miles away. Half way there I found a place to camp.

*   *   *

The next morning, February twenty-fourth, I started out heading northwest. Dodge City was that direction and I think it might be just far enough north to allow me to be directly underneath the band of swirling clouds. If I can find more food, a water supply and some shelter, I could stay a few days and see if the band is moving north or south. Although I don't think it is. It doesn't appear to be getting any further away, or closer to, the sun.

Still, a chance to kick back and just nap the day away for a couple of days would be nice, too. Most of the city parks had been relatively unscathed. A few picnic table pieces strategically stacked could provide suitable shelter. Plenty of grass for the horse.

Find food. Find water. Find shelter. The adventure of living. Although, I was nearly living that life before that night.

I was growing my own food, most of it. My water was a well and nearby stream. The shelter I built myself, and most of it survived that night. How's them apples?

Ha! I didn't realize that until just now, that my home is still pretty much standing. Everything else I've seen is either a pile of rubble, or only one corner is standing.

Sure, my kitchen is gone and there are cracks in all but one of the vaults and the dome has a hole, but it's still standing. I suddenly had a surge of pride ripple through me. All this destruction and my house stands.

I had veered northwest off the highway after leaving Pratt. Several hours later a smell hit me that was at once distinctive and unrecognizable, and cleared my mind. It stunk, but also had that alluring sickly, sweet smell. I couldn't imagine what was causing that smell, but it was getting stronger.

I came upon stream a little while later. When I first saw it, I thought it was the origin of the smell. But when I crossed it, the stream stank, but of sewage and chemicals, not the odor I had been smelling.

As I climbed a shallow but long embankment from the stream, the crest several yards away, the odor grew considerably stronger until I knew what it was - it was the smell of rotting human flesh. Plus, there was the odor of cow dung. I started to feel a little nauseated.

I was quite anxious to reach the top. I had the holster unlatched, the little gun in front, and the rifle in my hand. I wanted to know what was over the hill, then again, I didn't. I slowed the horse as we reached the top.

The land was flat. I could see a patch of downed trees in the distance off to the left. Tall grass stood drooped as far as

I could see. Spread out in front of me were about twenty head of cattle. Most were in clusters of two or three. They all had their heads below the grass line. The closest one, and the only one alone, was about twenty yards away in front of me. Either it hadn't noticed me, or didn't care I was there.

I got a firmer grip on the mane, then edged the horse forward. A few moments later, as I was about to see what the cow was doing, the cow made a noise that I believe was suppose to be a growl.

The horse stopped without my assistance. I knudged it in the ribs but it refused to move. I scooted forward, as far as I could on the horse, gripped the horse with my knees, and leaned forward while raising myself. Finally I could see what was engrossing these animals.

I nearly dropped the rifle. What I saw nearly made me turn and run the horse at full speed anywhere but there. The cattle were eating people. I sat back and just stared at the horses mane. I now knew where the scent of human flesh came from.

It was disgusting. What the hell could have caused all these people to have died, then the cattle to eat them? Were they eating the people for moisture because the stream is poisoned? It made no sense. It was, however, poetic. I couldn't help but laugh, then I shot the animal in front of me in the head with the rifle. The other cattle jumped but kept their attention below the grass line.

"I'll cook you first," I said as I got the horse moving and headed for the bovine I just shot. It has to be that car accident thing. I had to ride by and look closer at the person that cow was eating.

When I reached the body I was glad I hadn't eaten all day because my stomach heaved. I got a mouthful of bile and spit it out beside me. The cow had been eating on a little girl. The face was gone, most of the meat on her legs and arms was gone, and her belly had a few bites out of it. Her clothes were in shreds. Thankfully her pants still covered her hips. She couldn't have been more than ten. Maybe eleven. I had to get away.

I sipped some water out of the canteen and rinsed out my mouth, then swallowed a few gulps. I checked the clip in the rifle, it was four shy of a full clip. The extra two clips I had on my belt were full with fifteen rounds each. Forty-one shots.

I looked around and counted the cattle. Twenty-three. I picked one side of the small herd to start with, the next cow. This was actually going to be fun. I booted the horse in the ribs and we picked up some speed.

As we got within 'can't miss range', the cow I was approaching jerked it's head up. I yanked on the mane and the horse came to a sudden stop, almost sliding me off. I quickly regained my seat and knee grip, then leveled the rifle at the cow. Just as it started to move towards me, I pulled the trigger. It dropped where it stood. I looked over the rifle at the cow. Had it started to attack me?

All the heads of the remaining cattle shot up and looked in my direction. It surprised me at first, then I realized it was just instinct responding to the sound of the rifle. When they all started moving my direction a few moments later, I became concerned. Maybe they were like the rabbits and they did kill these people. Humans without weapons are helpless against large animals.

I held the horse still and aimed at the closest animal, fifty yards away. A squeeze later and the animal dropped in my scope. I found the next closest and did the same. By time I had downed five of them, I had to move. They were getting too close. I shot one to my left and headed in that direction.

I kept the horse at a slow pace and aimed at the nearest cow off my right. This one I hit in the neck and it dropped one shoulder for one stride, then increased speed. The others picked up their pace, too.

I stopped the horse and aimed. The bullet hit the cow between the eyes. It tumbled head first into the ground, the heels coming up and over an instant later. That didn't deter the rest of them, however. I turned the horse a little more and I sent another one to the scavenger cafe. Then I grabbed the horse's mane and kicked its ribs. It took off in a gallup, hitting full speed a few moments later, pulling away from the man-eating cattle.

My heart was racing. I was terrified, and angry. Cows eating people. Cattle chasing me for fodder. I glanced over my shoulder. They were still coming.

I turned the horse and started heading back towards the stampeding herd. I didn't have a plan, but I wanted to kill them all for eating my kind. Revenge, I guess.

As the space between me and the charging herd closed, I had a thought that they killed those people for their own revenge. I shook my head. No. Animals don't think that way. Animals don't have the same thought process as humans. They don't seek revenge. They were eating those people because of that night, the Equinox. It changed the rabbits, rats, pigeons, ticks. Why not cattle? If that was so, how many more animals have different traits than before? How many herbivores are now carnivores?

The cattle didn't hesitate any when I turned back towards them. They just kept coming. I slowed the horse and aimed the rifle. I downed one then changed clips. I shot another before veering off. The remaining herd turning with me. I headed for a small rise.

Once on higher ground, I dismounted from the horse and knelt for a steadier aim. I pushed all thoughts from my mind and aimed. This was going to be too easy. They were headed right for me, their big heads perfect targets. I pulled the trigger and the lead cow fell to the ground, the others behind it simply going around. What made them so unrelenting?

I fired again and another one hit the dirt, dead. Then the bovine did something that left me stunned. The remaining eight animals split up, three heading to my left, three heading to my right, two still heading straight for me. They were trying to flank me.

I scrambled for the horse, stumbling on the way. The horse was obviously agitated at the gunfire and the charging cattle and it took an extra couple of seconds to mount. Just long enough for one of the cows to reach me.

It knocked me down, the rifle flying from my grip. The horse bolted. I scrambled away, backpedaling from the cow and trying to get to the rifle. The cow stayed with me, inches from my feet, nipping at them. In a hurried fluster I unlatched my revolver and withdrew it from it's holster. I had to kill this cow and get up before the others joined it and I became fresh meat. Still backpedaling on the ground, I raised the revolver and put a bullet into the skull of the animal at my feet.

I stopped, rolled, and got to my feet just in time for another cow to hit me from the side, knocking the wind out of me. I hit the ground hard. How I kept a grip on the revolver I don't know, but I rolled with it and came up and shot the cow that had struck me. It fell inches from me.

I looked around this time before standing. The cows that were flanking me were heading for me, but I had time to get to my feet. There was no place to go. The area was open flat land. The horse was too far away to run to. I suddenly felt like an outnumbered matador.

I grabbed more bullets from their place on my belt and headed for the cattle on my right, yelling at the top of my lungs like I was some type of warrior going into battle as I reloaded. I started shooting a few steps later, bullet after bullet, repeatedly squeezing the trigger as I ran towards the oncoming cattle. One, two, all three cows down and dead. I released the spent shells and reloaded as I turned to the remaining cattle.

They were coming at me full speed, their mouths foaming and eyes bloodshot red. I ran straight for them, my warrior yell slipping into the distance as their grunts and huffs echoed in my ears. I shot two of the cows before the revolver jammed. There was just feet between me and the last cow. I threw the gun at it, striking it in the head. It didn't faze the animal. I pulled my knife, enraged with the fight, and jumped on the animal's back as we met.

The cow jerked and tried to buck me off, but I was determined to stay on. I squeezed with my legs and wrapped one arm around the animal's neck. I then plunged the knife into it's neck, over and over and over. After several minutes, both me and the cow soaked in the animal's blood, the bovine fell to the ground. I leaped off as it was going down, exhausted and sore.

I tried to walk away, but the adrenaline quit pumping and I collasped beside the animal. I sat there, my back against the blood soaked animal, and shook uncontrollably while the last breath of the animal slipped away.

By the time I could move, the blood on me was dry. I retrieved the revolver, the rifle, and the horse, then I went back to where I first found the cattle. Slowly I went from one body to the next. Ten corpses. The youngest was that little girl. There were three other children and six adults: three women and three men. All had been eaten to some degree. There wasn't a weapon near any of them. Nor was there any packs, bags, satchels or backpacks.

How naive were these people? This wasn't the world of restaurants, shopping malls and street lights anymore, although they did stay alive this long. Today was February twenty-fourth. Four months since the Equinox. And where had they come from? Had they just been roaming around?

I could spend the rest of the day trying to guess where these people came from and what they were doing. Instead, I cut a big piece of meat from one of the cows and continued on. I had about three hours of daylight left and wanted to be as far away as I could from all this dead meat by time night fell.

Chapter XX

I made camp that night in the middle of a field. The farmhouse that I presumed used to work it was back about four miles. It, like all the other buildings, was a pile of rubble. I thought some more about the people by the stream while I cooked the steak. Where they could have come from, where they might have been going, what they were doing without weapons or packs out there. Had they lived in that farmhouse? Did they come from the farms in the area? How did they survive this long?

Shortly after I finished eating, while cleaning the revolver, the blue firefly showed up. I quit thinking about the poor souls by the stream and drifted through memories of my time with Lisa before falling asleep.

By noon the next day I was on the outskirts of Dodge City. From the hill I was on I could see cattle grazing to the north. I wondered if they, too, were carnivorous. I headed for the town, keeping an eye on the cattle. I didn't want to go through another attack with those animals. As I neared the town, the cattle paid no attention to me.

"You there," a disembodied male voice called out to me. "Stop where you are."

I looked around, but saw no one. I kept moving.

"Stop, I said," the voice reiterated.

I stopped the horse and looked around again. The voice was coming from my left, but still I couldn't see anyone. "Who's there?" I called out.

Movement in a patch of tall grass caught my eye. A young man, dressed in jeans and a ragged t-shirt rose above the grass. "What's your business?" he asked.

I looked at him for a moment. He was in his early twenties, if that old, gaunt, but muscular. In his right hand he held a rifle, lever action. "I'm just passing through," I replied. "Heading home."

The young man walked out of the grass and headed towards me, his eyes darting to the cattle then back to me. "What's your name?"

"Name's Woods. And you are?"

He was close enough I could see his face, his expression. He was obviously nervous. "None of your business. Now dismount." He still held the rifle by his side.

"I don't see any reason for that. What are you doing out here hiding in the grass?"

He moved to bring the rifle up, but I had my revolver drawn and pointing at him in one swift move. He stopped, looked at the revolver, then me, then lowered his rifle. "This isn't going to go well for you mister."

"It hasn't been going well for awhile, now."

"You're going to end up like the group we banished if you don't stop pointing that gun at me."

Was he talking about the people I found back by the stream? "Come here, boy," I ordered.

He stepped cautiously towards me, eyes still checking the cattle in the distance. When he was close enough that I could hear him whisper I asked, "You sent those people out there without weapons or food? Four of them were children."

He straightened up as if proud of the accomplishment. "Damn straight we did."

We? "Who's we?"

"There's a hundred of us living in Dodge City. Those ten wouldn't do as we wanted, so we banished them to the grazing ground."

"You know the cattle are carnivorous?"

"I wouldn't know about that," he replied, eyeing the cattle behind me. "But they will kill and eat you."

I didn't believe there was a hundred of them. I did, however, believe that this little shit was a moron, and that he and his group sent those people to their deaths. "Where's the rest of them?"

He looked at me dumbfounded. "Who?"

"Your cohorts."

"Get down off that horse and I'll show you my cohorts," he threatened.

"Where's the rest of your group, you idiot." I cocked the revolver, not that it needed to be to fire, but it emphasized my point. His eyes grew wide and the color drained from his face.

"They're in town."

"Give me the rifle."

"No."

I had had the revolver close to me, but now leveled it at his head, pointing between his eyes. He stepped the few paces to me and handed the rifle up. I took it and laid it across my lap. "Lead the way, boy."

He turned and started walking towards the demolished town. I followed ten yards behind on the horse.

As we got near the town a figure stepped out of hiding. The figure remained motionless as we approached. Moments later I could see it was another man, older than the boy in front of me, probably late forties. A few steps later I could see recognition in the man's face at the boy walking, and concern when he looked at me. Several yards away from the man in the street I ordered the boy to stop. The man wore a holster and carried a rifle.

"This boy belong to you?" I asked.

"What are you doing with his rifle?" he countered.

"I don't like be threatened."

"He knows about the banishment," the boy said.

"Does he? And how would he know that?"

"He saw them."

The man looked down and shook his head. "How does he know they came from Dodge City?"

The boy looked to his feet and kicked up some dust. "I...I guess I let it slip."

"You stupid shit."

"I'm sorry, Mr. Spacer. He had his pistol pointing at me and..."

"Shut up, Kevin. Just shut up."

"Both of you shut the hell up. You, Spacer, drop your weapons."

Spacer glared at me, then slowly put his weapons on the ground. He let the rifle slip to the dirt, releasing the barrel after the stock was resting on the ground. Then he undid the buckle and let the holster fall.

There hadn't been any other movement in the area. Were these the only two? "Both of you, over there." I motioned to a pile of rubble to my right. As they walked over to it, I nudged the horse forward until it was over the rifle and pistol of Spacer. I scanned the area looking for more of the gang. I couldn't see anything or anyone. Something wasn't right. How did these two drive out the others?

"You there," came a voice from behind me, "on the horse. Drop your weapons and get off the horse."

"Oh shit," I muttered to myself. I climbed down off the horse and turned around just in time to see a board being swung at my head.

*　　　*　　　*

When I awoke it was dark, my head hurt something terrible, and I was tied up. My hands were lashed behind my back to something solid and my legs were straight out in front of me, tied at the ankles. What had I fallen into? I hoped it wasn't another holier than thou group.

As my eyes adjusted, it was clear that I was outside in the open. Feeling behind me and wiggling around I determined that I was tied to a wooden post, and it was firmly planted in the ground. I looked up but there were no stars or moon. Cloud cover. Great. It was going to rain again.

"He's awake." It was Kevin. The little moron had been right after all, things weren't going well for me.

"Well," Spacer said as he walked in front of me. He was carrying a torch that lit the surrounding area in a flickering dim glow. There were two others beside Kevin with him. "Woods, is it?"

I nodded.

"Just what are you doing here, Woods?"

"Just passing through."

"Uh-hunh. That's why you ambushed Kevin and threatened us, because you're passing through."

This wasn't looking good. He was twisting everything around to put the blame on me. "I suppose I sent those people by the stream back there to their deaths, too."

"I wouldn't doubt it. You appear the type."

I appear the type? This guy was either a salesman or a politician. "I found them dead after you banish..." A foot hit me in the gut and forced all the air out of me. I gagged and coughed. He wasn't going to let me speak the truth. But surely his little cabal knew what happened, unless there were more than what was here.

Wonderful. Just fucking wonderful. The world is almost destroyed, the human population decimated, and this group is already lying and twisting facts to gain power. Nothing has changed.

Lightning lit up the area for a moment. Dodge City was also in ruins. We appeared to be in a clearing, a dirt parking lot.

"We'll deal with you in the morning, Mister Woods."

Spacer looked to the sky. He and his little group turned and started walking away. Spacer looked back and added, "Don't get too wet."

As the others walked away, Kevin hit me in the face with his fist. "That's for calling me a idiot."

When they were gone from sight, I started struggling against my bindings.

Sometime later, the rain started.

I sat there getting soaked, the lightning illuminating the area in millisecond flashes. I tried to sleep, but my head ached from the board earlier, Kevin's slug making it worse. The rain wouldn't let me sleep, either. It was again fierce and hard, the wind driving it into my face.

Hours past and the rain chilled my skin. The night was warm, but the cold rain caused intermittant bouts of shivering. It was during one of those shaking moments that I noticed the post I was tied to moved.

It was only a little, maybe a fraction of an inch, but it moved where before it was rock solid. I pulled my knees up and started rocking, pushing and pulling the post from side to side and back and forth. I continued until a sucking sound told me that post was loose enough to pull out of the ground.

Grabbing the post by pulling it against my back, I slowly and with considerable effort, stood, bringing the post up and out of the ground with me. I was free, kind of.

The post was ten feet long and made me top heavy. I fell to the muddy ground with an, "Oomph". I squirmed and wiggled and made my way down the post until I was free of it. Then I pulled my legs through my arms, getting my arms in front of me. I untied my feet and stood, gnawing at the binds at my wrists with my teeth. The wind kicked up and shot the raindrops at my face sideways, making my efforts even more difficult. Moments later, however, I was free of the bindings.

I started looking for my horse and weapons, and the men who had done this to me. Revenge was coarsing through me like boiling water. I was drenched, but the chill and shivering had left; I was on fire with rage.

In the flashes of lightning I surveyed the area. They were somewhere, and so were my guns and horse. Then, in the darkness, I saw the flickering of light in the distance at ground level. I headed towards it.

The light was coming from a basement of a demolished house. They were living in the basements of the town. I approached with caution, crawling up to the window until I could see inside. I could also hear the occupants talking.

"...no one else can find out about the banishment. After the rain stops, we'll get that Woods fellow to tell us all he knows; who he's seen, where he's been, then we'll feed him to the cattle." It was Spacer. He must be their leader.

"What if he has friends? People waiting for him?"

"I just said we get him to tell us all he knows before we kill him. You are an idiot, Kevin."

I saw Kevin lower his head. The room was full. I counted seventeen people, all men, and there was still some I couldn't see. Maybe this revenge thing wasn't a good idea. I started to crawl away, then someone else spoke.

"We need to have more people working for us. I'm getting tired of looking for food, water, building places to live."

"Exactly, Bob. We are the elite now. We will be the ones reaping the benefits of everyone else's work. But we need to stick together when opposition rears it's ugly head. We need to establish ourselves and work for ourselves until we can get a base together."

"I say we put that Woods guy to work for us. Instead of killing him."

"No. We can't. He's too independent. He's too strong. He's been out there on his own for months now. If it wasn't for Larry's quick thinking, Kevin and I wouldn't be here now. We have to kill Woods."

The people in the basement all agreed in unison. I had to find weapons, my horse, then wait for dawn. I couldn't let these lunatics live. They were just like the ones that massacred Clint's camp. And, I wanted to kill them. Kill them like I killed the meat eating cattle. Kill them like you would an insect, without thought, without remorse.

I crawled away and started looking.

*   *   *

About a block away I saw a dim light in another basement window. Again I got on the muddy ground and crawled to it. The rain had not let up any and the water splashed in my face as the large drops hit the ground.

Looking in I saw their amory. It was full of guns: rifles, machine guns, pistols, military weapons. I could see one person on guard. I crept around the building until I found the entrance, then sneaked in. The area was dim, a short hallway that led to the room with the guns. Several candles lit the hallway and as I walked down it I noticed the items lining the hallway, stacked haphazardly. It was the basement of a church.

I kept my attention on being silent, but looked for something I could use as a weapon as I traversed the hallway.

I found a large, metal candlestick a few feet from the door. I hefted it, its weight feeling good in my hand, then gently turned the knob of the door. I tried to remember where the guard was in relation to the door, but couldn't. Then a crack of thunder gave me my opportunity and I shoved opened the door.

A boy, no older than seventeen, stood across the room, eyes wide and terror on his face. He started to pull the pistol from his holster, but I threw the candlestick at him and hit him on the shoulder. He cried out in pain and shock, dropping the pistol. It went off, putting a bullet through the window.

I crossed the room in a few steps and struck the teenager in the face, knocking him unconscious. The gunshot was sure to have been heard. I had to move fast and get out before anyone arrived.

I saw the guns I had been carrying thrown in a corner. I quickly gathered them up, putting on the holster, then grabbed some extra ammunition and headed out. The hallway was clear, but when I opened the door to the outside there was a man standing there. Without hesitation I leveled my rifle at him and fired. He flew back a couple feet and flopped to the ground.

The rain had not let up any, the large drops pounding the ground and me. A lightning flash showed the area clear, but I could hear the yelling in the near distance. They were all coming this way. I hesitated a moment, then went opposite the voices, not knowing where or which direction I was going. I ran, stumbled, got up and ran some more. The voices were following me. How they knew which way I went I didn't know, it was too damn dark to see anything. I reached a road and pushed with all I had to move faster.

Sometime later, exhausted and soaked with rain and sweat, I found a culvert to take shelter in and rest. Apparently I had made my escape, but I wasn't through with the Dodge City gang.

Dawn brought a dull glow, the rain still coming down in sheets. I had slept in fits, jerking awake with every clap of thunder. My clothes had dried but my feet were still wet. I had to have them in the water that flowed through the drain to keep the rest of me dry, resting and dozing in a reclined position.

As I checked my guns, I went through my options, deciding that I couldn't let those men back in town get away with what they had done, or they would continue to it. I realized I was making myself the judge, jury and executioner, but I knew that what I was doing was right. It felt right. That it had to be done or the human race was going to suffer like it had always done. A few enjoying the labor of the rest. They were the same breed that attacked Clint's camp. Megalomania wasn't going to rule the world this time. Not if I could help it.

I figured if I couldn't stop these men, then I didn't want to live on the same world as them. Eventually, the world would return to what it had been, a blind populace ruled by a select, greedy few. The ruthless ones. And I just couldn't be a part of that. I would rather die trying to stop the madness that permeated our former lives from occuring again, than to live, hidden in a corner of the world, hoping someone else makes sure the humans get it right this time.

I wondered how I was going to take on twenty or so men. I could probably kill a few by sniping, but then the rest would take cover. I tried to talk myself out of what I was planning, but couldn't come up with a good enough reason not to; even the possibility of my own death didn't deter me.

I went outside, almost instantly becoming soaked again. I had ran farther than I thought. I couldn't see Dodge City through the heavy rain.

Chapter XXI

There was no one watching the town in the rain. Didn't they think I'd come back? Maybe they didn't like getting wet?

In my search for them, I found my horse. I led it to the edge of town, the rain constant, then returned to exact my revenge. Due to the darkness the night before, I didn't know where I was going. If I could find the community room, or the armory, I could find the other. But I didn't know the location of either. I was going to have to a building by building search.

Halfway through town, the dim disc behind the clouds having passed its apex, I found the amory. Through the window I saw that it was unguarded. A closer look and I knew why, the place was about empty. Still, I crept inside and looked around. A couple extra clips and boxes of bullets would be nice. I found one box of bullets for my revolver, and a box of dynamite. A little more searching produced blasting caps and fuses. I had my advantage. Looking for something to cover the box, I found a long, canvas drover. Dark brown. It was a little large on me, but I wasn't swimming in it. I'd stay a little dryer now. I found another and wrapped the box in it, then went back outside to find a place to put the pieces together.

Two blocks away I found a corner of a building that had part of the roof left. It was dry enough to work the dynamite. I made two bundles of five sticks, hoping to catch a crowd in one room. These I put in the big pockets on the outside, one on each side. In the inside pockets I put two singles each. Along my belt in back I slide four more singles, then put one more through my belt in front, loosening the buckle to the second to last hole.

Leaving the armory I knew which way to go to find that room from last night. My heart started pounding, but it wasn't from fear. It pounded with bloodlust, thirsting for revenge for the humiliation, the intentions, and the death of the helpless. I wanted to run, but stalked instead. There should be just more than one room, and I didn't know where they could be. I didn't want to be seen first.

Agonizing moments later I could hear voices. Muffled, coming from on the ground. They were there, in the same room from last night and I was getting close. I slowed my pace even more, pulling out one of the packs of five over several paces. I dug out a joint, I didn't have any cigarettes anymore, and lit it. When I could see the window from last night, I lit the fuse off the joint. When it lit, I burst into a run, heading straight for the window. I drew the revolver with the other hand and watched for movement on the peripheral. A few steps from the window I saw a face staring back at me. I raised and fired the revolver in two steps, the man dropping from view. Another step and I unleashed the dynamite, starting my turn to lead me away when a bullet struck my left hand.

My hand shot backwards, spinning me and I stumbled to the pavement. Laying there in pain, half stupified and dazed, I realized that I was shot from someone in front of me. I slowly opened my eyes only to realize I had no idea which way I was looking. Then I heard screams from behind, coming along the ground. "Dyamnite!" a lot of them were screaming. I heard a door bang open, then a window burst out towards me on a blast of silvery light. I shut my eyes and moved both hands to my face, my left arm on fire with every move.

After the shock wave passed and no glass followed, I opened my eyes to see a hole in my left hand. Through it I could see the flames in the basement window. I thought I saw someone moving, but quickly dismissed it as shadows and smoke. Then a bright figure moved off to the right. It must be the guy who had opened the door right before the blast. A shot from in front of me dropped the burning man backwards. Death instantaneous.

I quickly turned, my hand throwing blood several feet, to see a whisp of smoke above a basement window a block down. I fired off three rounds at it, then stood, getting off one more on the way up. A flash from the window informed me a moment before the crack of the shot reached me, that I had been again fired upon. I have no idea where that one went. But the next two came really close, I could hear the buzz through the raindrops, those metallic mosiquitos. I fired off two more rounds, then dove behind some rubble on my right. I reloaded the revolver. I noticed the dynamite, thankful that it wasn't hit. The joint was gone. Washed down the street by now. I didn't have another one ready and it was too wet to roll another.

With the gun full, it went into it the holster, and out came a stick of dynamite. I lit it with the lighter, waited as it burned down a few seconds and withdrew the revolver, then jumped up, shooting the revolver with my left hand, grimacing after each shot. I got off two then had to throw the dynamite or faint. I more fell than anything back to the ground.

When the dynamite went off, I tried to head off to the right, but was overcome by dizziness and only got a couple steps. I was still behind cover, just not where I intended to be, nor how I intended. I took all the dynamite at my waist and put it in the empty pocket on the outside of the coat. Then, I removed my belt and wrapped up my hand, pulling it as tight as I could stand it. I closed my eyes and waited impatiently for things to stop spinning. As my heart rate dropped, I thought I heard voices.

"Was that dynamite?"

"That was dynamite. Who the fuck left the dynamite?"

"Christ."

That was three seperate voices. How many did I get with that first blast? I tried to remember if I could tell how full the room was before I threw those sticks, but all I can see is that one guy staring back at me.

"Larry?!"

The volume made me jump.

"Larry!?!"

"Oh, for Christ's sake...**What!?**...fucking idiot just told him about me."

For Christ's sake, Larry was close! Like, on the other side of the rubble, close.

"Have you seen 'im?!"

I had another stick out, lighter too.

"No!"

I lit the fuse. Then a low, long, gutteral rumble of thunder, hid the hiss of the fuse. If only it would last a few more seconds.

No. The thunder quit, but there was still too much fuse left. He could throw it back. I hoped the rain would cover the noise, sounding similar. With about two seconds left on the fuse, I flipped it to the other side of the mound. I heard,

"Oh, shit."

Then boom. I ran.

This time I made it up and across the street, behind another demolished building. This one had been bigger, hence the taller pile. I should be able to get down the remants of this building, then get around behind them. I tossed another stick of dynamite towards the window and ran, turning left at the next street.

The corner was just under half a block away. That should be far enough. I turned left again at the corner, then tried to decide where to cut up at.

Picking the least threatning yard, I turned left again and slowed my pace. I still knew of three, but that didn't tell me if that was all. I would've walked right into Larry if his moron friend didn't rat him out. I still didn't know how many I was left dealing with.

Three piles of rubble up, I heard voices.

"You think he left?"

"Would you?"

"Yeah. Duh."

"When the rain stopped, we'd come hunt ya' down."

Cool. This window. I lit the other bundle of five. Just before it split into three separate strands, I shot out the window, the dyanmite following the glass to the floor. Then I ran.

Not fast enough, though. The blast caught me from behind and flipped me forward. I landed face first in a muddy yard, the breath knocked out of me. I gasped and got a mouthful of muddy water splashed up by the rain and coughed. Then gulped down a few breaths of air before coughing again.

Then a metallic mosquito whizzed by.

I rolled to the closest curb and waited. Another whizz. Overhead, from right to left. I was pinned down. Another shot buzzed over me. The only way I could go was backwards, back to the corner.

I started the gut scratching crawl, every so often a shot whizzing somewhere close by. I made the corner and the shots stopped. I peeked above the curb several feet down and discovered I was behind another pile of building. I pushed myself up and stumbled over to the edge of the rubble. That crawl really scratched up my belly and chest. And I think one of those shots might have nicked me in the ass.

Yup. Damn. Not deep. Stings, though.

My hand, however, was throbbing to burst. I had to find out where they were, without getting shot. I went down to the end of the rubble and cut up. My patience was getting thin. I wanted done with this. I wanted to move on.

I stopped at the next former building and fought to curb my impatience, instead focusing on finding a better bandage for my hand. Remants of cloth was always around in the towns. A short while later I found a long strip stuck in the debris by the curb. I unwrapped the belt, then wrapped the wet cloth as tight as I could around the wound and tied it off. I put the belt back around my waist, . My patience, and bleeding, under control, I moved two more piles of rubble to the right, then cut up again.

I paused when I heard voices. They were two buildings away. If they would just shut up, I wouldn't be able to find them so easy. I couldn't figure out why everyone talked so loud. A few more paces and I could see the entrance, a slanted entry into a cellar. I pulled out a stick of dynamite and the lighter as I crossed the debris strewn street. Halfway there I lit the fuse. At the door the fuse was still a few seconds too long, so I stood there and watched it burn, trembling with fear, excitement, and rage.

When it was ready, I moved towards the door but it was opening from inside. My heart pounded, yet I casually sidestepped with the door, drawing the revolver as I moved. Just before pulling the trigger, I saw that it was another young man, early twenties. He fell backwards into the room, dead with a bullet through his heart. I tossed in the dynamite, fired another couple rounds, then slammed the door shut and turned away. I heard chairs sliding across the floor, then someone yell, "Dyna...", then boom.

I waited several seconds after the blast before opening the door and making sure everyone was dead. The room was dark, but there was enough light coming through the windows and open doorway that I could see that all six men had been killed by the blast. The room was small, half the size the building due to the collapse. But as the sight sunk in and things settled a bit more, I finally understood why they talked so loud.

The rain was pounding, like being inside a drum. The structure amplified the raindrops that hit the debris above. It was almost deafening.

Outside the rain seemed quieter than before. I stood motionless as I waited for my hearing to return. But the rain had calmed a little. The wind was now a stiff breeze. The drops were smaller and noticeably fewer. And the town seemed quieter. Was that the last of them? I told myself it was and headed for the horse. It was time to go.

I was nearly out of town when someone called me from behind.

"Woods!"

"Shit," I muttered. I stopped and turned around to see it was Spacer.

"I can't let you leave, Woods."

"Sure you can. Just turn around."

"Can't do that, Woods. Can't have you telling the world about what you saw here."

"Get a clue, Spacer. There is no world left. It's going to be hard enough without the likes of you trying to turn it back to like it was. It's never going to be like that again."

He stopped walking. Easy shooting distance. "What the hell are you talking about?"

"Your own little kingdom. Your own little fiefdom. People working for you while you just enjoy it all."

"You get a clue. It's been done like that since before we learned how to use tools."

"Not anymore."

"And you're going to stop everyone that tries? Who made you God?"

"Some would say God himself. When he chose me to survive."

He looked shocked. Like I stole his line. "You know how crazy that sounds?"

"Actually, yes, I do. I met up with the likes already. Scary folk."

"Were they now?" he sounded almost proud.

"Yup. Claimed to talk to God and I was just suppose to believe them. Well, why the hell can't God talk to me? Only take a second. Just a quick, 'Forrest, God here, follow these nice people and do what they say. They know what's best.' That's all it would take, but, nothing. He ain't said a word."

"What the hell are you talking about?"

"I gotta feelin' that you're one of those people who talk to God."

I saw his shoulder drop as he went for his holster. I hadn't reholstered mine and simply it raised it and fired, dropping Spacer where he stood. "Please be the last one." I walked over to him and checked, then fired one more shot into his head. I stood there and stared at the body, waiting, listening, for someone else, for one more.

Several minutes passed while I re-loaded the spent cylinder. Nothing. Maybe he was the last. I turned and headed for the horse, then grabbed some supplies.

Chapter XXII

The rain was still coming down the next day when I hit Liberal, Kansas on the twenty-eighth. My hand was throbbing, but the fire was gone. I could almost use it already. As I scrounged around the rubble, hoping all the rain had uncovered something I missed the first time through, I heard a voice.

"Is somebody there?" It was a female voice.

I stopped digging.

"Anybody there?"

It was to the left of me. Across the street a corner of a building still stood. The voice came from over there. Cautiously I crossed the street and peeked around the edge of the building.

In the corner, under cover from part of the seconde floor, was a young woman tied to a table so she would be...accessible; spread eagle, naked below the waist.

"Oh please be a decent human being," I heard her

whisper. "I've been raped so many times I don't care what you do, just cut me loose when you're through."

I almost laughed, but whoever left her like this, knew what he was going to put her through. I pulled out my knife and cut her loose, helping her stand as I cut her arms free. When she was steady I removed the drover and wrapped it around her. "How long have, uh, you been there?"

"How the fuck should I know?" She dipped and I caught her. "Thanks. I'm sorry. I don't know. A week. A few."

It must have shown what I thought.

"They would give me something to eat and some water, so I'd stay fresh for next time. They came back again and again."

"When was the last time you saw any of them?"

She shrugged.

"How many?"

Again a shrug.

"That doesn't help."

"There's a lot about it I'd like to forget, okay."

"I'd like to know what we're up against."

"Help me find my pants and we'll just get out of here."

We found her jeans nearly buried in the mud under the table. They were thick with mud. She took them to the street and let the running water rinse through them. I scanned the area, but no one or movement.

"There was six. The one that tied me up never came back."

"Is he in that six?"

"No." She looked past me. "Is that your horse?"

"Duh."

"Can we get outta here?"

"Get your pants on and we're gone." I waved at the horse and it came, arriving as she was snapping her jeans. I helped her up on the horse, then jumped up behind her.

"Wouldn't be better if I was behind you?"

"When you're stronger. Now lean forward." I reached around her and grabbed the mane. A gentle nudge in the horse's ribs with my heels and we headed out of town. She felt good beneath me. Warm, wet, vunerable. I pushed the thought from my mind and scanned the area. No one, no movement.

Suddenly, a bullet whizzed behind us. I went to kick the horse but it had already broke into a run. I pushed the woman down further onto the horse, lowering both our profiles.

Another bullet zinged overhead. The first one was to the right and in front of us. This one was just to the right of us. We were passing whoever it was. I looked to the right and saw a whisp of smoke above a window. I pulled the revolver and emptied it at the window as we passed.

The street veered to the left a half block down and we rounded the bend without further incident. I reloaded when we straightened out, rising to a more comfortable position, the horse slowing slightly. The woman rose moments later, stopping only when she was leaning against me.

"You gotta name?" I asked.

"Claire."

"I'm Forrest."

We rode in silence for quite a while. Turning off the road a few miles outside Liberal, we rode fast across open land for several hours, the rain stopping while we rode. We stopped at a creek several hours later and watered the horse and ourselves. The Texas border was a few hours ride south of us. New Mexico was a day and a half east. It was close to two weeks to reach home.

Claire waded into the water knee deep and splashed water on her face. I knelt beside the creek and splashed water in my face and over my head. I tasted it. It was okay. I drank several palmfuls. The sun had started its rapid descent and this looked like a good place to camp.

"You hungry?"

"Starved," she said, then headed back to shore.

"I got some canned goods. Don't know if we'll get 'em heated up with everything wet like it is."

"Anything will be good. Dig it out."

When she plopped down beside me, I grabbed her closest arm and put it in my lap. I pushed up her sleeve and looked at the wound the ropes had caused. The other three wounds were just as bad.

The sun was nearly to the horizon by time I had her bandaged up and we started eating.

We ate peaches, yams, and beef brisquets that she said was dog food. The paper label was long gone. It tasted okay, she just thinks it was dog food. It could be dog food. Before the event I remember feeding my dogs similar looking meals.

While we ate we watched the sun disappear behind the horizon. With no clouds to reflect the sun's rays, night fell quickly. Soon only the star's dim glow lit up the night into dark shadows and ill defined silhouettes. I went over to the horse and removed the bedroll. It was two wool blankets. Thin blankets.

"One a piece," I offered as I held up the blankets, one

in each hand.

"Or we share."

"Or you could stand watch." If we shared, we would spend the rest of the night trying not to touch each other. Not that I wouldn't be attracted to her, later. But right now, so soon, after what she's been through. She probably doesn't want me touching her, anyway. And I don't think I could pull it off. She's still dirty to me. She'll have to stay out in one of the rains, from start to finish, to feel like any of it has washed off. She'd have to use a river to douche.

Maybe that's what she was thinking when we first arrived; standing knee deep in the creek just to get a drink. She didn't wade out there to cool off. It wasn't that warm. Not after the rain.

"You stand watch. You're the man."

Oh jeeze. "You guys were emancipated early last century. You stand watch. They're after you."

She looked hurt. I thought she might cry. "That's not funny."

"Wasn't meant to be."

"Then why'd you say it?"

"Besides being true, I just met you and would rather not have you sleeping right next to me. I don't know if I can trust you. Whoever did that to you back there might have had a valid reason."

"Oh really?!" She was close enough that I could see her silhouette move. I had said something wrong. "And just what would you consider a valid reason?" she dared.

"Oh...shit," I muttered, thinking. "A spy. To show everyone that you can't be trusted."

"A spy?"

"Yeah. Check out the prey ahead of time. They send you in to get cozy. Find out if he'd be worth the effort. Then you'd just disappear one evening. Later, the guy would get attacked and robbed"

"Me? A spy?" Her tone had gotten defensive. "Is that why you think I was put there?"

"You asked me for a valid reason. I simply gave you one. You're the one getting all put in a tizzy."

"I'm not a spy."

"Never said you were. But, uh, why did they put you up there?"

"Will I have to stand watch if I tell you?"

"That depends on what you tell me."

"After that night everything was destroyed, I was stranded on the highway, miles from anywhere. After sitting with the car for two days, I started walking to the nearest town."

"Liberal?"

"Hunh-uh. Ganon. Oklahoma. I didn't get to Liberal until a few weeks ago. A guy I met in Ganon took me up there. He said we were going to join some others and start a community. What he didn't tell me is that I was to be a big part on the community starting part."

"What? Whoa. What?"

"Yeah. This group of men were taking turns trying to get me pregnant. Then they planned on keeping me pregnant and spewing out babies until I couldn't anymore." I heard her take a quick breath. Then another. "I even overheard them talking about getting another one."

"If not more."

"What?"

"Can't these guys come up with anything better than that? This is the third time since the Equinox that I've come across this shit."

"What shit?"

"This behavior. It's like the rabbits eating horsemeat or herds of ticks sucking you dry while you sleep. Something's causing these imbeciles to snap and somehow seize power in their little communities." I didn't mention that I had killed all the ones I came across, or that I felt zero remorse for any of the people I've killed. That was something I would work out later. "I'm beginning to think it has something to do with the Equinox. I'll have to go back."

"Go back? What the hell for?"

"To make sure they can't find someone to replace you."

"Shit," she muttered. Several moments later she stirred. "Where's the rifle? If I'm standing watch I want a goddamn gun."

"Here." I hit her in the chest with it, her small breasts bouncing into the back of my hand. "Sorry. There's one in the chamber."

"Thanks. How long you want sleep?"

"How long you want to stand guard?"

"I'll wake you in a couple hours."

"Wanna a watch?"

"You gotta a watch?"

I quickly put a few twists to the spindle knob, then handed her the pocket watch.

"Cool. Is it right?"

"It's close enough."

*   *   *

Dawn brought a clear sky and a warm sun. Claire's head was laying on my chest, her right arm draped across my waist, the rifle between us. Some guard. It felt good, though. The rifle, however, was poking my ribs. When I moved to clear the rifle, she jerked awake.

"What? Halt. Wait. Who goes there?"

"It's morning, Bright Eyes." Her eyes were a light blue that reflected the sky. They looked made of opal, looking into them only caused you to look deeper. I have no idea where bright eyes came from; perhaps sarcasim on her guard duty, maybe affection.

"What?" She looked at the sun just past the horizon, it's heat already warming the air. "Oh shit." She sat up, then stood. "I meant to wake you. I was up for about three hours, I think." She held out the watch. "This thing is hard to see at night."

I sat up and took the watch.

"I was so tired," she explained, "and you looked so cute laying there. I just wanted to lay next to you for a minute. I guess I was more tired than I thought."

"Apparently, so was I. I didn't wake up until the sun hit my eyes. I didn't even know you were there 'til I woke up. 'Bout scared the shit outta me."

"Oh, I did not."

"Well, I was startled to find you there."

"Imagine my surprise."

"Yeah. Right. Roll up the blankets."

"Me?"

"I unrolled them last night."

"I'm gonna take a bath first."

"Oh, jeez. I'm gonna lay back down, then."

She waded out into the creek, splashing the cold water onto herself as she went further out. "Hey?"

"What?"

"What's with that equinox thing you kept mentioning last night?"

I sat up, catching a glimpse of her breasts under the open shirt before she turned around. She waded out a little further, until the water was up to her waist, then removed her pants. She knelt, then turned around and said something to me, but I couldn't hear a word of it. She was too far out and the water just too loud. I threw up my hands and shrugged.

She struggled under the water for several minutes, then finally stood, wearing only the shirt. It fit her like a small dress. Claire rolled up the sleeves as she made her way back to shore, her jeans draped over her shoulder. I pulled out the date book and checked off another day. Today is the first of March.

"What's this equinox thing?" she asked as she walked out of the creek. "And what are you writing?"

I put the date book away. "Marking off days." I pulled off my shirt and handed it to her. "Here. Wear this while yours dry."

She leaned towards the extended garmet and smelled it. "Uh, no thanks. I smelt better than that going into the water."

I pulled the shirt back and took a whiff of it. I threw it into the water and stood. "Did you put the soap back in the dish?"

"Yup. Don't forget to rinse the tub when you're through."

"Funny girl."

"Hey, what day is it?"

"March first."

I grabbed my shirt on the way out before it floated away. The water was cold, but bearable. I waded out until it reached my crotch, then slid into the water and started swimming. I went a little further out, then turned towards the current. I used Claire on shore as my marker and checked every few strokes, swimming against the current for resistance.

The exercise felt good. Invigorating. I wondered if the creek back home had cleared. Wondered how the garden was doing in the increased heat. Wondered if Claire will stay. Wondered how long before the weather settled. Wondered how many more groups of morons I'd run into if I just kept roaming around. Then I wondered what was going to happen when we reached the other side of the gravity wave.

Some minutes later, having wondered that and more, I angled towards shore. Several yards later I stopped swimming and stood. It was easier to walk than swim. My arms were spent. They felt like weights instead of arms. I wrung out my shirt, dunked it under water a few times, then wrung it out again as I continued to shore.

I sat down beside Claire and explained what I had been told about the Galatic Equinox. We were dry by time I finished telling her, the sun a third way up the sky. It was time to go. I rose and went to my horse.

Just as I was going to get on the horse, Claire asked, "We are going back, right?"

I let go the mane and turned to her. "I thought we made that clear last night?"

"Just making sure."

"How many did you say there were?"

Chapter XXIII

Five days later, after watching what use to be Liberal, Kansas for four days, we discovered that there were eight of them. They seemed a little agitated, presumably over losing Claire, and appeared to be keeping a watch for traffic during the day. At dusk they met in one place until well after dark.

I had grabbed twelve sticks of dynamite back in Dodge City before I left. I put four of them together, wrapping them in strips of cloth and twisting the short fuses together. No standing by the window this time, waiting, counting.

As we waited for sundown, Claire got awfully close before saying anything. I was in kill mode. My thoughts about the deed ahead.

"Why are you doing this?" she asked.

How much do I tell her? The junkyard, where I find a boy who rapes his own sister? Clint's camp, where a bunch of self-proclaimed elite massacre a peaceful group of people and kidnap the baby makers? The Dodge City gang who send the unwanted defenseless into the prairie? Alf? "Let's just say that I don't want to think about them finding someone else, either."

"You the law, now?"

"Don't think of it that way."

"No? How do you think of it?"

"Just trying to save the world from ourselves this time 'round."

"And you think by killing all of those that oppose your beliefs..."

"Phfft! My beliefs are few and still open for interpretation. I could care less if anybody likes what I think. But man being man isn't going to cut it this time. We're going to evolve, or become extinct."

"Forrest Woods, the philosopher, judge, and executioner."

"Shut up." I didn't tell her that I liked killing. It was easy killing people like this. Ones that mean to do others harm. Ones that mean to oppress, enslave. Ones that mean to exploit.

"Ooh. Touchy."

We spent the next hour or so in silence while night crawled over the land, waiting and counting until all eight were inside. When we could see the light in the window, we moved into position. I gave Claire the rifle and she scurried over to where she could see my approach, the door, and the window. I went to the street and headed for the target building.

A block from the building I lit the fuse. I broke into a full run as soon as I put the lighter away, the short fuse giving me only a few seconds to get away. I focused on the glow from the window, pulling the revolver on the way; one shot to break the glass.

I hit one of them in the leg with my shot through the window, seeing his surprised face as he spun around from the hit. As I released the dynamite I glimpsed above him and saw a naked woman tied spread eagle to a bed, one of the men on her. I turned away as a shot whizzed behind me from Claire.

I cut again and was almost a half block away before the blast went off. The shock wave hit, knocking my feet from under me and slamming me back first onto the pavement, knocking the wind out of me. I was gulping for breath as a dismembered arm sailed over me. Small rocks and plaster hit me in the head and I closed my eyes against the debris.

I didn't open them until I didn't hear anything else fall from the sky. I turned my head, brushed the dust off my eyelids, and slowly looked around. I heard shots fired and I snapped my head to the building I just blew up. Claire was at the doorway to the room, spraying the room with bullets with the machine gun.

I got to my feet, brushed off while my head cleared, then headed for Claire. She had re-loaded and was still firing. She could re-load two more times before I reached her, if she had all the clips.

As she was changing clips the second time, I called out to her, "Claire! Claire! They're dead Claire. Stop wasting ammo. They're dead. Clair!"

She locked in the third clip and resumed firing. I quickened my pace, which wasn't very much, my back was screaming obsenities at me, but I reached her as she pushed in the fourth clip.

"Claire." I grabbed her arm with a firm grip. "Stop

wasting ammo."

"They're not dead enough, yet."

"They're as dead as they're ever going to get." I looked into the room. The floor above had collapsed in one big piece into the room. You couldn't see anybody who had been in the room below. She had actually been shooting at the floor from above.

"Did you see," she asked, "before the blast, what they had in here?"

She did see. "I saw her. Just as I let go of the dynamite, I saw her."

"When you shot that guy in the leg and he went down is when I saw her. I shot her right after that."

"I wish we had known. We could have gotten her out."

Claire just started crying. She dropped the machine gun and fell into my arms. I pulled her close and let her sob on my chest. I scanned the area as she wept, looking for anything, anyone, any movement.

As I scanned, my thoughts returned to the woman through the window, the look of terror, then relief, as she watched me throw in the dynamite.

A tear slid out of my eye. If I had known she was there, we could have gotten her out the next morning. If I had seen her a moment sooner. If I had not seen her at all. But I had. Claire had, too. The tear turned into a trickle. Soon there was a steady stream dripping on Claire's head. She just held me tighter and cried a little harder.

When I got so teary that I couldn't see, I gently pulled away from Claire. "We need to get going," I said as I wiped away tears.

"I did the right thing? Didn't I? Shooting her, like I did. That was right? Right?"

"You were in her position. What would you have wanted?"

She thought about that for a moment. I could see her ease up a bit, relax a little. Apparently this helped her. I was now wondering how guilty to feel, knowing that the woman was dead before the dynamite went off.

We spent the rest of the night hiding, and waiting for anyone else to show up. We didn't talk about the woman in the room. We didn't talk at all the rest of the night. The blue firefly showed up just before the Eastern sky started to lighten. Claire was asleep. The insect had come from the Southwest, hovered in the area, then disappeared back the way it came. Home was that direction.

When dawn arrived and no one else had come wandering into town, I nudged Claire awake. "Hey."

"Hey."

"Feeling any better?"

"No. Not really. I wish we had known. You really think we could have gotten her out?"

"Sure. No problem. We would have waited 'til dawn and let her go while they slept off their party."

"We could've burst in there with guns blazing last night. They would all have had their pants down."

"If we had known she was there, Claire, if we had known, we would have saved her."

"We would've had, too. Like you saved me. We would have rescued her."

"Yes, we would have."

"I got her right in the head, Forrest. I watched the blood splatter on the headboard. She was dead that instant."

"When I first saw her, she had just seen the dynamite. There was this intense terror on her face, then it's like she realized what was going to happen next and relaxed; like it was the lesser of two evils; like it was a relief."

"I wish we had known." She fell into me, her head thumping against my chest.

I put my arms around her and pulled her tight. She felt good, comfortable, feminine. I hoped she didn't start crying again. "Me, too, Claire. Me, too."

"I wish we had known," she mumbled into my chest.

"We did what we had to. It was right." I squeezed her gently in a few short squeezes, kinda shaking her. "Now come on, we need to look for supplies before we head out."

She sat up, straightening her shirt and hair. "I know where two of them hide their shit. Water, cans, ammunition, guns."

I looked at her stunned. Why didn't she tell me this before? "Let's go."

By noon the horse was loaded down with food, water, and ammunition. We would be walking this trip. It would take a month by foot to get to Bagdad, but the weather wasn't changing. It's been nearly five months since the night of the Equinox and the temperature has just now started to level out. I didn't think we had anything to worry about weather wise. The rain didn't bother me any more.

It was human contact that worried me the most. Even the animal attacks weren't as bad as human contact. At least with the animal you knew their intentions straight off. I was concerned with who else was out there. I had come through Liberal on the way here, even did some scrounging, but missed those men that first time, and Claire, too.

I shook my head. I had to stop those guilt trips. Things happen. You don't find anything and you move on. And if she had made any noise that first time, I would have heard. It's awfully quiet most of the time. Mostly you hear your own footsteps and breathing.

This was going to be a long walk.

*   *   *

Eight days later we came across Las Vegas, New Mexico. Felix wasn't kidding, a whole mountaintop did slide on top of the city. The only sign a city was there was the road leading up to it.

We turned south and headed down Interstate Twenty-Five for a day and a half before turning westerly and back across open country. We found Albuquerque three days later.

*   *   *

We spent most of the day in Albuquerque scrounging. We had come across a police station and I wanted to find their evidence room. We were heading back into tick country and I wanted a good quanity of marijuana on hand. Claire just laughed when I told her what I wanted it for. She did say she would smoke it with me. She didn't care if it kept ticks away.

I don't care that she laughed. As long as she smokes it. Once a day. Maybe I'll tell her about Felix someday.

While I dug in the precinct, she roamed around and found some bottled water and unmarked cans. Probably more dogfood.

A little past noon I found what I was looking for; marijuana. Fifty pounds of it, all neatly wrapped. I grabbed ten pounds worth and headed back for Claire and the horse.

Claire was laid out by the horse, soaking up some sun. Her shirt was tied tightly just below her breast, her arms out of the sleeves, baring her shoulders. I hated to disturb her, wanting instead to lie down beside her and start kissing that neck. I shook my head. "Eh-hmm. You awake?"

"Hunh? Oh, yeah. Just resting, waiting for you." She slid back into the shirt, buttoned a few buttons near the top, then untied it. "Oh, you found some."

"About ten pounds, still good. There was fifty."

"Ten pounds? And we're leaving forty behind. Why not take it all?"

"It'd just be too much for the horse."

"Hell, I'll haul fifty pounds myself."

I thought a moment. "We'll split it if we can find a way to carry it."

Back at the precinct we found our choice of packs in the evidence room, got everything loaded, then headed out of the city.

"I can roll a joint if we stop."

"We're not stopping. Not 'til night."

"I can roll one if I can sit on the horse."

I looked at the horse. It was already burdened with about two hundred pounds. "It can wait."

"It'll take ten minutes."

"What is wrong with you?"

"I like it. I haven't had any since months before that night. Now we got fifty pounds. I just," she shrugged, "want some."

I scanned the area. We weren't even past city limits yet. "Can it wait 'til we get outside the city?"

She looked ahead. "How long you figure that'll take?"

"I dunno. There's not as much rubble. Soon."

"Outside city limits I can roll us a doobie?"

I thought about it for a moment. She'd probably forget. "Sure. Why not."

*   *   *

Two miles past the city limit sign, Claire spotted a place we could rest and she could roll up a marijuana cigarette. She didn't forget. I thought about the idea of smoking while walking, but we've been walking for ten or so days and haven't run across anyone so I didn't see the harm. We had a full cache of food and water, and we were both armed to the gill. "Half hour. Remember, I have a watch."

"I'll have it rolled and ready to smoke in ten minutes. Where's the skins?"

"I'm gonna eat something. Want anything?"

"Yeah. If you come across a double-cheeseburger and onion rings, I got dibs."

"I saw a McDonald's back a few miles."

"Where's the skins?"

I fished the rolling papers out of a pack on the horse. "Skins," I muttered as I handed them to her.

"What?"

"You call them skins. Haven't heard it in awhile. How long you been smoking?"

"Started while I was in college. Haven't quit. You?"

"Off and on for about twenty years."

"Fifty pounds, dude. That's like a year or more of getting high."

"It'll last more than a year. We only need to smoke a joint at night."

"Need, sure. Want, now that's a different story. Fifty pounds. I could stay high all the time, everyday, for a year."

"You're a pothead."

"I consider myself a stoner. And what's the matter with you? Have you ever seen fifty pounds of weed before? I haven't. I'm all a goose-pimply."

"No, I haven't. It's just not that big of deal anymore. If I don't smoke the ticks will kill me while I sleep. Now shut up and roll."

"Oh. Ticks. That's right. And I suppose now you want some?"

"After all that blabber about it, what self-respecting toker wouldn't?"

"Blabber about it? Shit. All that weed got me excited."

I looked at the sun. We had two hours of daylight left. "You about done? I want to find a good place to camp before it gets dark."

"You mean before we get too wasted."

"Can you start a fire stoned?"

"What kind of fire you want started?"

The way she said it caused a stir in my crotch. I knew

exactly what kind of fire she was insuating, and so did my groin. "Shut up and roll."

A few minutes later she declared her task complete. The joint was rolled. We started walking again. "You got a light?"

*   *   *

An hour later we came across an old, adobe structure. The roof was gone and so was one complete wall and part of another. But it would work for camp. Besides, I was really getting into my buzz and wanted more, or sleep. Claire said she would roll another while I made camp.

The fire was going and the stew cooking when Claire finished. She came and sat beside me and held up two joints. "One each? Or you want to share 'em both?"

I shrugged. "After we eat, okay?"

"What is it?"

"Stew."

She peered into the can. "Dog food. How about we smoke one of these before we eat? It'll make it taste better."

"It's stew."

"I'm telling ya', it's dog food. Use to feed the exact same stuff to my dog. She loved it."

"It's stew."

"Hunh-uh. Look at it. Way too much meat, too few veggies. It's dog food."

"It's stew."

I looked at the contents of the can. It was dog food. "Light one up."

She put one of the joints down, then lit the other with a stick from the fire. She inhaled deep, then handed me the joint. As I inhaled, she exhaled.

"So, this tick thing. Is it really true? They suck the blood out of while you sleep?"

I nodded. I held the smoke as long as I could. If that was dog food, I wanted a really good buzz. "Uh-hunh. Seen the results a few times, but saw it happen overnight once. The guy was alive when we went to sleep, dead the next morning. Sucked dry." The joint came around again and I filled my lungs with it.

"This happen before you knew about the weed, then?"

"Hunh-uh. Just a few weeks ago. Dumbshit refused to smoke a joint. Hell, just half of one would have saved his stupid ass, but he was dead set against it. Wouldn't have any part of doing something that was illegal just a few months ago. Fucking idiot."

"Still kinda bothers you?"

I took a long hit and held it, passing the joint back to Claire. "He was an idiot. If he had taken a few tokes, he'd be alive today. Instead I find him the next morning looking like all of the air had been let out of him. I didn't think the ticks were around, or I would have pushed him to smoke harder. I thought I had a couple of days to talk him into it. But they got him that night." An involuntary shiver shook me. "It rattled me for a few days, too. Don't know why. I had only just met the guy."

"Maybe because it could have been you?"

I remembered the fine combed sand and shuddered again.

"You okay?"

"Yeah. Just remembered that they did come visit me that night, too. Got real close. Maybe that's why I can't get all excited about hauling around fifty pounds of weed. It's a necessity."

"So, how come you didn't have any when you ran into me? You run out?"

"Let's just say I ran into some trouble in Dodge City."

She handed me the joint, then pointed out, "Can's boiling over."

                    *   *   *

As we ate I told her about Dodge City and the man-eating cattle. I was ready for her to call me crazy or something when I told her about the cattle, but she just said,

"Are all the animals crazy? I saw a flock of sparrows attack and kill a housecat. It was a big housecat, too."

"I've seen rabbits eating carrion, pigeons killing rabbits, rats killing coyotes and men. Everything is crazy. And it seems most of the people I've run into all have a god complex of some type. 'I survived. God loves me best.' Fucking idiots."

"Maybe it's got something to do with magnetics. I'm sure the pole shift changed the magnetic field around the Earth. It's bound to fuck things up. Hell, we still got that band of clouds going around us lickity-split."

"Lickity-split?"

"Faster than the everything else."

"I never heard anything about magnetics affecting behaviour. That don't mean it can't, obviously. Although, they did think that migrating birds use the planet's magnetic field to navigate those great distances. Perhaps it does have something to do with it. But turning herbivores into carnivores? That's a bit of a stretch."

"You got a better theory?"

I shrugged. "Light that other joint."

She handed me the fired up joint. "Do ya'?"

"Um-m-m-m; a government lab cracked open that night it shook and let loose some wicked biological agent."

"Oh, that's a nice thought."

"Hey, I came out this way to check on a nuclear plant. To see what happened to it."

"What happened to it?"

"It's under water. I'm pretty sure."

"Where was this?"

"Wolf Creek, Kansas."

"Where's that?"

"South of Topeka."

"And you know it's under water..how?"

"Wichita is under water. Deep water. I'm assuming most of the Plains states are under water."

"Assuming? How far did you go?"

"Little town named Viola. About twenty miles west of Wichita. That's the furthest east I could get. That's were the beach was; just a few feet from the highway going north through Viola. I went as far north as Highway Fifty-Four. The beach, as far as I could see, kept on going north."

"You really think Topeka is under water, too?"

"At least. Have you ever been to an ocean beach?"

She nodded.

"It was like that. You can see Catalina island on clear days from L. A., and that's twenty-two miles. I couldn't see anything but water."

"Holy shit."

"A lot has changed." I went on and pointed out the things in the heavens, the sun, moon, stars. Evidence of the pole shift. I told her about the new coastlines to the south and west. I told her about the earthquake and how the ground just fell away at my feet, taking those women with it.

The blue firefly winked its existance, hovering in the direction we were heading. Claire finally saw it and we got to talking about Lisa, then Roberta. I didn't say how old Berta was, but when Claire asked, I didn't lie. I told her Berta was seventeen. She didn't even flinch.

"How'd she die?"

"Freak accident during a storm. A branch hit her in the head. She never regained consciousness."

"I'm sorry."

"Me, too."

We finished the joint, sand scrubbed the empty can and utensils, then laid down and watched the fire burn out. When it had turned to embers, Claire crawled over to me. I turned my head when she got close.

"Can I lay with you? I got cold last night."

"Sure."

As she settled in next to me, the sky lit up in greens and blues. "What the hell?" I demanded as I sat up, rolling Claire off to one side.

She righted herself and said, "That's the Aurora's."

"The what?"

"The Aurora Borealis. They usually don't get this far south."

I stared skyward for several minutes before saying, "So that's them. Far out. Must be that magnetic change you were talking about."

"Far out?"

"Cool?"

"At least you didn't say nifty." She pushed me back down and laid her head on my chest.

"You know," I said hesitantly, "I slept without a blanket last night. It was probably in the mid seventies. Like it is now."

"How about lonely? Would you settle for lonely?"

"Is it the truth?"

"What? What else would it be?"

"You're scared."

"And what? You're my protection? You're an ass." She got up and moved back to where she was.

I'm an idiot. And now, a lonely idiot. We watched the lights in the sky dance and sway for awhile, her on her blanket, me, ten feet away on mine. Then I scooted over to her. "Can I lay with you?"

"Wha'sa'matter, you scared?"

"No, lonely."

She rolled over to face me, then got up on an elbow. "You're not fucking around, are you?"

I shook my head. "No. I've been laying over there thinking about what's ahead. I really wouldn't like having to go it alone."

"I just want someone to hold. No sex." She looked at

my feet. "I'm...I'm not ready for that."

"Furthest thing from my mind," I lied. "I wouldn't think you'd be ready for anything."

"I'm ready for someone to hold me."

"I can do that."

I put my arm around her shoulders. She laid her head on my chest, then I felt her relax. We laid on both blankets, the warm night air perfect for under the sky sleeping. As she fell asleep on my chest, I lay there amazed, watching the lights swirl and dance in the sky. My thoughts drifted over the last few months and how many men I've killed. Still, I felt no remorse, no guilt. Nor did I feel satisfaction or pleasure. It was more disgust. A disgust that I would need to kill people like that after what everyone had gone through. That people like that would even try to impose what we had before infuriated me. The top down heirarchy that only benefits those at the top wasn't going to fly this time around. At least not around me. I didn't feel any remorse. Just a saddness that we haven't changed as a species. We're still so petty.

The lights in the sky started to recede, then fade completely away. I was awed. I started to wonder if I should worry about someone coming after me for all those men I've killed, then was distracted by Claire's little purr of a snore. A few moments later I saw the blue firefly.

It came to within inches of my face and hovered briefly, then increased altitude, as if trying to see Claire. Seeming satisfied, it returned to eye level, hovering in a back and forth arc. As always, I felt the presence of Lisa. My thoughts floating back to her as another woman lay beside me. As my mind drifted, the firefly flew away, leaving me with

Claire and memories of Lisa.

Chapter XXIV

"This is your place?" Claire whispered.

It was the eleventh of April. We were peeking over a rise, the sun was behind us, still low in the east.

"Yup."

"Pretty cool house."

"Thanks."

"Looks like you got company. Ya' know 'em?"

"Nope."

My home was inhabited by a family of five: Mom, Dad, two boys and a girl; the daughter the middle child. By the looks of things, they had been there several months: there was a crop coming up in the garden, laundry was strung on the south side, the cracks in the vaults looked filled, and there was work being done to the hole in the dome.

"What are we going to do?"

"Meet the new owners." I scooted back down the hill to

grab the horse.

Claire came running behind me. "We gonna kick 'em out?"

"Hunh? No. We're not going to kick them off the property. I've been gone six months. I pretty much took everything I wanted with me when I left. They can have it. I'll let 'em know it was mine and it's now theirs."

"Then where will we live? And in what?"

"There's some nice land a few miles north. There's a stream close. There's room for a couple acres of crops. We'll have the first vault up in two months."

"Two months?" She looked up the rise, a completed home on the other side.

"We'll be okay."

"You're kidding?"

I shook my head. "Nope. "

"How far away is this land you mentioned?"

"A good days ride."

"There's a stream?"

"Yup. Well, uh, there was. Before the Equinox there was. Only one way to find out."

"You better hope there is."

A moment later we were headed down the other side of the rise.

"Morning," I called out when we were about half-way down. The adults snapped their heads our direction, the mother quickly shooing her children into the house, following behind them. The man started walking our way, with a distinct veer towards the house. Moments later the woman returned with two rifles, handing the man one of them. She ducked back behind the house as the man continued on.

Claire and I stopped.

"Name's Forrest Woods," I yelled to him.

"Wha'd'ya want?" the man demanded.

"Just passing through. Use to live in the area."

"Ain't nothing around for miles. '

"I know."

"What?"

"Can we come down there? I'm getting tired of yelling at you."

He eyed us for a minute, then called up, "Leave the horse and the woman there."

Claire stood by the horse and stroked it's mane while I headed down the slope at a steady pace.

"That's good," the man ordered when I was about twenty feet away. He was relatively young. Early to mid-thirties. "Who are you?"

"I'm Forrest Woods."

"Forrest Woods? The photographer?"

I was shocked. I had no idea my work had become that popular. "Uh, you've heard of me?"

"Wife's got all of your calendars." He pointed the gun to the ground and walked over to me. "Didn't know if you survived though. We were beginning to think no one else but we did."

"There's a few more," I said flatly. "Uh, you are?"

"Oh, shit. My bad. I'm Jarod Komes."

"How long have you been here, Jarod?"

"About three months."

"You got water?"

"There's a well close by. Most days it's fine. After the rain though, it's undrinkable for a day or two."

I looked the place over. "Looks good. You do good work."

"Most of it was here when we got here. I just patched things up." He turned towards the house, then back to us.

"Come on inside and meet the family. The wife has coffee brewing and I'm sure Denise will be thrilled to see you. She just loves your pictures."

I waved to Claire to come down. As I waited for her reach me, I gazed at my old home, suddenly with an urge of wanting it back. But these people had childern, and I was still in decent health. The hole in my hand has healed nicely, except there is always going to be a hole there. It'll make a great pencil holder. And Claire is in her late twenties, she won't tell her exact age, only 'around thirty'. The rope wounds on her ankles and wrist are starting to drop scabs. She's got a good head on shoulders, and doesn't take crap from anybody, including me. We will have little problem building our own home.

When Claire reached us I grabbed the horse and led it to where the pen had been, thinking at least I could tie her up there.

As we walked, we talked.

"So," I hesitated, "you plan on staying with me?"

"I thought that was a given?"

"I...I just wasn't sure. You do know we got some hard work ahead?"

She looked back to the house. "Sure looks that way." She turned to me. "Is that the only kind you know how to build?"

"I'm afraid so. But, it survived the 'Equinox with relatively minor damage."

She looked again to the house, studying the patches. "That's a plus."

We took a few more steps. "What would you think about becoming nomads?" I proposed.

We took a few more steps. "You mean hunt the type of animal we dealt with back in Salina."

We were at the corral. I wasn't surprised to find it rebuilt, but I was surprised to see eight other horses. I unloaded the horse, then herded it into the corral. I grabbed the bags we needed for the night and headed for the house.

"Maybe," I sighed. "Maybe after seeing my home squatted on, I just don't feel like settling down."

"Yeah, maybe."

We were almost at the front door. "Maybe, what?"

"Maybe that's a reason."

"Yeah. Maybe."

We went in through the open door and put the packs by the wall. "Hel..."

"Mister Woods!" It was Denise. She was excited.

We followed the voice around the corner and nearly ran into Jarod's wife.

"You must be Denise," I offered to shake her hand.

"Denise, this is Forr" Jarod, sitting in my recliner, started.

Denise, giggling, took my hand and squeezed it quickly once, but wouldn't let go. "Forrest Woods," she kinda whispered & giggled at the same time.

"Nice to meet you, Denise."

She giggled some more, released her grip on me, then turned to Claire. "And you're just lovely." She extended her hand. "And you are?"

Claire reciprocated the handshake. "I'm Claire Samuels."

"Nice to meet you, Love," Denise responded. "Come in and sit down. Then she went and sat down next to her husband on an ottoman. I wasn't sure what to do. I never met a fan before. Then Claire waved for me sit next to her on my couch.

Their children came into the room a moment later and Denise introduced them. "This is Kyle, our oldest. He'll be seventeen in a few months. Abigail just turned fourteen and Jeremiah is eleven."

"Abby, Mom. You know I like Abby."

"Hi, Abby, Kyle, Jeremiah." Claire said.

"Hey, kids," I muttered.

"Hi," they all said.

"All right, back to doing your chores," Denise ordered.

"Good looking kids you got there, Jarod."

"Thanks, Forrest."

"Yes, they're beautiful," Claire said to Denise.

"I think so, too."

After several moments of awkward silence, Jarod surprised me by blurting out, "So, Mister Woods, you want your house back?"

I'm not sure why it surprised me. There was a year of pictures of my home in calendar number three. I looked at Claire. She leaned over to me.

"Where else can we go?" she whispered into my ear.

"I told you I know a few places. Unless you want to

evict them. Then we could just stay here."

"Of course not."

I turned to our host. "Jarod, the place is yours."

Denise squealed in glee, thanking me repeatedly.

"I really feel funny about taking your home, Mister Woods. We thought you were..."

"Eh," I shrugged.

"Let me give you something for it."

"Like what?"

Jarod shrugged. "I don...I don't know. We don't really have all that much."

"How 'bout a couple horses?"

He seemed taken off guard. "Oh, a couple horses? A couple of horses. Yeh, that could be arranged."

"One to pack, one for Claire to ride."

She smacked me on the arm. Hard, too, for not listing her first.

*   *   *

We left Jarod and Denise the next morning. They gave us some extra food, fresh vegetables from the garden, and Denise had cooked a rabbit that Kyle had shot the night before and she gave us half of that. We went to the stream and turned north.

As the sun was nearing it's apex, we heard voices. Loud, male voices, then horses hoofs. We headed for a short hill, scooting behind it and dismounting, holding the horses still. What seemed like hours later, but was only several minutes, a group of men passed us on the other side of the small rise. There was quite a few because I couldn't discern less than four voices, and there was definitely more than four. I guessed there were fifteen or twenty by the sound of the hoofs. They were still talking as they passed.

"I don't care how old she is or what she looks like, the next bitch we come across I'm fucking 'er brains out," a voice stated.

"That won't take long. Anyone screwing you won't have much brains in the first place," a second voice responded.

"Shut up, asshole."

"Make me."

We heard a gun cock.

"Put that away," a third voice commanded. "You frigging idiots. This is all life and death now. I could shoot you both right now and nobody would care. Nothing is going to be easy anymore. I thought I got that through your thick heads already?"

"Yes, sir," came the first two voices in unison.

"Besides, the first pussy we come across, I get her. You morons can have her when I'm through."

Claire made a motion to move and I stopped her. "Shhh," I whispered. "We don't know how many there are."

"But..."

"No. We wait."

We waited impatiently for several more minutes until we couldn't here the hoofs or voices before Claire spoke.

"Do you think they'll find Denise and Jarod?" she whispered.

"Nah," I said in hushed tone. "They're following the stream south. They'll miss 'em by a few miles."

We waited several more minutes, then continued our journey north. By nightfall we found a place to call home and unloaded the horses.

*   *   *

Three days later, while we were staking out the dimensions of the dome, the youngest son of Jarod and Denise stumbled his way into our camp. It was obvious something was terribly wrong. He was all scractched up, his clothes were in tatters, and it looked as if he hadn't slept in days.

"What happened?" Claire asked, reaching the boy first.

"They," he paused and wiped his nose on his ripped sleeve. "They killed Daddy and Kyle and took Mommy and Abby."

"They? Who's they?" I asked, already knowing the answer. I had been wrong a few days ago. Dead wrong. They didn't follow the stream.

"Men on horses. They came after you left. They found Abby at the stream." He wiped his nose again. "Daddy and Kyle tried to fight them away, but," he hitched his breath, holding back a sob, "they shot 'em down."

Claire glared at me. I looked to the ground, feeling more guilt then when I was with Michelle while Lisa died. How was I suppose to know they would run into a member of the family at the stream. There was no solace that they had followed the stream.

"We have to go..." Claire started.

"Not we," I interrupted. "I'll go. You need to stay here with Jeremiah."

"No." She stood. "We all go."

*   *   *

When we reached my old home, we found Jarod and Kyle in front of the house. Kyle had been shot once in the chest, Jarod in the right shoulder, abdomen, and head. All the horses were gone, the house was in shambles. It looked like they had gone through it and took everything of use.

While Claire and Jeremiah sorted through the mess inside, looking for anything we could use, I found their trail.

The sun was descending in the Western sky when I went back to house and found Claire comforting Jeremiah. "We'll get your mommy and sister back. I promise." I heard her tell him.

'And kill the fuckers who did this,' I thought.

What Jeremiah said stunned me, stopping me in my tracks. "I wanna help kill 'em. Daddy showed me how to shoot a gun after that Bad Night. He said I was a natural. Whatever that means?"

"That means you're good at whatever from the git-go. But me and Forrest will take care of those bad men." She paused for just a moment, then added, "You can count it."

"So," I said as if I just walked in, "did you find anything?"

Jeremiah ran over to me. "We found some bullets. I'm going to help kill those bad men."

I put my hand on his shoulder. "Killing isn't fun, Jeremiah. I wish it didn't have to happen, but with men like the ones who took your mother and sister, sometimes it's necessary."

"I know. Daddy taught me about killing. He said, 'Killing for food, as a necessity, is an acceptable evil. Killing for fun or sport is just evil.'"

I looked over to Claire. She just shrugged. I looked down at Jeremiah. "Your father was a smart man, son. But unless it's absolutely necessary, me and Claire will take care of the men who took your mother and sister."

"No," he commanded. "I'm going to help. I'm a good shot; was from the git-go."

I looked at Claire again. Again, she shrugged. "We'll see how it plays out," I told him. "With any luck there won't be any shooting at all."

"I doubt it," he said to the ground. "These men are just bad."

"That's apparent."

*   *   *

We spent the night in my old home. Jeremiah didn't sleep well, and for that matter, neither did Claire or I. It seemed all of us were itching to get moving; to catch up with and rescue Denise and Abby.

The next morning, curious to how well Jeremiah could shoot, he and I left Claire sleeping and headed over the hill. I brought along the M40.

Jeremiah surprised me by hitting the target within a five inch pattern. He was a natural.

By the time we made it back to the house, Claire was awake and standing outside, looking in our direction.

"Did we wake you?" I asked when we were close.

"How could you not?"

"Sorry. I was curious to how well the little guy shot."

"Uh-hunh." She looked perturbed. "So?"

"So, what?"

"How good is he?"

I paused. "He's almost as good as you."

"Jeremiah, go gather your things," she told him. After the boy was inside she turned to me. "So, you're going to let him kill?"

I looked to the ground. "Not if we can help it." I looked her in the eye. "But if we need his help, and there are quite a few of them, he's a good shot.

"Now whether or not he can kill someone, that's a different story all together."

"I can kill those men," Jeremiah said. He stood in the doorway. How much he heard is anyone's guess. "After what they did to my dad and brother, I won't have any trouble killing them."

Claire and I looked at each other. We had a young man on our hands, not a boy. "We'll play it by ear, son," I stated.

"I'm going to help get my mom and sister back," he said flatly. "You can't stop me."

"We'll see," was all I could come with.

*   *   *

As we headed out, I looked up to the band of clouds. They were still swirling and churning, but had not moved neither north or south. I scanned the horizon for clouds and another three day rain, but besides the band of clouds, the skies were clear.

Jeremiah, being the smaller of us, carried the most cargo on his horse. He had the food, water, bedrolls and marijuana. Between Claire and I we carried the weapons and ammunition. Jeremiah did have his father's Russian Dragunov sniper rifle in a sheath on his horse. It was the only weapon those men didn't find. He wouldn't tell us where he had it hid.

We didn't talk as we rode. I had the lead, following the trail of the men. They had made no attempt to hide their tracks, apparently oblivious that someone may follow them. It was obvious they had that god complex. That they were better than anyone else because they survived. My rage was on a slow boil. I thought about how ineffective I was before the Galactic Equinox in changing anything, helpless as those in power took more and more. But thing were different now. I could change the course of the future by eliminating those who had illusions of grandeur, of power and control. I wasn't going to let how the world was before come into being again. We would either co-exist as equals, or not exist at all.

The first night out we made camp in a clearing, the land flat and surrounded by trees that had been snapped in half by the shaking months ago. While Jeremiah tended to the horses I got the fire going. Claire came over as the fire caught and asked, "How far ahead do you think they are?"

I shrugged as I poked at the fire. "Hard to say. At least four days if they've kept moving, maybe more."

"We're still on their trail, aren't we?"

"Oh yeah. Jeremiah could follow the tracks they left."

"Do...do you think they've...uh..."

I knew what she meant; if they've raped Denise and Abby. "Definitely."

"Maybe we should ride through the night."

"We have a boy to take care of. Riding all night isn't going to help him."

"Yeah, well, taking days to catch up with them isn't going to help Denise and Abby."

She was right. Each day that passed meant more terror for the two. "I know. But we can't jeopardize Jeremiah's well being, or ours."

She looked over to Jeremiah, then back at me. "Having his mother and sister with that bunch of animals isn't doing his well being much good, either."

I stood up. "Look, there's fifteen or twenty of them. Maybe more. And just the three of us, and one of us is only an eleven year-old boy. You really think pushing us to the extreme and rushing in there will do any of us any good?"

Claire looked at the fire. "No. I...I just don't want them to go through what I did."

"Neither do I. But we have be careful or we'll all be dead."

"You got a plan?"

I gazed at the fire. "No. Not yet."

"Look," Jeremiah called out as he headed towards us. He was pointing behind us. "It's a blue lightning bug. I've never seen a blue one."

Claire and I turned to see. There it was, hovering at the edge of camp, blinking blue. "She's still watching me."

"Who's she?" Jeremiah asked.

"My late wife. That thing showed up after she passed

and has been with me ever since."

"How long ago was that?"

"Going on four years now."

"You know those things don't live that long."

"Sure they do."

"No. They only last about a week as lightning bugs."

"How do you know so much about them?" Claire asked.

"My Dad told me. He really liked nature."

That put a new twist on things. If Jeremiah was right, then the blue firefly really was Lisa's spirit. A chill ran down my spine and I shuttered in a quick shiver.

"What?" Claire asked me.

"It really is her."

She watched the firefly another moment. "Apparently." The blue firefly then left the area. "You think she approves of me?"

I thought about that night outside Albuquerque in the old, adobe house and how the firefly had hovered over her and I. "Yeah, I think she does."

"Is the food ready?" Jeremiah queried.

Chapter XXV

Early the next day the trail we were following turned eastward. After several more hours following it, it became clear they were headed for Phoenix. They had turned to follow Highway Ninety-Three. I wondered if that was where they came from, or if perhaps they were just checking on what was left?

The wind picked up around noon and my left hand gave out a low whistle if I held it just right in the wind. Jeremiah thought it was funny.

"How'd you do that?" he asked.

"Happened in Dodge City. I'm lucky that's all that happened."

"Is it a gunshot?"

"Uh-hunh."

"Bet it hurt."

"That would be an understatement."

"A what?"

"It hurt like Hell."

"Oh."

Claire rode up beside us. "They turned, didn't they?"

"Yup. Looks like they're headed to Phoenix."

"Didn't you tell me there's nothing there?"

"Yup." Then I remembered Alf and Becky. "We're going to have to increase our pace."

"Oh yeah? Why now?"

"Jeremiah. Ride ahead and look for a place to camp."

"Sure, Mister Woods."

"Forrest. Call me, Forrest."

"Yes, sir."

After Jeremiah was out of ear shot I told Claire about Little Phoenix and what happened there, then about Alfred and Becky. She listened in silence, asking one question when after I finished.

"You sure you want to make camp tonight?"

"I just did that so I could tell you about Clint and his group. We're not stopping 'til we get to Little Phoenix."

* * *

As we nibbled on lunch, I studied the map of Arizona, periodically glimpsing up at the Sun, trying to determine the quickest route to Phoenix and Alfred and Becky. We had stopped following the tracks of the men who had Denise and Abby shortly after I told Claire about Clint's group, turning more eastward. I was sure they were heading for Wickenburg. In fact, they could be there at this very moment. We would cut north of it, hopefully reaching Little Phoenix before they reached what was left of Phoenix.

I was hoping we had time on our side, even though they had several days lead. They wouldn't be rushing to get anywhere, where we would.

While Jeremiah readied the horses after we finished lunch, I turned to Claire. "If they get to Phoenix before we do, at night they'll be able to see the campfire of Little Phoenix. That's how we found them the first time."

"You and Berta."

"Me and Berta." I felt of pang of sorrow. She was so young, so vibrant, so full of life and optimism.

"You miss 'er, don't you?"

I thought for moment. "Yeah. Guess I always will. Just like I'll always miss Lisa."

She thought for a moment. "I can live with that."

"I sure hope so. It has nothing to do with how feel about you."

She scooted a little closer to me. "And just how do you feel about me?"

I watched Jeremiah with the horses. Actually, I didn't know. I knew I liked her. That I was attracted to her. I liked her personality, the way her hair moved in the wind, her eyes - I could fall into those eyes and never look back. But to describe how I felt about her in one word, like love or like, I just didn't know, but I had to tell her something. "I think I could fall in love with you."

She seemed taken aback. "You think you could fall in love with me? You think?" She was almost indignant. "Well, Mister Woods, I got some news for you. I do love you," she spat. A tear slid down her left cheek. "I have fallen in love with you. It happened after you rescued me. You were kind, respectful. You have integrity." Another tear slid down the same cheek. "The way you took care of me after that, the way you've taken care of me since. It's all made me love you even more."

It was my turn to be surprised. The first thing that came to mind was the patient falling in love with her doctor after saving her life. But, deep down, in my gut, in my soul, I knew it was far more than that. I felt guilty for letting her down. Saying that I did love her now wouldn't work. First, because I wasn't sure if I did. Second, she would consider patronizing. After several moments at looking at the ground I said, "Well, don't stop. Because what I think and what I feel are often two separate things."

"What?" she sniffed. "What the hell is that suppose to mean?"

I looked her straight in those light blue eyes of hers. "It means that I have feelings for you, deep feelings. That I'm comfortable around you. That...that I would miss you, too, if I lost you somehow."

She nearly pushed me over when she threw her arms around, pulling me into her. She felt good. Safe.

"Are two going to screw?"

"Jeremiah!" we said in unison.

* * *

We rode all that night, using the stars the best I could to stay on course. It was actually rather simple. As the stars rose from the Eastern horizon, I made note of where a bright star was and kept it to our right. It was, however, a little difficult to recognize particular constellations because they, too, had been affected by the 'Equinox.

We crossed Highway Seventy-One late that next morning. We were making good time, but I could see the toll it was taking on Jeremiah. We stopped for lunch early, letting Jeremiah sleep for several hours before moving on.

Late that day, as sun was racing towards the horizon, we reached the old mine at Black Rock. I decided we would camp for the night. It was ten miles to Wickenburg. After Claire and the boy fell asleep, I slipped away to see if I was right about the men with Jeremiah's mother and sister.

*   *   *

Two hours later I was sprawled out on a hilltop, studying the campsite below. They were on the outskirts of Wickenburg, the fires glowing embers. I couldn't make out the girls, but counted at least twenty people down there. Two of them had to be Denise and Abby. I contemplated picking off a few, but quickly decided against it. I didn't know where the girls were.

Then I had an idea. A stupid, foolish idea, but it may just work. I tied the horse to a bush, then made my way on foot towards the camp.

Half an hour later, at the edge of their camp, I was surprised that there weren't any sentries. I laid still for nearly another half hour as I watched the camp up close, thinking the pounding of my heart would surely wake everyone. But there was no movement. Everyone was asleep. I crawled to the edge of camp and found one of the men covered in ticks.

I quickly moved on, coming to another man and quietly slit his throat. I had never done it before and was surprised how difficult it was to cut through his windpipe. He jerked once as the knife cut his trachea, but he made no sound. I was sure the pounding of my heart would alert the rest. But they all slept through what I was doing without a stir.

I slithered to another, doing the same, this time using more force so the cut was quicker. By the time I had cut the fourth throat, I reeked of blood. Two more men met their death before I came across Denise and Abby.

I put a hand over Denise's mouth before I woke her. She nearly struggled away from me, thinking I was one of the men who had abducted her, looking to rape her.

"Shhh," I whispered. "I'm not going to hurt you. I'm here to rescue you. Jeremiah is a couple hours away."

Her eyes were wide with astonishment. When I felt she understood my intentions, I pulled my hand away from her mouth. "Wake your daughter. Quietly. We have to sneak away. There's only me."

"Mister Woods?" she whispered.

"Forrest, please."

Without a rustle, she woke Abby. I headed them in the right direction towards my horse, then crawled over to the next man and slit his throat. I did two more, then followed the girls, peeling off two horses and letting the rest of them go before heading to rendezvous with Denise and Abby.

* * *

When we reached camp, I woke Claire while Denise readied the horses and Abby woke Jeremiah. When the boy awoke, he nearly screamed out in joy. I rushed over to him and knocked him over trying to squash his enthusiasm. "Shhh," I hissed out. "Sound carries miles out here. You have to be quiet."

"You got Mom and Abby back," he gushed.

"Shhh," I repeated. "We have to go. Now."

I knew those men would be infuriated, enraged, pissed, come dawn, and I wanted to be as far away from Black Rock as humanly possible before the sun peeked over the horizon.

While they broke camp, I mulled over an ad hoc plan of meeting up with Alfred and fighting off the rest of the men I left at Wickenburg. I didn't think about how Alf might react. But I also knew that they were headed to Phoenix and would no doubt find him anyway.

"What did you do?" Claire asked after we were on our way.

"I rescued them."

"No shit. But how?"

I slowed my horse, Claire doing the same. Jeremiah had the lead, his sister and mother close behind. When they were far enough ahead, I gave Claire the details.

"So that's what I smell on you. Their blood. Death."

"First water we come across I'll wash it off."

She was silent for a while.

"What was it like? I mean, killing somebody like that."

"You wanna know the truth, or some philosophical babble?"

"The truth."

I thought about it for a moment. I remembered as I left their camp I felt empowered, almost God-like, for getting away with murder with such ease. "It was nerve-racking. I thought the sound of my heart beating in my chest was going to wake up everybody.

"But as I made my way out of camp, with no one the wiser, I felt a power I've never felt before. Like...like..."

"Like what?"

I shrugged in the dim dawn light. "I dunno. Almost...god-like."

We rode in silence for a while before she spoke. "I remember hanging on that table back in Liberal. I felt so helpless. So, vunerable. So, powerless." Then she stunned me. "I wish you had taken me with you."

After several more minutes of silence I said, "They'll come after us, you know. I'm sure we left a trail."

"Then we won't stop."

"It's going to be a rough next couple of days."

"I wouldn't have it any other way."

Chapter XXVI

Late into the night on the second day after rescuing Denise and Abby, we reached Little Phoenix. Alfred and Becky were asleep in one of the homes I helped construct. I pounded on the door until a light was lit inside and Alfred flung the door open, pistol at the ready.

"Forrest!" He was obviously startled to see me, especially with the others behind me still mounted.

"Morning, Alf," I said calmly.

"What the hel..." he turned inside. "It's all right, Bec'. It's Forrest." He turned back to me. "What the hell are you doing here?" He looked around me. "And who did you bring with you?"

"We got trouble coming, Alf."

In the dim light I saw his face harden. "Like before?"

"Worse. These guys are mad."

"How do you know?"

I motioned for the other to dismount and follow me inside. "You got a joint rolled?"

While Becky tended to her univited guests, Alf and I sat out front toking on a joint as I filled him in on what had happened Wickenburg.

"Holy shit, Woods. What were you thinking? Leading them here."

"They were headed this way, anyway, Alf. I knew that if they were in Phoenix at night they would see your fire. You'd be dead and Becky in the hands of those madmen.

"So, when I saw my chance back at Black Rock, I had to act. At least there's eight less of them."

"So, how many are left?"

"Denise told me there were twenty-two when they raided their home." I rapidly calculated in my head. "There's fourteen left."

"You happen to know what kind of firepower they got?"

I shook my head. "No idea. But we know they're coming. We know the terrain. We should be able to do away with them without any losses." I looked towards the door. "Little Jeremiah is a hell of shot." I turned back to Alfred. "If he can shoot a man, I don't know. But Claire is a good shot and will stand up under fire. I imagine Denise has some revenge she wants to extract. We should make it through this.

"Pass the joint, eh?"

Alfred took a hit, then passed the marijuana cigarette. "Maybe," he exhaled, "we should catch them down in the rubble?"

"The rubble? Oh, Phoenix." I inhaled deeply, handing

the joint back to Alf while I held the smoke in my lungs. I thought about his suggestion. It would be safer if they didn't know about Little Phoenix. "You might have an idea there, Alf."

Claire, Denise and Becky joined us then.

"The kids are asleep," Denise mentioned.

"I brought some more weed," Claire announced, then sat next to me on the log.

Becky sat close to Alfred, Denise on the other side of her. We could all feel her pain, even in the starlight, we all knew she was hurting, physically and emotionally.

"You okay, Denise?" I asked.

"Yeah. Just tired. That was a long ride."

"Why don't you go sleep with your kids, then?"

"No. I want to know how you're planning on killing the rest of those fucking animals."

"With your help."

"You can count on it. Jarod," she paused for a moment, his loss still acute. "Jarod showed me how to handle a gun after that night."

"Galactic Equinox," Alfred pointed out.

"I don't give a shit what it was," she spewed. "It changed everything. Jarod and Kyle are dead because of it. My life is ruined because of your equinox."

Becky put her arm around Denise. "It's all right, Honey. We all lost something that night." She looked at me. "Or afterwards. We gotta keep on, though. We gotta stay strong or those animals will win."

Denise fell against Becky, sobbing quietly. Becky stroked her hair. "Shhh. It'll be all right. You're with friends here. Everything will be all right."

Alfred nudged Becky, handing her the joint. Becky took a quick hit, then handed it to Denise.

"Hunh? No. I don't smoke that shit."

"You need to," Denise explained. "It keeps the ticks away."

Denise sat up straight. "What? I don't need to worry about ticks."

"Yes you do," I pointed out. "They go around in hordes of millions and find you while you're sleeping. They'll suck the life right out of you."

"He's right," Alf added. "They got my wife while she slept. Awful thing to see afterwards." He shuttered, as if a cold hand was laid on him.

"No shit," Denise said.

"No shit," Alf confirmed.

As she took the joint from Becky, she glanced towards the door. "What about my children?"

"They'll need to take a few tokes a day as well," I said.

"But," she hesitated, "what will it do to their development?"

I shrugged in the darkness. "Dunno. But without it, they'll be tick feed."

Claire hit me in the arm.

"Ow."

"Be nice."

"Just being honest."

*   *   *

We all woke up late the next day. The sun was halfway to its apex by time we ate breakfast. The rest of the day we spent cleaning guns and readying ammunition. It seemed Alfred had been busy during the time I was gone. He had retraced the trail we followed before and scrounged up several hundred rounds of ammunition, some pistols, Uzi's, and a few more rifles. Some of the firearms came from the camp, what they had use to try to defend themselves.

Denise and her children separated the rounds while the rest of cleaned rifles, Uzi's, pistols and revolvers. I liked revolvers because they were more durable and dependable. Besides, I thought they looked cool.

"Will have to go without fires at night for the next few days," I said to Alf.

"Sounds like a good idea."

"And nobody leaves here."

"We don't have much to eat. We were planning on foraging soon."

"We'll have to make do with what we have. We don't know where those men are."

"I thought you said they were headed for the Rubble?"

"It looked like they were before Black Rock. Far as I know, they've been tracking us." I holstered my revolver. "But we came through Phoenix. They should have lost our trail there."

"Then how do plan on attacking them?"

"I expect they'll make fires at night. We should be able to see 'em."

"Yeah, we should."

"Let's hope so."

Claire came over to us then. "What are you two talking about?"

"Strategizing," I said.

"That mean you got a plan?"

"Working on one. How's Denise?"

"She's going to be fine. It's Abby I'm worried about."

"Why's that?"

"You saw her at breakfast. Not a word out of her. She hasn't said anything all day except, 'Mmm mmm. She either nods her head, or shakes it."

"Make sure she stays around her mother. That should help her get through this." I looked over to where they were digging in the rounds. "Does she know what we have planned?"

"Revenge? Oh yeah. Her eyes light up when we talk about it."

"We'll have to make sure she understands why we're doing this."

"She understands. She understands that no one has the right to do what they did."

"How do you know this if all she says is 'mmmm'?"

"Woman's intuition."

I picked up my M40. "Oh. That thing."

She punched me in the arm.

"Ow."

"Oh quit crying."

I leaned over and kissed her on the shoulder.

She put her hand under my chin and lifted my head, then kissed me on the lips. "I do love you."

"Yes, I know." I couldn't bring myself to returning the

admiration, even though I was sure I did. It just didn't feel right. Maybe it was too soon after our little discussion about it.

"You love me, too," she offered.

"I do, do I?"

"Yes, you do."

"Don't tell me. That woman's intuition."

"You got it, Buster."

"Hmph."

Abby came over and sat down beside me. "Mister Woods?"

"Forrest."

She looked to the ground. "Um, Forrest, I want to thank you for saving Mom and me."

"It was my pleasure, Sweetheart."

"Was it really?"

I was a caught off guard. "Uh, hunh?"

"Was it really a pleasure killing those men to rescue me and Mom?"

"No," I lied. "It's just an expression. But it was a necessity. I had to do what I did or they would still have you."

"A necessity. Right. I see."

I looked over at Claire. She only shrugged.

"Listen," I started, "some people are just evil. They do bad things because they can; because they think they can get away with it. A lot of people that were in government before the 'Equinox were like that. That's why wars were started and waged. That's why so many people lived in squalor. Because people in power are selfish. They thought that by keeping other people down, they were more powerful when, in reality, they were more pitiful."

Abby gazed at me, as if I had said something profound. I felt my face blush. It wasn't profound, but something that had been going on ever since Man began organizing, perhaps before. I didn't know how to tell her that, if I had anything to say about the course of humankind from this point forward, men would not be allowed to get away with it again.

"How'd you get so wise, Mister Woo...uh, Forrest?"

I know I blushed then. But before I could say anything, Claire said, "He's not wise. He just likes to kill."

I didn't know what to say then. Claire was right, I did like to kill men like that. But maybe it was because before the 'Equinox there wasn't anything most people could do about the abuses of power and the privileged. They had their jobs to worry about. They had mortgages, bills, tuition to worry about. They just hoped that those in power would make life a bit easier for them, while life was a breeze for the privileged.

Or, perhaps, maybe the magnetic shift affected me, too. Maybe I liked killing for the fun of it. Because I could get away with it, have gotten away with it. I looked Claire in the eyes.

"No, I don't like to kill." I turned to Abby. "I wish I didn't have to, but I will kill anyone who thinks they are better than the rest; anyone who thinks he can enslave others; anyone who hurts another like they did you and your mother."

Abby threw her arms around my neck. "I want to kill those men, too. Thank you, Forrest."

I was lost. "Thanks for what?"

She stood. "For helping me understand that it's not just revenge. That there is something more to this senseless killing we're getting ready for."

I looked over at Claire. She nodded.

"Glad to be of help."

Denise showed up just then. "Was she talking? I thought I heard her talking. Is my baby going to be all right?"

"She's a young woman. And she's going to be fine."

"Go help your brother." She shooed Abby on. When Abby was far enough away, Denise turned to me. "What did you talk about?"

"About the necessity of killing."

Denise looked shocked. Her mouth dropped open a little and her eyes grew wide. "You did what?!"

Claire spoke up then. "After what she's been through, it's like Forrest said, she's a young woman now. She understands that what we're going to do we have to do or those men will keep doing what they did to you and her."

Denise gazed at the ground for a moment, then looked at me. "Thank you, Forrest. I don't think I could have done what you did; either when you rescued us, or just now." She turned and quickly walked away.

I watched her until she reached her children, observing as she hugged Abby briefly, then got back down to business sorting rounds.

Claire leaned over and kissed me on the cheek.

"What was that for?"

"For being such a good man."

My mind raced back to Michelle while Lisa was dying. "I'm not too sure about that."

"I am."

"Yeah, if you knew what happened while Lisa was dy..."

She cut me off with a peck on the lips. "Shhh. Your past doesn't matter. What matters is what you do today, tomorrow."

"Yeah, but..."

She pecked me again. "Shhh. It doesn't matter. From what I've seen you do, you're a man of integrity."

I pulled her close and just held her until Alfred came over a few moments later.

"Hey," he said, "if you two want some privacy go inside."

As Claire and I pulled apart I whispered, "I love you, Claire."

She halted and stared at my face, in my eyes. "You ass."

"Bitch," I whispered.

She punched me in the arm again.

"Ow."

"Wuss."

"You about ready?" Alf asked.

"Yeah," I said. "I've got my revolver and rifle cleaned and loaded. Three forty-five's are ready, so are four Uzi's and another rifle."

"When do you think they'll show up?"

I shrugged. "Tonight, tomorrow. We'll have to post watches until they do."

"I'll go check with the others, then draw up a schedule."

"Sounds good. Let me know."

"Will do."

Chapter XXVII

Two days later everyone was getting tense with anticipation. The night before was long without a fire, and dinner that night was barely eaten by anyone, except Jeremiah. He had the appetite of a growing boy and ate an entire bowl of berries.

The day after was filled with sitting around fiddling with the firearms, tending to the horses, and keeping watch for movement as far as we could see in the direction of Phoenix, the Rubble.

It was now late afternoon on the second day after reaching Little Phoenix and I had a feeling of foreboding. I knew those men would show up in Phoenix sometime today and made arrangements with Alf to get first watch after nightfall, then talked Claire into taking a nap with me before dusk arrived.

*   *   *

Claire sat with me as dusk turned into night. We were
facing due West, watching as the sun slid behind the horizon.
Neither of us spoke, just watched as we leaned back against a
log, waiting for it to get dark enough so we could see fires
burning below.

"You have a plan for this?"

"For what?" I knew what she meant, but needed her to
say it.

"For attacking these guys."

"No. Not really."

"What is that suppose to mean?"

"It means I don't really have a plan. When they show
up, we'll see where they are and try to get setup before sunrise."

"Sounds like a plan to me."

"If it is, it's not much of one."

"Maybe so, but it's still a plan. Say it again."

"Say what again?"

"That you love me."

"I thought woman's intuition had that covered?"

She punched me in the arm.

I leaned over, pulling her to me, and kissed her long on
the lips. "I do love you, Claire. I really do. You be careful
through all this."

"Count on it."

Then I thought I saw something and sat up straight.
"There. Do you see it?"

Claire sat up and looked in the direction I was. "There's
a...there's a glow."

"It's a fire. That glow is a fire."

"I'll get the others."

*   *   *

Two hours later, a full moon to light our way, we were all headed down to the Rubble, as Alfred called it. Alf had the lead, followed by Denise, her children, then Claire, with me bringing up the rear.

Two more hours brought us to the camp of the men that had abducted Denise and Abby and killed Jarod and Kyle. We made our camp about a mile away in a small clearing of rocks and brush. Alfred and I made our way as close as possible, spotting sentries standing at the perimeter of the fire's glow. We studied the situation for sometime, then made our way back to the rest.

"There all bunched up around the fire," I explained. "There's four sentries, one at each compass point. We'll get into position before dawn, then at first light we'll take them out."

"Let's ride in there and take them while they're sleeping," Denise offered.

"No. It's too dark. Some of them could get away," I paused, "or worse, they could get one of us."

"I see," she said.

"It'll be better to wait. Position ourselves around them, then, like I said, at first light, we simply open fire and kill them all. Couple of minutes and it'll be all over with."

"When do we leave?" Denise asked.

Alfred looked to the east. "Won't be for a few more hours. We should probably get some rest."

"I'm not tired," Jeremiah chimed.

"Good," I stated. "You can stand first watch."

"No he can't," Denise complained. "He's too young."

"Nothing's going to happen," I said. "He'll be fine."
Then I turned to the boy. "You hear anything you wake me up
before doing anything else. Understand?"

"Yes, Mister Forrest."

"Just Forrest."

Alf and Becky snuggled up next to a rock, Denise and
Abby laid down on a blanket, and Claire and I curled up close
to the horses. I kept an eye on Jeremiah as long as I could,
when several minutes later, after everyone else was asleep and
I was about ready to doze off myself, I saw the blue firefly.

"Forrest," Jeremiah whispered.

"Shhh. I see it."

"Want me to catch it for you?"

I nearly leaped up. "No," I whispered harshly. I took a
breath, then sighed. I felt Claire move. "Come here."

Jeremiah eased over to us, trying not wake Claire, but I
was pretty sure she was awake now. "I didn't mean to make
you mad," he whispered.

"I'm not mad. It's just, well, there's just no reason to be
hurting or capturing any living thing unless it's necessary."

"What would make it necessary?"

"Did your parents ever take you to a zoo, or a circus?"
He nodded in the darkness.

"Well, those animals don't normally live that way.
They were taken from their homes for our enjoyment, for profit
of the people who caged them. It wasn t a necessity. We all
could have easily done without zoos and circus'."

"But I liked to go."

"I understand. But do you think those animals liked it?

Were they necessary for you to eat, drink, breath?"

He was silent for several moments, mulling it over. "No, I guess not. But I did like seeing the animals up close."

"Yeah, I like animals, too. But we have to respect the other creatures that share this world with us. Just because we can capture or kill them, doesn't mean it's the right thing to do."

"What is the right thing to do?"

"Just let them go their own way."

"But your lightning bug, it's not real."

"It is too, real. You saw it."

"Well, yeah, but it's not natural. They don't live for years. I told you that."

"So then, the blue lightning bug is supernatural. That makes it even more special and due our respect."

He was silent again. "Yeah, I guess you're right."

"You still okay to stand guard?"

"Yes, sir."

"Then get to it and let me sleep."

"Yes, sir."

He walked to the other side of the camp and plopped down on a rock. I closed my eyes, hoping what I had said made since to him.

"You're pretty good with kids."

Claire's voice startled me and I jerked. "That's not funny."

"It wasn't meant to be."

"I mean scaring me like that."

"Yeah, right. I scared you. You knew I was awake."

She was right, I knew. I had just forgotten while talking to Jeremiah. "I suppose."

"You really think that lightning bug is supernatural?"

"You heard Jeremiah. They only live a week or so. I've been seeing it for years now. We've been seeing it for months."

"You really think it's your late wife?"

I kissed her on the forehead. "Yup. She's watching over me."

"Us."

"Us."

I drifted off to sleep moments later, the last few days having taken a toll.

*   *   *

I was back at the cabin at Cathedral Peak.. Lisa and I were sitting on the front porch, watching a spectacular sunset. As we sat in silence, the sun slowly slipping in and out of clouds, I had the feeling that this never happened. That what was happening was something surreal, ethereal.

"They all look up to you, you know," she said.

I knew instantly who she was talking about; Claire, Alf, Becky, Denise and her children. It was then I realized I was in a dream. I didn't want it to be a dream, though. Even with my deep feelings for Claire, I still missed Lisa and wanted her back. "I wish they wouldn't. I'm not that good of a person."

"Don't be an ass." That struck me like a slap in the face. She had never used a harsh word the entire time I knew her. "You've saved all of them. You've helped them all through this difficult time. Without you, evil men would be spreading across the remains of your world. You've put a stop to many of them." She paused, letting that soak in for a moment. "But there still are many more. Your journey has just begun."

"But what about those I couldn't save?"

"Simple. You couldn't save them." She turned her head to me. Her brown eyes deep and rich as ever. "You can't save them all. But you must save those you can. The world needs it."

"What's that suppose to mean?"

"You have a chance of shaping how the world turns out, how mankind evolves. You, my dear Forrest, are a good man. You have integrity, honesty, a kind soul, and, you like animals."

"I hate ticks."

"They're bugs. I've seen what they do. You just keep smoking your weed and you'll be fine."

I was stupified. When we were married she had made me quit. "What changed your mind about weed?"

"The ticks, moron. Besides, since I've been on this side, I can see that what had transpired before about weed was all bulshit."

"Uh, what else can you see?"

"That you have a chance to make the world what is always should have been, before evil began it's reign."

Just then a thunder clap burst from the clouds on the horizon. It sounded like a gunshot. I jerked awake.

"What the hell?" I barked.

"I'm sorry, Mister Forrest. It was coming right at us," Jeremiah explained.

"Forrest. Just call me Forrest," I reiterated. "What was coming?"

Jeremiah pointed past Alf and Becky. Everyone was

awake. In the waning moonlight I saw the wolf, dead on its side. "It was headed straight for them."

I cursed under my breath, knowing the men below heard the shot. "Good shot, boy. Thanks."

"Yeah, thanks," Alfred added.

I stood. "Everybody. We've got to get moving. They know we're here."

"Shit," Denise exclaimed.

"Mother," Abby astonished.

"Shut up and get on the horse," she ordered, then turned to me. "What do we do now?"

I thought for a moment. The sentries heard the direction the shot came from, they knew the general direction we were. We had to move. "We need to get away from here," I said, then had an idea. "But we still have a chance at surprise. Everyone, come here."

Ten minutes later I sat alone, the dead wolf lying a few feet away from me in the clearing, my horse behind me, facing the direction the men would come. I had started a small fire so they would come straight to me. It only took them twenty minutes to reach me.

"Yo, the camp there," came a voice from the brush.

"Who's there?" I called out, moving my rifle off my lap and unholstering my revolver.

"Name's John. I heard a shot. Are you all right?"

John. Right. And I suppose his last name is Smith. "I'm fine. Had to shoot a wolf," I answered. "What do you want?"

Seven men came into view then. I knew what they wanted; whatever I had. I rose, leaving my rifle against the log. My revolver was in my hand by my side.

As they neared, John asked, "You alone?"

"Been alone for months. What do you want?" They were close enough to shoot with my revolver.

"Just heard the shot and were curious." They all took another step. "But we want whatever you got."

"Kinda figured that," I said, then raised the revovler and shot the closest man. That's when my comrades opened up. Five more dropped in an instant and I was moving to my right, taking down another before the last man could raise his weapon. Another shot from one of my comrades and he dropped where he stood. It was all over in less than ten seconds. We wouldn't be this lucky with the remaining seven.

Moments later all but Alf entered the clearing. "Alf go check for the others?" I asked Becky.

"Yup. Just like you told him to."

"Good. Let's get moving.'

We checked the corpses. They were all dead. Again, I felt no guilt. I looked at the faces of the others in the pale light. I wouldn't call what I saw elation but there was no sorrow, especially from Denise, Abby and Jeremiah. Revenge was theirs.

We gathered the horses and headed due north, away from the Rubble and Little Phoerix. I wanted to make sure they didn't find out about Little Phoenix, in case something went wrong in the next few hours.

"Where we going, Forrest?" Jeremiah asked. He had stayed with me after we left, the others only steps ahead, Alfred again in the lead.

"I dunno. Alf said he knew someplace we could wait for the rest of those men. He said it wasn't far, that we should be there by dawn."

"Oh."

We rode in silence until the eastern sky started to glow with the loom of the sun, then Jeremiah said, "I liked killing those men. It was easy."

I nearly reprimanded him, but didn't. "You'll think different about it in a few days. Right now you're just flushed with adrenaline."

"No, I really liked killing those men for killing my dad and Kyle, and hurting mom and Abby. I want to hurry up and kill the rest."

So did I. I wanted it over with, to go back to Little Phoenix and escape in Claire and a fat joint. "It'll come soon enough. Only this time it's going to be harder. This time they'll be shooting back."

"Not if we surprise 'em again."

"We can't count on that."

"But you said..."

"Nothing is certain, anymore. Never was."

An hour after sunrise Alf led us into a box canyon. He stopped at the entrance. I rode up to him. "This is it?"

"Wha'd'ya think? Think we can take 'em out here?"

I surveyed the canyon. "If I was them, I wouldn't follow us in."

"They're not you."

"No, but they did only send seven back there to check out the shot. They have some brains."

He looked into the canyon, then at me. "You got a better idea?"

I looked around at the surrounding area, then at our

little group. "No. Not at the moment." I wished for a cigarette. "Let's get setup and hope their stupid."

Chapter XXVIII

We paired off in two's. Jeremiah went with Claire, Abby with Alf, Denise with Becky, and I took a high place by myself. They were to wait for me to shoot, aiming at the closest target to them respectively, then open fire. If we were lucky, it would again be over in seconds.

We waited three hours, me keeping track with the watch I took from Felix. When the men arrived, they hesitated at the entrance to the canyon for only a moment before following our tracks into it. As I watched them through the scope on my rifle, I thought how stupid they were, allowing revenge to control them that way. Then a shot rang out, minutes before we would have had the advantage of a crossfire and certain death to them all.

I looked to my right to see the whiff of gunsmoke coming from where Becky and Denise were positioned. I knew it was Denise who had fired the shot. "Damn her," I muttered, then took aim and dropped the closest man to me. The other five had turned their horses and were headed the short distance to the entrance of the canyon and escape.

I stood and draped myself over the boulder I was behind and shot another man off his horse. Then through the scope, I saw Abby running towards the remaining four men, shooting wildly as she ran. Before I could get a bead, one of the men turned and shot her in the chest. She spun completely around then fell face first into the Arizona sand, dead.

I heard Denise scream in defiance and disbelief, then saw Jeremiah stand and shoot the killer of his sister. Claire then reached up and pulled him back behind the rock as a shot was fired in his direction, kicking up a puff of dirt directly behind where he had been standing. I finally had a another one in my crosshairs and pulled the trigger, shooting one of the horses in the shoulder, it and the rider hitting the ground hard.

Then a volley of shots came off from my left, Alfred shooting without aiming to keep the men from returning fire anywhere. I took careful aim and put the farthest man from me, the closest to the canyon entrance, in the dirt with half his head missing. A shot came again from my right and another man backflipped of his horse. I knew it was Claire.

I saw movement off my right and glanced over to see Alf standing. He brought his rifle up and fired, just as a bullet from below struck him and sent him careening backwards. I looked through my scope again to see one man on horseback galloping out the entrance to the canyon. I held my breath, then gently squeezed the trigger. The recoil blurred the sight through the scope for an instant and I thought I had missed, but when the rifle settled I saw the last man tumble off his horse as the horse continued on. I closed my eyes and exhaled heavily. A moment later I heard Claire yelling for me.

"Forrest! Forrest! Denise is going after the man down."

What? I peered through the scope. The man who's horse I had shot from under him was on his feet, his weapon raised and pointed at...I moved the rifle in the direction he was pointing. Denise. She was running full speed at him, screaming at the top of her lungs that she was going to kill him for what he had done. Before I could put my scope on him, I heard a shot. Then my scope was on him and I saw the puff of smoke from the barrel of his gun, then heard another shot and an instant later a crimson spray exploded from his chest. He fell face first into the ground. I thought Alf had shot him, but I later found out it had been Jeremiah.

They were all dead now. All the men that had killed Jarod and Kyle and abducted Denise and Abby were dead. So too, were Abby, Denise and Alfred.

Reluctantly, the rest of us made our way down to the canyon floor. I checked each man as I reached him, putting a bullet into the head of the second man I came across.

"She's still alive!" It was Alf. Alf? I looked over to see him kneeling beside Abby. I broke into a run, putting a bullet into the head of the third man I passed for good measure. By time I reached Alf and Abby, Becky and Claire were there.

"How is she?" I huffed.

"It went clean through, just below her right shoulder," Becky diagnosed. "If we can stop the bleeding, she'll be okay."

I looked at Claire, then to the other bodies scattered across the ground. "Them?"

"Denise is dead. So are all of them."

We only lost one, I thought. It could have been worse, but we didn't need to lose anyone. If Denise had only waited a couple minutes more.

"You okay, Alf?"

"I'm fine, considering."

"I swear I watched you get shot."

"Hunh? Oh that, no, I wasn't shot. But I saw his muzzle blast aimed right at me, I went to move and tripped over backwards. No harm done."

I merely stood, thankful that he hadn't been hit. If she had only waited two more minutes, there would not have been any return fire. Seven for seven. Two, three seconds tops, and it would have been over with. "Glad to see you okay."

He stood. "Think she knows about her mother?"

I shrugged. "I thought she was dead."

"Let's get her back to Little Phoenix. I'll get the horses."

"I'll give you a hand," Claire offered.

With our horses ready for the ride back, Claire and I dug a grave for Denise while Alfred and Jeremiah retrieved the horses the men had rode. Becky tended to Abby, reworking the bandage and cleaning her face. She had stopped Abby's bleeding and the color was returning to the girl's face, her pulse stronger. Alf and the boy returned with five of the horses while I was finishing lashing the travois together, Claire helping Becky get Abby wrapped up for the long, bumpy ride.

Minutes later we leaving the box canyon, nobody talking now, the clopping of horses hoofs on the sandy ground and the occaisonal moaning of Abby the only sounds. Jeremiah stayed close to me, the riderless horses leased out behind him. I didn't know what to say him, so I said nothing.

*   *   *

Abby stayed unconscious the entire ride back, the occasional moan a cruel way to know she was still alive. She didn't wake until after Alf and I carried her inside and she felt the cool air

"Where is everyone?" she muttered.

It was only us three inside, the others were taking care of the horses and starting a fire.

"Outside," Alf started, "with the horses."

"Where's Mom?"

Alf and I looked at each other. Pausing.

"She's dead, isn't she?"

We looked to the floor. I had the absurd thought that it was woman's intuition. "Uh, yes she is," I said solemnly. "She died saving you," I added, as if it would help.

She turned away. "No, she died because I acted like a revenge-crazed lunatic."

"I'll go get Becky," Alf volunteered, then briskly walked out.

I almost said, 'She died because she fired too early', but didn't. Instead I said, "You didn't know what was going to happen. Nobody did."

"I wasn't thinking. I saw the man that shot Kyle and...and I just...just lost it."

I knew she had lost it back there, her mother had, too. But I couldn't blame nor condemn either one after what those men had put them through. "You're what? Fourteen? Fifteen?"

"Fourteen."

"Well, for being fourteen you're holding up pretty good. Don't beat yourself up over this. Nobody is always in control."

Becky came in and paused when she heard us talking. "She's awake? Is she lucid?"

I nodded at Abby, "You'll be okay. I already know you're pretty tough. You need anything, let me know."

"Thanks, maybe."

I smiled. "If you need anything..," I let it trail off and gave her a quick nod. I turned to Becky, "To answer your questions: Yes, she's awake, and no, crazy as a loon." I headed for the door, pausing with Becky for a moment. "She's going to be okay. She's pretty down to Earth. Already trying to blame herself for her mother's death."

"Thanks, Forrest. I'm going to check her bandages."

"Take your time. As long as she's awake I think someone should be in the room."

"You think she'd try something stupid?"

"Hey, you two quit talking about me. I'm awake, you know. I can hear every word."

I turned her direction. "Oh you can not."

She lowered her voice an ocatve. "'As long as she's awake I think someone should be in room.' What? You think I might 'try something stupid'?"

"Actually, I thought it'd be a good idea that you had someone around, in case you needed to talk. Or maybe get out of bed."

"Get out of bed? I've been shot, man."

"In your shoulder. Not your legs or ass."

"Watch your mouth."

I turned to Becky and whispered, "Sassy."

"Sassy? I'll show you sassy. Mmph. Ow. Help me out this bed and I'll show you sassy."

"Better go check her bandages." I rolled my eyes. Becky smiled.

"Shit. I'm bleeding again."

Becky almost sprinted to her, I watched for moment, in case Becky needed something. A moment later she looked my way and nodded. I turned to leave when Abby whispered to Becky, "He's okay." I smiled and went outside.

They were all hanging around the doorway. Alf and Jeremiah were sharing a joint, Claire grabbing hits as it was passed around. I stopped. "She's going to be okay. She's pretty sassy already."

From inside, through the open window I heard Abby say, "I heard that."

The joint came around to me and held it, taking a hit and holding it and the joint. I wanted to catch up. After three hits I motioned for Jeremiah to come over. I took once last hit, then handed him the joint. "Make sure your sister takes a few hits."

"How many?"

"More than three."

"Okay."

I walked over and sat by Claire as Jeremiah disappeared through the doorway. "How's he doing?"

Claire leaned against me. "He's tougher than I am."

"You're pretty damn tough, girl. Don't kid yourself."

The sun was almost at the hoizon. She stood. "I'm

going to go roll another joint and start supper." She looked me in the eyes. "Dogfood?"

"Stew, if you can find it."

I watched her walk away, feeling a stirring in my groin.

"Dogfood?" Alf queried.

"She thinks some of the cans are dogfood." I shrugged. "Tastes all right to me."

"Hope she brings two joints now that I know we're going to be eating dogfood tonight."

Chapter XXIX

Claire and Jeremiah went out each day to get food, every few days they would shoot something: rabbit, squirrel, coyote. Alf and I made a corral over the next two weeks as Becky tended to Abby. The day we finished the corral, Abby was up brushing horses. That night, after a coyote dinner, Claire and I sat out several hundred yards from Little Phoenix sharing a joint.

I thought about my brief dream at the cabin. I had thought about roaming around, seeing who and what was left when Berta was alive. I was certain she would have joined me. I thought I'd better tell Claire my intentions, though. I was certain the dream was confirmation. I wondered if I'd ever see the blue firefly again.

Claire nudged me then, it was my turn. I inhaled deeply, handing it back as I held my breath. As I exhaled some moments later, I began. "I'm going to need to get going soon."

"Going where?" she back breathed as she inhaled the smoke.

"Guess go check out what's all left."

"Oh yeah? How long you think that'll take?"

I shrugged. "Dunno. Depends on how much is left." I pointed towards the rubble of Phoenix. "A couple miles south of that is the ocean. Further on, a couple days is ocean. A few days more east is more ocean." I shrugged again. "Few months. Few years. Just dunno."

We finished the joint before she asked, "Mind if I come with you?"

"I was hoping you would ask."

"When do we leave?"

"Next couple of days. I'll tell Alf tonight. You can tell Becky and the kids."

"Thanks."

I leaned over and kissed her on the lips. "We'll do just fine out there."

"I know we will."

We sat there several minutes in silence. I looked to the sky, checking the progress of the stars. "It's starting to get late. We better head back."

"Wanna smoke another joint first?"

"You got another?"

She reached into a breast pocket and retrieved a joint. "You got a light?"

When she passed the joint to me, she asked, "You think we'll find more evil men out there?"

"God I hope not."

Two days later Claire and I left Little Phoenix, Alf

telling me then that Becky was pregnant. I promised we would be back for the birth.

We headed north, intending to turn west when we reached the band of swirling clouds. At camp the first night we saw the blue firefly. I knew then I had made the right choice. We reached the band of clouds the following day and rode on the shadow line until we ran into the ocean, then turned north again.

* * *

It has been quite an adventure. Two years ago we had grown tired of roaming around and settled down. Plus, we couldn't find any more evil men. We made a lot of friends out there, and hopefully, all of our enemies are dead.

We didn't make it to the birth of Becky's baby, but we saw the boy a few months later. They named him Forrest. Abby and Jeremiah had pretty much got back to normal, Alf and Becky their adopted parents. I felt a litte strange, though, when Jeremiah and Abby called Claire and I, 'Aunt' and 'Uncle'.

A lot has happened in the six years. Claire and I saved, and killed, a lot of people. A lot of times we had help from those we rescued. There weren't as many evil men out there as I had anticipated. I was surprised, happily surprised, but still surprised. We have children of our own now. Clint, four years old, and Jarod, nine months.

What's left of the continent isn't much. Most of California is gone. Only the eastern pieces at each tip, the rest is under water. We didn't get much further north than southern Canada. It just got too cold. The coastline in the east, along the newly dubbed Plains Sea, runs pretty much north and south. We followed it south straight to Dallas, clipping off the eastern side of every state straight down. We don't know about the eastern half of the country. From what we can see, there's no shore looking across the Plains Sea. We thought we could see islands along part of the southern coast, but it appeared that most of Mexico was gone.

The band of swirling clouds still zips along at a good pace west to east. In fact, that's where we made our home, right along the shadow line. Our food dome sets in the shadow. It's two days ride to Little Phoenix and we visit about once a month.

But now, six years later, as I stand near the front of our home, our eldest, Clint, playing in the front, Claire in the house readying breakfast, our youngest, Jarod in my arms as I watched the sun rise, the ground shook with a violent jolt.

"Get to a clearing and wait," I yelled to Clint. I stepped away from the structure and towards him as another jolt knocked me to the ground.

"Is this it?" I heard Claire yell from the inside of the house. She came running out, headed for the middle of the clearing in front of the house.

Claire reached Clint first, hugging him tightly through each jolt.

"Has it been seven years?" she asked when I reached them, little Jarod still asleep in my arms.

I shrugged. "What month is this?"

"August."

"Sure?"

She nodded.

"It's a couple of months early."